BURNING

ALSO BY ELANA K. ARNOLD

Sacred

BURNING

ELANA K. ARNOLD

DELACORTE PRESS

Text copyright © 2013 by Elana K. Arnold
Jacket photograph copyright © 2013 by Eva Kolenko

All rights reserved. Published in the United States by Delacorte Press, an imprint of Random House Children's Books, a division of Random House, Inc., New York.

Delacorte Press is a registered trademark and the colophon is a trademark of Random House, Inc.

Visit us on the Web! randomhouse.com/teens

Educators and librarians, for a variety of teaching tools, visit us at RHTeachersLibrarians.com

Library of Congress Cataloging-in-Publication Data
Arnold, Elana K.
Burning / Elana K. Arnold. — First edition.
p. cm.
Summary: In the scorching Nevada desert during the Burning Man festival, a small town boy meets a Gypsy girl, when both are at crossroads in their lives.
ISBN 978-0-385-74334-1 (hc) — ISBN 978-0-449-81076-7 (ebook)
[1. Coming of age—Fiction. 2. Love—Fiction. 3 Romanies—Fiction. 4. Deserts—Fiction. 5. Burning Man (Festival)—Fiction. 6. Nevada—Fiction.] I. Title.
PZ7.A73517Bu 2013
[Fic]—dc23
2012025726

The text of this book is set in 11.5-point Goudy.
Book design by Stephanie Moss

Printed in the United States of America

10 9 8 7 6 5 4 3 2 1

First Edition

For you, Honeyman. I burn for you.

We are all
wanderers
on this earth
our hearts
are full
of wonder
our souls
are deep
with dreams

—*Gypsy proverb*

Mountains do not meet, but people do.

—*Romani saying*

CHAPTER ONE

BEN

Pete, Hog Boy, and I were spending Monday afternoon screwing around on our skateboards on the shipping dock at the deserted drywall plant. The place was creepy these days, and I could tell from Pete's stupid jokes and Hog Boy's extra-loud guffaws that they thought so, too, but none of us was saying it out loud.

It was ridiculously hot, well over a hundred degrees, and the air was so dry and electric that my hair felt like it was standing on end. Every breath I took burned the whole way down, hot and dry and painful. I watched Pete almost land a heelflip but miss, his board instead shooting out across the flat expanse of the concrete shipping dock and banging into a ten-foot stack of drywall sheets.

Hog Boy snorted, "Smooth!" and I caught the unconscious quick hunch of Pete's shoulders as he jogged over to his board and flipped it up with his foot.

Pete's board had dented one of the bottom sheets. I ambled over and examined the stack, kicking at it before kneeling down and pushing my finger into the hole his board had created, scooping out some of the gray-white powder that had been pressed together to make this sheet.

Gypsum. Our town was built on it—built *because* of the wealth of it in our landscape, and named after it, even: Gypsum, Nevada. And it was gypsum, too, that was ending it all, because of our town's reliance on it.

The housing bubble had burst. That was how the journalists put it, as they observed the rise and fall of the lines on their charts with detached impartiality. *Pop.* Just like that. No one's building anymore, not when there are so many perfectly good abandoned, foreclosed homes all across the country.

When no one's building, no one needs drywall. No drywall, no need to mine. No mine—no Gypsum.

So we had the shipping dock to ourselves this afternoon as the sun stared down at us, unblinking. Silver lining, I guess. This was a great place to skate.

"Hey, Ben," called Hog Boy. "You gonna stand around all day jerking off or are you gonna skate?"

For Hog Boy, everything was about jerking off or getting laid or getting air. Truth was, I didn't much feel like skating. My family—Mom, Pops, my little brother James—they were home packing boxes. I should have been home helping them. I didn't feel like doing that, either.

I felt like getting in a fight.

But I took a deep breath like the high school counselor had told me to do and I focused my gaze on my board. The grip tape across its deck was worn and peeling in places. I'll replace it when I get to San Diego next week, I told myself, then threw the board in front of me and jogged toward it, jumping on and curving just before I crashed into Hog Boy.

He didn't flinch. He never did. He just grinned that goofy grin of his, and I had to smile back. Hog Boy.

I'd known him and Pete forever—we were all Gypsum to the core. If you cut one of us open the white dust of crushed gypsum rocks would probably pour out instead of blood.

All our dads had worked at the mine—Hog Boy's dad and my pops had been laid off along with everyone else back in January. Pete's dad would have been laid off, too, if he hadn't already been dead.

Hog Boy's face was an almost cartoonish shade of red. He didn't tan and he wouldn't wear sunscreen or a hat, so his skin was turning to leather. A crop of white-blond hair, tightly shorn, capped his head. He wasn't all that fat, but he was big. Packed solid. Like a well-fed hog.

I carved across the platform of the shipping dock, heading for the three-foot ramp we'd built right after the plant had closed for good back in May. I rolled up the ramp and ollied off the back side, but my heart wasn't in it.

I felt the sticky press of my T-shirt against my back. Damn, it was hot. On days like this, it was like the sun was literally bearing down on me. I felt like some sort of depraved Atlas holding the weight of the sun on my shoulders instead of the world. I felt myself compressed by the weight of it, by the weight of everything.

"Let's drink the beer," I suggested, and I didn't get an argument. We rolled to the shaded port of the shipping dock, where we'd stashed our cooler.

It was maybe a few degrees better there. I looked around the large, rectangular port. I'd been here lots of times—every summer since freshman year, until this one, I'd helped out at both the plant and at the quarry, too, just a few hundred yards from the shipping dock we were skating on. This place had been packed—forklifts, men everywhere, tall stacks of drywall being loaded onto flatbeds and carted off all across the country.

Pete handed around the beers. I pressed mine against my forehead and shut my eyes. Better. With the icy can against my skin and my eyes closed, I could imagine for just a second that I was already out of here—in Southern California, at UC San Diego, salty ocean breeze and gorgeous blondes in bikinis, every color of the rainbow.

When I opened my eyes, Pete and Hog Boy were watching me. I got the guilty feeling they knew where I'd gone for a minute—somewhere they didn't have a ticket to.

I cracked open the can and took a long drink before squatting to the concrete.

"So you leave in a week, huh?" Pete asked.

I nodded. He already knew the plan. But he kept coming back to it, again and again, as if he were looking for some loophole that could keep it from coming true.

"Yep," I said. "I'll help my folks get their stuff to their new place in Reno, and then they'll drop me off at the bus stop."

Strange to think of my family without me, and in a new city. All my life I'd seen them in the same context—in the boxlike wood-planked house we'd always lived in, two bedrooms, one bathroom, and a postage stamp of a living room where we ate and watched TV. But the mining company owned all the houses in town. They owned the only store, too, and even the two churches, one Baptist, one Protestant. And nothing—not our homes, not the schools, not even the churches—was exempt from the town closure. In a week it would all be boarded up. Fat rolls of chain link waited just at the edge of town. Once we were out, the entire town would be surrounded by it.

And then what? Our lawns would die, first of all. The smartest people had already left over the last year or so, knowing that our country's bad economy spelled bad news for our gypsum mine. Those of us still here were the die-hards, those who hadn't wanted to believe the writing on the wall until it was too late to ignore it any longer. We kept watering and weeding and mowing even though we all knew our days here were numbered. Once we left, the desert would reclaim our little plots of yard in no time. By the end of September there'd be no green left.

Without fresh paint our houses wouldn't look neat and tidy for long, either. Desert weather is merciless. The buildings would splinter soon enough.

Then the sidewalks we'd ridden our bikes on and the streets where we'd learned to drive would crack and buckle and disappear into the desert landscape, too.

I tried to turn my thoughts to less depressing things. I pictured the road map in my head, the one I'd studied many times since reserving my seat on the three p.m. Greyhound bus out of Reno: the first stretch, west from Reno on Interstate 80, then a transfer in Sacramento at six-thirty in the evening. I'd sleep on that second bus, and when I woke up the next morning I'd be in San Diego. New day, new life.

My friends didn't want to hear about my road trip, though, so I turned to Pete. "What about you and your mom? Did you guys figure out what you're going to do yet?"

Pete shook his head and bit his lip. It was a bad habit of his, one he'd had all his life. I remember him doing it back in kindergarten, picking at and chewing on that same spot on his lip until it bled. There was a permanent divot there in his bottom lip, right in the middle, from all the times it'd broken open and scabbed over.

Other than that, Pete was definitely the best-looking guy in our little school. He was romantic-looking, I guess, in a way girls seemed to go crazy for. The only one of us with a steady girlfriend, he was tall and kind of angular, not really muscular but well built anyway, and I'd heard Cheyenne and Becca talking about how his eyes were "smoldering."

Maybe they were. I sure as hell didn't know about that. But if they *did* smolder, it was probably on account of all the shit he'd crawled through in his eighteen years.

We all knew each other's stories in Gypsum, and no one in town seemed opposed to mulling over what should have been the secret lives of its residents. So no one thought twice about discussing how Pete's dad, Jerry, had fought a long, ugly battle with lung cancer, taking way too long to die, or how his mom, Kathy, had distracted herself from her sadness by friending her old high school flame on Facebook. Everybody knew—and had a definite opinion about—how Kathy had been out of town the weekend Jerry had finally taken his last breath just over three years ago. Pete had found him.

The town was divided over whether or not Kathy should have moved away from Gypsum after that. The mean gossips said that the Facebook guy had dumped her, so she had had no choice but to stay in Gypsum. The nicer ones held the theory that Jerry's death had snapped her back to her senses, and that *she* had dumped *him* so she could focus on raising Pete and seeing him graduate high school.

Pete wasn't saying, and I can't say I really wanted to know the truth. When you grow up in a town of 489 people, you get pretty tired of hearing about everyone's dirty laundry. But I couldn't ignore the look that had come into Pete's eyes during the months that surrounded his father's death.

And neither could the girls; I guess there's something about suffering that turns chicks on.

We drank our beers and didn't say much for a while, just watched the sky as clouds began to roll in, slate gray and smokelike and not thick enough to offer any real hope of rain.

It was Hog Boy, of course, who broke the silence.

"Knock, knock," he said.

Pete rolled his eyes and refused to bite, but I decided to throw him a bone.

"Who's there?" I asked.

"Ben." He grinned.

This couldn't be going anywhere good. But I replied gamely, "Ben who?"

"Ben over and lick my ass," he said, and snorted.

Pete shook his head. "Nice, Hog Boy."

"You're just jealous you didn't think of it."

"Hog Boy, I've heard versions of that same joke about a thousand times. You didn't make it up. You couldn't make anything up."

I laughed. I was going to miss these guys.

We shot the shit while we drank our beers. Hog Boy told us his favorite story, the one about the chick he'd met last summer at Burning Man. I gave the story about a fifty percent chance of being true.

"It was better than Christmas! Naked chicks everywhere, tits flying, a fucking *cornucopia* of drugs and booze. Burning Man was, like, exactly what you'd get if you looked inside my sick little fantasy world. I shit you not, there's no place like it."

Pete and I had to take Hog Boy's word for it. Of the three of us, he was the only one with parents permissive enough to let him go.

Other than the gypsum mine, our town didn't have a lot going for it. There was Burning Man, though.

Picture this. Gypsum, Nevada, was home to just under five hundred people. Burning Man, a weeklong event atop the playa just twenty minutes outside our town, had attracted over fifty thousand people last year. Fifty *thousand*. They show up—artists, musicians, druggies, hippies, ravers, nudists—from all over the world, they park themselves on the playa the week before Labor Day, and they party for seven days straight. On the Saturday before Labor Day—two days before they close up camp and drive away, back to their real lives for another year—they burn an enormous wooden effigy. That's Burning Man.

It was another reason some of the Gypsum families were still in town—to keep our local store open and make a few more bucks while we still could.

It made sense that Hog Boy thought Burning Man sounded like heaven. Ever since we were kids he's been the one to try and get the party started, smooth talking the girls in hopes of getting them to show him their panties. He was a social animal. His family—like mine—was relocating to Reno, just about a hundred miles from Gypsum. Now that he'd graduated high school, Hog Boy would be looking for full-time work.

"She was painted hot pink, all of her, and the way she moved . . ." Hog Boy shook his head, reminiscing, maybe, or losing himself in his own fantasy. "She was crazy for me, too. Couldn't keep her hands off me. Course, who could blame her?"

Pete and I shared a glance. His doubtful expression mirrored my feelings exactly. A sexy, naked, painted chick desperate to get her hands on *Hog Boy*?

This was the last year the three of us would ever be like this, out here in the desert, practically walking distance from the festivities. I could almost feel the pull of them, the fifty thousand outsiders just down the road, people who had come to our playa from all over the *planet* practically. It was in the air—the migration, the invasion, whatever you want to call it, all those people—and nearly half of them women.

"I still don't see how you talked your parents into letting you go to Burning Man," Pete said, his voice tinged with envy. "I mean, don't they have any idea what goes on out there?"

Hog Boy shrugged. "I can be very convincing," he said. "And I had a fake ID. But this year I don't need one. I'm eighteen—we all are. We should totally go."

But even as he said it some of the wind seemed to go out of his sails. Admission to Burning Man was $360 a ticket. Pretty steep even when times weren't so lean; with the mine shutting down and the impending move on everybody's mind, the three of us shelling out a combined thousand bucks to go to a festival of wackos sounded far-fetched, even to Hog Boy's ever-hopeful ears. So close, but still a world away from us.

"What a bitch," he mumbled. "I fucking hate being poor."

No argument from me and Pete. Of course, as we nodded our agreement and tipped up our beers for the last sips, a pang of guilt shot through me. Because even though my pockets were as empty as Hog Boy's and Pete's, there was a gigantic difference between their situations and mine.

A scholarship.

There's not a lot to do in Gypsum, but there's a hell of a lot of room to do it. I came by running naturally: My parents had both been on their high school's track-and-field teams in Reno. That's where they met and got married, and where they made the decision to move to Gypsum when the mine was booming.

It's not bragging to say that I'm fast. It's just true. My

times speak for themselves. It's a good thing I'm into running and not some sport that requires a lot of equipment, like lacrosse or football. Our tiny high school in Gypsum has never had a budget—or a student population—large enough to support those kinds of programs.

And one of the guys my dad went to high school with went to UCSD back in the day, so when my dad sent him my times, he gave us some suggestions about qualifying for a scholarship. But UCSD doesn't give enough scholarship money to its athletes to cover even close to all its costs. Luckily I had good grades, too, and of course the fact that our entire town was closing down must have impressed the scholarship committee, because all I have to pay for the first year is my bus ticket.

I tried not to talk about this stuff too much with Pete and Hog Boy. No reason to rub salt in their wounds. Hog Boy would end up working at a gas station or a mini-mart; maybe Pete would get lucky and get a job at a casino.

The beers were gone. We'd brought a six-pack—two cans each—and that was enough to take the edge off, I guess. Hog Boy, though—he should never drink. It always turns him into an even bigger asshole than he already is. You wouldn't think that two beers could have any effect on a guy his size, but maybe the beers are just an excuse to let his inner douche bag really shine.

After he finished his second beer, he smashed the can flat with his foot and started kicking it around, trying to keep it up in the air like a hacky sack.

"How's your girl, Petey-boy?" he asked, even though we'd

all seen Melissa just before we headed out to the mine to skate. She worked at the store in town, and this week she was too busy to do much else since Burning Man was in full swing and each day brought new busloads of half-baked partiers jonesing for Twinkies and soda.

I knew from the twitch of Pete's jaw that Hog Boy was skating on thin ice by starting in on Melissa. Pete was probably going to marry her, and he didn't like Hog Boy opening his fat mouth about her.

"She sure is pretty, that Melissa." Hog Boy was singsonging now. Sometimes I hated that fucker. It wasn't really what he said so much as how he said it.

"Uh-huh," said Pete. I watched his fingers curl into a fist and relax again.

"Too bad she doesn't have a sister," said Hog Boy. "A twin sister. Boy, if she did . . . I sure would like to dig into a piece of that pie."

Pete was up in a flash, and he leaned forward menacingly.

Hog Boy laughed and held up his hands in a gesture of surrender. "You misunderstand me, my friend. Not *Melissa*, I would never *dream* of sticking it to *Melissa*, she's *your* girl. Just . . . you know, hypothetically, if Melissa had a twin. I'd be happy to stick it to her *twin*, you know . . . if she had one."

I had stood up, too, though I didn't remember doing so, and I had angled myself between Pete and Hog Boy just in case Pete lunged at him. I knew who would win that fight— Hog Boy, no doubt in my mind. Pete's eyes may be smoldering, but Hog Boy knows how to throw a punch, and even though he has a hard-packed gut already, it doesn't seem to slow him down any.

Luckily, Pete decided to see the humor in the situation. "Hog Boy," he said, "it's a good thing that fantasy world of yours is so rich, because you're *never* going to get laid in real life."

"I told you, the pink chick at Burning Man last summer . . ."

I left them to bicker it out. The situation was defused, I could feel the difference in the air, so I kicked my board back onto its wheels and meandered around the shipping dock, turning smooth, wide curves, just paddling because there was nothing better to do, enjoying the sound of the wheels against the cement.

There was more moisture in the air now, or maybe it just felt that way since there was more moisture in *me*. But the clouds seemed thicker, too, like maybe they were considering turning into something more like rain. The weather here is fast to change. I knew that just because it had been sunny a couple of hours ago, that was no guarantee that there couldn't be a storm before tonight.

I looked back at Hog Boy and Pete. They were playing kick the can together now, argument forgotten, and laughing together about something I hadn't heard.

I skated over toward them. "Hey," I said. "You guys about ready to head back to town?"

Hog Boy looked up at me, still laughing. "You're still a goofy-footed bastard, aren't you?"

Hog Boy is one of those people who derives pleasure from pointing out any differences he might happen to notice. So I ride with my right foot forward instead of my left. Big frigging deal.

"Always have been, always will be," I said. "You guys ready to go?"

"I wonder," Hog Boy said to Pete in his best pseudo-intellectual voice, "if there is any sort of positive correlation between being goofy foot and being a homo."

The smile dropped off Pete's face. "Ben," Hog Boy said, still enjoying himself, "maybe you can shed some light for us. Is your little brother goofy foot, too?"

And that was when the school counselor's deep-breathing technique stopped being effective. It seemed amazing to me that Hog Boy could *still* get off on pushing that particular button. Un-frigging-believable. Just as I had stepped between Pete and Hog Boy earlier, now Pete tried to wedge himself between the two of us. But I pushed him aside.

"You opened your fat mouth one time too many, Hog Boy," I said, and then I split open my knuckle on his front teeth.

It hurt like a bitch, but Hog Boy just stood there laughing like an idiot as blood trickled down from his lip. Then he rushed me, his refrigerator-like body knocking me hard to the ground. I felt the back of my head connect with the cement, and sharp pain radiated through me. Later, when I was alone and calm again, I'd be able to rationally explain Hog Boy's drive to piss me off. He was angry that I was going somewhere better than he was, and he wanted me to pay for it. But flat on my back at the shipping dock, I wasn't thinking in words. Just a red explosion of anger, and reaction, and a desire to break something. Preferably Hog Boy's fat face.

I brought my hands up to push Hog Boy off me. He's like a heavy wheelbarrow: hard to get going, but once he's in motion he just rolls along. I flipped him on his back and hit him again, this time in the temple, and Hog Boy wasn't laughing now. I wanted to hit him again. And again.

But Pete grabbed me then, underneath my armpits, and hauled me up.

"All right, all right, enough," he said, and he shook me.

Hog Boy lumbered to his feet and brought his hand to his temple. For a minute I didn't know if he was going to attack me or not, and I could feel myself all coiled up inside, ready to react, *hoping* he'd come at me so I could fight some more and knowing that Pete couldn't hold me back if I really wanted to get loose. But then that shit-eating grin spread across Hog Boy's face and he said, "Damn, Stanley, you're getting strong. Big Bad Hog Boy sure is proud of you."

There was an instant when it still could have gone either way, in spite of Hog Boy's half-assed attempt at making peace. It was up to me. And even though there was a roar in my head that drove me forward, I forced myself to take deep, clearing breaths, and I felt myself slowly unwind.

Three years earlier I wouldn't have been able to control myself. But then I hadn't had so much to lose.

I wasn't ready to smile back, though, not yet. I shook Pete's hands off me. "Not my brother," I said. My voice was quiet but clear. "Talk whatever shit you want about me and Petey here, but not James."

"Hey, hey, whatever, man," said Hog Boy. "You know I just like to joke. But okay, I won't mention the little man, if it means so much to you." He held out his hand. After a minute, I shook it.

"No hard feelings, right?"

I nodded. No hard feelings. What was the point, anyway? Just a few more days, and then I'd be gone. Hell, I might never see Hog Boy again.

We climbed into Pete's piece-of-shit pickup that his dad had left him. I took shotgun, forcing Hog Boy to clamber into the open bed with the skateboards and our cooler. He didn't say anything, just shook his head and laughed his Hog Boy laugh before swinging himself up into the back.

Pete managed to get the engine going after just a couple of tries—better than usual—and we pulled away from the shipping dock. The cab of the truck was sweltering. I felt like I was sitting in an oven until the truck got moving and the wind pushed through the open windows. It cooled down a little then, enough to make it bearable, but just barely. The road back to Gypsum is straight and flat, and we watched the town grow larger as we sped toward it.

There it was—all our lives, everything we knew, just days from becoming a ghost town, a memory, a graveyard. And we were driving back toward it. What did that make us? Mourners? Or ghosts?

CHAPTER TWO

LALA

We had been parked in the godforsaken desert for twenty-four hours, and already I thought I would most likely die here.

It was unthinkably hot. Probably it wasn't so bad for the men; they came and went as they pleased, driving into the little town we'd passed for supplies and distraction, but for the women—my mother, my sisters, and me—the heat was oppressive and crushing.

The first day had been the worst. Certainly it was a clever idea; my sister Violeta's husband, Marko, is a clever man. He had heard about the festival the *gazhè* call Burning Man and had learned that it took place not far from Reno, where we travel each year to purchase inventory for our family's used car business.

Marko had explained to my father, who had heard nothing of this "Burning Man," about the kind of *gazhè* who would attend—how fifty *thousand* of them would make their way up this two-lane highway in the desert on their way to a spiritual festival, and how certainly a large number of them would be interested in stopping to have their fortunes told.

Marko was eager that my father should take his advice, and eager that that advice should prove to be solid. He wanted very much to please his new father-in-law, to prove his cleverness.

Because the territory did not already belong to any of the other Roma *kumpànya*, we would be stepping on no one's toes if we left a few days early and earned some extra cash before heading into Reno. We would have to travel several hundred miles out of our way, but if Marko was correct and the *gazhè* were willing to pay, we would be more than adequately compensated for our efforts.

It sounded like a fine idea, as we drove out of perpetually rainy Portland, where we made our home. It sounded like a good idea still as we drove south through the length of Oregon. But now, I felt that no amount of money could make up for the discomfort of living for a week in the mouth of hell.

The river of cars on the highway looked almost like a hallucination brought on by the heat; there was no logical explanation for why so many would want to come here, to this flat, barren land, in the middle of the hottest season.

But Marko was right, and my father was pleased. Many of the drivers, upon seeing our signs, pulled to the side of the road and waited in a line in the heat to have their fortunes told.

Most wanted to hear the same thing—that they would

find love, that they would be transformed, that freedom and joy awaited them just up the road.

We took turns sitting in a tent behind our camp, seeing customers one after the other. Some preferred the cards; others wanted their palms read. It made no difference to me.

The heat was the worst, I suspect, for Violeta. Heavy now in the seventh month of her first pregnancy, the heat had to feel like an even greater punishment to her than it did to me. She is better than I am, though; she complained little.

A great change had come over her since her marriage. Before she was married last year to her Marko, she was slow always with her work and often found a reason to pass it off to me.

Now it seemed she took particular joy in washing the laundry and preparing the evening meal. She wore a smile on her face. Perhaps it was because now the clothes she washed, the foods she prepared, were her husband's.

Maybe too she was particularly happy because unlike most newly wedded Gypsy brides, she was not at the moment under the thumb of her husband's mother. Having paid a bride price of close to twelve thousand dollars for her, naturally Marko's parents were not entirely pleased that Violeta and Marko were traveling with my father's *vitsa* rather than theirs.

Usually a young couple stayed with the groom's parents at least until several children had been born, and for the first few months of their marriage Violeta and Marko had done just that. But Violeta had a temper, and everyone knew that Marko's mother, Clara Nicholas, did, too.

It wasn't very long before the household had been re-arranged and my little sister Anelie and I had been forced to give up our room to Violeta and her groom. Now we slept on the hide-a-bed in the living room, as sharing a room with our brothers would have been unacceptable according to our customs. This was almost a blessing, since Alek was close on thirteen now and bossy, and little Stefan was still terribly spoiled even though he was now almost three and a half, and he had learned from Alek the fine art of acting like a little prince. At least in the living room, Anelie and I could whisper to one another at night.

It was even worse out here in the desert. Here Violeta and Marko traveled with their own little tent, but the family's motor home was far too small to sleep the rest of us. Anelie and I gave up the bunk beds to the boys and slept in the fortune-telling tent, rolling out our mats each night after the final customer had left.

The only town within walking distance—or driving distance, for that matter—lay about three miles behind us. I had been surprised when I'd seen the name of it: Gypsum, Nevada.

I wondered, Might it be a good omen, or bad, that the nearest point of civilization other than the temporary city the crazy *gazhè* had erected on the playa had a name so similar to that of my people?

Gypsum—Gypsy. Of course, among ourselves, most of my people preferred to be called Roma, or Romani. Even more often, we preferred not to be called anything at all, but to blend in. We did not correct teachers in our grammar school when they assumed we were Italian or Mexican; we did not offer our cultural story to the neighborhood children who shared our street but were never invited into our homes.

There was a simple reason for this: most people hate us and distrust us, the Gypsies. Across the world this is true. For some reason most *gazhè* do not know—or perhaps it is more to the point that they do not *care*—about my people's oppression.

In the years I attended public school, up until I was eleven, my real education, the history of my people, I learned only from my family. Inside the walls of the school I never heard a teacher speak of the five hundred years the Roma had spent enslaved throughout much of Europe. No one taught the children in my classroom about Hitler's treatment of my people, how a quarter of a million Gypsies had perished at the hands of his Nazis.

One of my strongest school memories came from my first-grade year. The teacher was pretty, with blond curls. She was unmarried even though she was at least twenty-five or twenty-six. She wore pants like a man but wore a lovely floral perfume as well.

Every day after lunch she would read to us from a book of fairy tales and we children would sit in a semicircle at her feet like obedient puppies. Her name was Miss Cameron. I adored her.

One day she read to us a story titled "The Princess and the Gypsy." I had been so excited to hear it—a story about a Gypsy princess! Perhaps it would be like the stories my mother told us at night.

But the story began at the bedside of the little princess, who looked nothing like any Gypsy I had ever known. Her hair was flaxen, her eyes sky blue.

And the Gypsy was a bent old crone just like the evil queen who gives Snow White the poison apple.

In Miss Cameron's story, the Gypsy stole the princess from her cradle and whisked her away to a drafty, leaky old caravan, where she raised her as her own, training her to pick pockets. The climax of the story occurs when the Gypsy sends the little child into a crowd to steal, but rather than taking coins from pockets as she's been taught to do, she puts flowers in them instead. The king and queen hear about this marvelous child, take one look at her, and realize she is their long-lost daughter. The Gypsy crone, of course, is hauled off to some uncertain—but certainly terrible—fate, never to be heard from again.

The happy queen pictured at the end of the story, reunited with her little princess, looked just like Miss Cameron. The girl in her arms looked nothing like me.

I think that was the day I truly began to understand the difference between *us*—my people—and *them*—the *gazhè* we walked among. It was then that I began to hide.

But there were times when it was to our benefit to play the part the *gazhè* expected of us. This week, for example— lines of people would not be waiting to have their palms read by Italians or Mexicans. They wanted Gypsies, the real thing.

With us they got them. The White family—and the

Nicholas clan, too, Marko's people—both of our families could trace their roots back many generations, to Eastern Europe.

We knew when to blend in, chameleon-like, and we knew when it paid to embrace the stereotype. So today I was dressed the way I should be to impress the *gazhè*: I wore a full skirt with many pockets that came in handy, strappy sandals, and a low-cut white blouse that gapped open when I leaned forward, and my hair, despite the terrible heat, was unbraided and loose.

My hair. Thick, dark waves of it tumbled across my shoulders, down my back, pulling on my scalp, heavy and hot, like a cape I wished I could shed.

I would have liked at least to pull it back into a twist, but each time I tried Violeta pulled it free, admonishing me, "The *gazhè* like to see you with your hair loose. And," she added slyly, "Romeo likes to see it down, too."

Romeo Nicholas—Marko's younger brother, just weeks older than I, and my fiancé. He was traveling with us, too, in the hope that he would learn from my father about buying cars. It had been decided between his father and mine that next month, when I became of legal marriageable age, he and I would wed.

My mother was proud that the bride price I had fetched was fifteen thousand dollars. That was more than any other Gypsy girl in our circle of relatives and friends.

I could not help but feel pride, also, though as the wedding date drew nearer, this pride had become tempered with another sensation, one I did not like to name. The bride price is compensation paid to the bride's family for the loss of her future earning power. At telling fortunes, I was fantastic. The Nicholas family hoped that I would bring a lot of money to their *vìtsa*.

We would share with them, of course, the money Violeta was earning on this little side trip into the desert. And being with her, at least, made me happy. Even in the middle of the desert, Violeta and Anelie were my best friends.

I would feel very sorry for any girl who did not have a sister. I was fortunate to have two—one older, one younger—and I was the bridge between them. I had watched Violeta ahead of me become a woman, become a bride and a wife, and also I had the privilege of guiding Anelie toward womanhood. She was eleven and still just a child, and what pleasure it gave me to watch her giggle and play with the other children.

She did not have much longer to enjoy this freedom. I could tell by the slightest beginning swell of her nipples, visible only when she was undressed, that her womanhood was almost upon her.

And then everything would change.

I sighed and stood up from my place in the shade cast by the tent we'd erected. Hands on the small of my back, I leaned first one way and then the other, enjoying the pleasant sensation of stretching my body.

Mother and Anelie were in the tent with a client. Anelie would be sitting quietly in a corner, unobtrusively watching and learning as I had done for years. Violeta was in the motor home with Stefan trying to get him to eat something—he was irritable because of the heat, as we all were.

Father, Marko, Romeo, and Alek had been gone for close to an hour. Soon they would return with food, and I would begin to prepare dinner.

Romeo, if he was as similar in behavior to Marko as he was in looks, would make a fine husband. And, Violeta liked to tell me, giggling, that I should hope Romeo resembled his brother when it came to lovemaking as well.

I did not want to think about this—not now, not yet. So I reached into the folds of my skirt and extracted my phone.

My family, like all Gypsy families, has very strict rules about what women can and cannot do. Unmarried girls cannot go out unchaperoned. Women cannot have sex outside of marriage. Women must do all the housework, for it is women's work. A woman must not sleep with others when she has her monthly blood, for during this time she is unclean. In very traditional families, like mine, a woman cannot show her legs, but she may show her chest, for the body from the waist up is clean, from the waist down, unclean.

But there are other areas where the rules are less clear. Probably because the rules were made before modern inventions like television, radio, movies, and my favorite possession, my phone, complete with a screen and Internet connectivity.

We can listen to music, we can read what we like, we can interact with others through Facebook, email, and texting—though our parents assume that the people with whom we are speaking are our people.

My parents never told me I *could not* have an email account, or that I *could not* download American books. Of course, it was very likely they didn't know that this was even a possibility. But parents do not need to know everything.

At home in Portland I was rarely truly alone—our house was always full of cousins, aunts, uncles, and friends stopping in to confer with my father, to bring something to my mother. And anyone who entered had to be offered food. So I was often busy preparing for and serving and cleaning up after the guests.

And with only a thin wall separating my bed on the couch from the room where Violeta and her husband nightly renewed their love, even at night I felt not alone.

Perhaps that was another good thing about this trip into the desert. Here there was space—so much of it. I could spread my arms wide and spin and spin and never bump into anyone or anything—if only it wasn't too hot to move. I could crouch in the shadow of the tent and read *The Catcher in the Rye* on the tiny screen.

What a strange boy, that Holden Caulfield. I did not understand him. He had a sister and a brother; that was something to be happy about, even if death had claimed his other brother. And he had parents who seemed to love him. But his family was disjointed like so many *gazhikanò* families are. Perhaps that was his problem.

The book begins when he is at a school far away from his family—a sleepaway school. Right there we know that something is wrong. What kind of a family sends its children away for an education? My people, we understand that the best education is gained from living and working *with* the family.

In the very first chapter Holden says this: "It was that kind of a crazy afternoon, terrifically cold, and no sun out or anything, and you felt like you were disappearing every time you crossed a road."

I read those words and then closed my eyes and tried to create that sensation: *Terrifically cold. No sun out or anything.* I ignored the line of sweat trailing down my back under my hair and pictured in my mind a place that was terrifically cold. Fantastically cold. If I sat still enough I could almost feel it.

And then I considered the next part: *You felt like you were disappearing every time you crossed a road.*

For this, I opened my eyes. In front of me the faded strip of highway broke the desert into two nearly identical sections, running for miles in either direction until it disappeared. Almost without intending to I stood, my skirt billowing about me, and stepped to the edge of the highway. Behind me I heard Stefan beginning to cry and Violeta singing to him an old melody we had been sung ourselves as children.

A faint wind stirred my hair. It felt almost like a hand at my back, urging me forward. To feel like I was disappearing, just by crossing a road . . . to become invisible . . . the possibility of invisibility appealed to me. Always in my life I was seen. Everywhere I was watched, weighed, valued, measured.

I transferred my weight to my right foot, extending my left out over the asphalt.

And then far off in the distance, but growing each second,

came a vehicle from the direction of that broken little town, Gypsum. I hesitated, then brought my left foot back and settled it next to my right.

The horn honked as the car grew closer. It was my father's Jeep, which we had towed behind the motor home.

The men had returned.

"Lala," called Romeo as he hopped down from the backseat of the Jeep. He was handsome; that, no one would argue with. He wore his dark hair combed back from his brow, and his smile seemed to be hiding something, some secret he wished he could tell me. "I brought you fruit," he said, holding out a paper bag.

Happily, I reached for the bag—but Romeo pulled it back, just out of my reach.

"A peach for a peach," he said. "Just a little kiss?"

My breath caught in my throat. I did not know what to say—how to react, where to put my hands or my eyes. I felt like a fool, reaching out for the bag Romeo was withholding.

But my sister saved me. Violeta must have heard him, for she walked up to us and swept the bag from Romeo's hand. "Oh good," she purred. "I have been craving something sweet."

I saw a flare of anger ignite in Romeo's eyes, but he rearranged his mouth into a smile. "Anything for my baby nephew," he said.

"It might be a girl," Violeta said. "I think it is."

"Either way, it will be a beauty like its mother," said

Marko. He swept his arm around Violeta and kissed her, murmuring into her mouth, "I missed you."

I recalled something else that Holden Caulfield said— "You take a girl when she really gets passionate, she just hasn't any brains." Watching my sister swooning in Marko's arms, I made a little silent prayer that I would never be as ridiculous as Violeta.

And then my gaze glanced over to Romeo, watching his brother kissing my sister. I knew with sudden cold clarity that my prayer would be answered.

CHAPTER THREE

I was only home for about ten minutes after Pete dropped me off before I had to get out of there. My mom was up to her elbows in the newspapers she was using to wrap our dishes and Pops was out in our one-car garage separating the tools worth packing up from the rusty saws and loose nails that had hidden for years in the dusty corners. The old motorbike still leaned against the far wall.

It blew my mind that Pops insisted on clearing out the garage so thoroughly. When he was done, there wouldn't be a loose nail or lost drill bit in sight. But it wasn't like he was getting the place ready for new tenants or anything. We were the last family this house was likely to see.

That was just the kind of guy Pops was, I guess. Honest. Hardworking. Full of integrity. My mom liked to tell me and James about Pops back in the early days, back before his years in the gypsum dust had turned his skin chalky and pale, back when he was robust and strong, back before lines were carved in his face like a road map to nowhere.

"I fell in love with your father during the first track meet of freshman year," she told us. "He was faster than any of the other boys—upperclassmen included. But when Bobby Carter tripped over his laces and fell down on the track, it was your father who helped him up. He lost the race that day, but he won my heart."

It was impossible to know if Mom's story was the truth or an insipid morality tale meant to teach me and James that there's more to life than winning. Pops would just smile when she got to talking about his greatness, and I knew from years of trying that no amount of pressure from me would make him confirm or deny her story.

I probably believed the story when I was a kid—maybe until I was twelve or so and running in earnest. After I won three blue ribbons at my first meet, I knew there was no way I would have slowed for Bobby Carter unless he was having a full-on seizure. I would have leapt over him and kept on flying.

Nothing against the Bobby Carters of the world. . . . It's just that you don't earn full rides for dusting off skinned knees. And watching Pops rearrange his garage for the last time, it seemed pretty clear what the long-range outcome of that kind of selflessness was.

I shouldn't blame Pops for what had happened with the mine. It wasn't his fault that the housing market had taken such a dump; how could Pops have predicted what would happen when he linked our lives to the gypsum company all those years ago?

Still, it was anger I felt as I watched him swipe his push broom across the hard-packed dirt floor of the garage. I hated myself for it.

"Hey, where are you going?" my mom called as I let the screen door slam behind me.

I didn't answer. I was already running.

It didn't take long to lap our town. It was basically a rectangle, all the streets perfectly straight and flat. North–south, the streets were numbered: First, Second, Third, and Fourth. That was it. East–west, the streets were all named after flowers—pretty ironic out here in the desert, where anything other than a cactus flower had to be trucked in from a less arid climate and fiercely protected, watered every day all summer long.

There went Apple Blossom, followed by Bluebell, then Crocus followed by Dahlia, and finally Freesia. I guess there aren't any cool flower names that start with E.

My normal run took me over to First Street from our house on Bluebell; from there I ran up to the corner of First and Apple Blossom before I began my grid pattern: down Apple Blossom, right on Fourth, right on Bluebell, left on First, left on Bluebell past our house, and so on, back and forth until I'd weaved my way through the whole town. Most of it was residential—about a hundred and twenty houses—with the few stores and our churches clustered on First Street, which was really just State Highway 447 renamed for the length of the town before it widened again slightly after Freesia. Freesia was home to a couple of small apartment buildings.

People in town were used to seeing me on my runs. Usually they waved at me and called out things like "You're gonna get heat stroke running on a day like this!" But today the few people I did see barely acknowledged me with more than a lift of the chin.

They're just busy arranging their lives into cardboard boxes, I told myself. It's nothing personal.

Still, I felt a twinge. The line was clear—there was me, Ben Stanley, going off to college—and then there was them. The good people of Gypsum. Off to . . . well, nowhere I'd want to go.

On First Street I saw Pete leaning against his truck, waiting outside the Gypsum Store for Melissa to get off work. It was almost six o'clock, quitting time. Pete's hand shot up in a wave. I waved back but didn't break stride.

Pete and I numbered among the seven seniors of Gypsum High's last graduating class. There was Hog Boy, too, and then the four girls—Allison, Becca, Hannah, and Cheyenne. Pete's girl was going to be a junior, so she'd be transferring to a new school in the fall. Her folks were moving her to Reno. I wondered briefly how she'd take the transition from small country school to big city high—and it occurred to me that Pete must be pretty worried, too. Reno High: school population 1,800. That makes about 900 guys. Maybe half of those upperclassmen. Say 450 potential dates for Melissa. I wondered if those numbers were part of the reason Pete had been so itchy with Hog Boy out at the factory today.

I know Cheyenne had done the math when I got my acceptance letter from UCSD. She and I had dated off and on—mostly on, I guess—since sophomore year.

The numbers didn't look good. UCSD's student population made Reno High look like a pond, and I'm pretty sure the fact that it's located in a California beach town didn't make Cheyenne feel any more confident about the chances of the two of us surviving a long-distance relationship.

And honestly, a long-distance relationship—with Cheyenne, with anyone—was the last thing I wanted. What I wanted was to earn my scholarship. I wanted to run hard, I wanted to study hard—I wanted to make UCSD glad they'd handed me a golden ticket. I sure as hell didn't want to end up married and stuck in Reno like I was pretty sure was going to happen to Pete.

So it hadn't been all that hard for me to turn down Cheyenne's suggestion that we "take our relationship to the next level" by sleeping together. Of course I *wanted* to sleep with Cheyenne—what guy wouldn't? She was cute enough, her pretty brown hair smelled good, and she had this way of tilting her head and saying my name like it meant something . . . I don't know, something *great.*

It had been in April that she had asked—"Do you want to do it?"

We were already fooling around. It was at her place, on a Friday night. Her folks had driven into Reno to get supplies at Costco and she was supposed to be watching her little brother Gabe. But he didn't really need watching—the TV and Wii pretty much kept him busy.

We were on her bed, kissing and stuff, and I was hard, really hard, and kind of pushing against her thigh, my hands up under her shirt.

My first reaction was crazy joy—was she kidding? Did I want to do it? It was all I wanted, in that instant, all I had *ever* wanted.

But then I remembered why I'd come over to her house that night in the first place—to tell her my news, my good news, the best news I'd ever gotten. That UCSD wanted me. And I remembered the look she'd given me when I'd told her about it. She'd smiled, but it was flat, not a real smile so much as a quick upward jerk of her lips. Under the smile there was something else—anger, maybe, or jealousy?

And then suddenly it seemed a little suspicious that it was this night, of all the nights we'd been alone together, that Cheyenne finally wanted me, too.

I felt cold then, a little shiver, and my dick went soft and I mumbled something about having to get home.

After that, I was real careful not to be alone with her again.

Sunset in the desert is a beautiful thing. The mountains lose all their dimension; they look like a flat black shadow on the horizon. Above them the sky looks unreal, like spilled paint mixing together, red and orange and blue and gray all swirled and striped. The size of it—all of it, the sky, the mountains, the flat expanse of the desert itself—it does something to me. It makes me feel small, but in a good way. Like whatever happens to me, it doesn't matter so much. No matter how bad I blow it, the desert isn't going anywhere.

I sprinted the last long block, all the way down Freesia, my arms pumping and my hands cutting through the air so fast they felt like a blur. My feet were hitting the ground but I didn't feel them. I felt the burn in my chest, the good, real feeling of a hard run, and I raced against the fading fire in the sky.

I wasn't in a hurry to wake up the next morning. It was Tuesday, which meant we now had six days before we had to vacate. I lay in bed with my pillow over my eyes and listened to the sounds around me.

James was awake already. He and I shared a room, twin beds on opposite walls with a desk separating them, an overcrowded closet stuffed with all our crap. My eyes were still closed, but I could tell from the sound of a heavy box being dragged across the floor that James was moving his shit around.

James. What kind of twelve-year-old boy wants to go by *James*? How about Jim, or Jimmy, or Jim-Bob? Not for my little brother. It had to be James, or he wouldn't answer.

I waited until I heard him open our door and head down the hall to the kitchen before I threw back my sheet and sat up.

I felt kind of angry with myself for spending the last few days I'd be with my family doing my damnedest to avoid them. It wasn't that I wouldn't miss them; I *would*.

Maybe that was the point—maybe I was weaning myself off them.

The smell of bacon got me moving. My stomach rumbled and I shoved my legs into my running shorts and pulled on a gray T-shirt from my side of the closet. I ran my hands through my hair, wondering if it was worth the trouble to get it wet, and decided it probably wasn't.

I picked up my wallet from the desk and looked inside, as if the tooth fairy might have decided to make a midnight visit and shove a few extra bills into it, just for old times' sake. It was as empty as it had been the night before—just my ID and a couple of condoms Mom had given me a few months ago, her eyes appraising me as she said, "Just in case."

I *did* have some money, though; I'd saved every penny I could from my last couple of summers working at the quarry with Pops. It was deposited in the Reno branch of the bank; I didn't make a habit of carrying around any cash. If I did, no doubt Hog Boy would come up with some pretty strong arguments about how we should spend it.

Mom was transferring the bacon from the frying pan to a plate lined with paper towels. There were scrambled eggs, too, and James was buttering bread as it popped out of the toaster. His hair, sandy blond like mine, was neatly combed and parted, freshly trimmed around his ears. I ran my hand again through my own unruly mop and shook my head.

Pops looked up from the newspaper he had spread out on the table, opened to the Help Wanted section. I don't know why, but I looked away kind of fast, like I'd seen something I wasn't supposed to see.

"Hey there, Pops," I said, but my voice sounded overly cheerful, like I was faking it. That's how I felt—like a fake.

"You slept late," he said with a grin. "Getting ready to grow again?"

I shrugged. At six foot one, I was already a couple of inches taller than my dad, so I figured I'd pretty much reached my max, even though some guys grow until they're twenty or something. "Just tired, I guess."

"Maybe you'll have enough energy to help me tear down the old fort before it gets too hot?"

Oh, come on. Was he for real? "Jesus, Pops, are you serious? No one cares if we leave the fort."

I could tell from his expression that he wasn't budging on this one. "It doesn't matter if anyone *else* cares," he said. "The agreement with the mine was that we would leave this property in the same condition it was leased to us in. When we rented the house, there was no fort in the yard. So when we leave next Monday, there will be no fort in the yard."

I sighed and pulled out the chair across from him. James brought the toast to the table. "I'll help you tear it down," he offered, and he sat down, too.

Pops smiled and ruffled James's hair. He didn't seem to notice when James yanked his head away and smoothed his hair back into place. "Atta boy," Pops said. "Way to pitch in."

I poured myself some juice. "All right," I said. "After breakfast."

Mom's bacon and eggs considerably improved my mood.

I slathered three pieces of toast with apple butter and polished them off, too.

"Pops," I said, "you know there are better ways to look for work than the newspaper classifieds."

"Yeah, I know," he said. "But I found my last job in the classifieds, so maybe it's lucky for me."

"How long ago was that?"

He laughed. "Before your time, big man."

"I could help you out," I offered. "You know, post your resume in a few places online, set you up a profile on LinkedIn, stuff like that."

He finished his last piece of bacon and stood up. "You just worry about getting packed for college and shaving a few more seconds off your times," he said. "Your old man can find himself a job."

I'm no actor. The doubt I felt must have shown on my face, because Pops looked pretty irritated as he headed out the door and back to his garage. "Thanks for breakfast, hon," he called back behind him.

Mom hadn't said more than two words all through breakfast. Now I noticed that she'd barely eaten.

"You okay, Mom?" I asked.

Her lips were pinched together in a tight line, but she nodded and faked a smile. "No problem," she said.

At least Mom had a job lined up. She'd been the school nurse up until our school closed in June. That's why they were heading to Reno: a grammar school there had hired her. I think the principal at Gypsum was buddy-buddy with the principal there and had pulled a few strings.

Between her salary and Dad's unemployment checks, they would probably be all right even if it took Pops a while to find a job. But he was the kind of guy who never took a sick day unless he was coughing up a lung, and I couldn't picture him pushing the vacuum and folding laundry while Mom brought home the paycheck.

I was about to offer to do the dishes before tearing down the fort—I guess the bacon had made me feel generous—when I heard Pete's truck rattle up the street and stop in front of the house.

A minute later he and Hog Boy crashed through the door and into the kitchen.

"Hey there, Mrs. S.," said Pete. "It smells good in here. Got any more bacon?"

"Sorry, Pete. It's all gone. Hello, Randall."

"Hi, Mrs. S.," said Hog Boy.

Even most of our teachers had long since forgotten that Hog Boy's real name was Randall. But my mom refused to call him that. She thought it might hurt his feelings. I had tried to explain that to *hurt* Hog Boy's feelings, he'd need to *have* feelings.

"Dude," said Hog Boy, his grin splitting his face, "you've *got* to see this. Out on 447, a couple of miles before the entrance to Burning Man—"

"Randall," interrupted my mom, "I hope you boys aren't spending time out there. All the drugs and alcohol—"

"No, Mrs. S.!" Hog Boy was all wide-eyed innocence now. "I'd never go to Burning Man. It wouldn't, you know, mesh with how my family raised me."

My mom narrowed her eyes. I could tell she wasn't swallowing Hog Boy's bullshit.

I guess he could tell too, because he tacked on, "Besides, we can't afford the tickets."

She nodded, satisfied, and began to clear the table.

"We were out there this morning," Pete said. "You know, just taking a peek to see how the playa looks this year. They say it's the biggest crowd ever. But before we made it out there all the way, we saw this RV pulled over on the side of the road." He lowered his voice as if he didn't want my mom to hear him. "Dude," he said. "There was this chick."

"Oh, yeah?" I laughed. "Was she covered in pink paint Hog Boy?"

"Pink paint?" asked James.

"Never mind," I said.

"Ben, this chick was hot. I mean *smokin'*. Not like a normal chick. You've gotta check her out."

Honestly, I didn't really feel like driving all the way out to the playa just to ogle some girl parked on the side of the road. "I can't," I said. "I've gotta pull down the fort out back. And I haven't started packing or anything."

"You're tearing down the fort?" Pete sounded almost insulted. "*Our* fort?"

"It's not like we've even used it in the last few years," I said, "and we can't pack it up and take it with us." I didn't say the other part of my thought—that we were heading in different directions, anyway.

And thinking about it—tearing the fort into pieces, heading off without Pete and Hog Boy—all of a sudden, maybe it didn't sound like such a terrible idea to drive out on 447 to check out the hot chick the guys were so stoked on.

"Mom," I said, "you mind if I head out for a couple of hours?"

"What about the fort?" James's voice sounded whiny, younger than it should, and inwardly I flinched at the sound of it.

"We'll get to it later," I said.

"We're running out of 'later,'" James called after me as Pete, Hog Boy, and I headed outside.

I felt it, the weight of his words, the pressure of time running out at my back as we climbed into the truck. And driving through town I saw that the exodus of the remaining town residents had kicked up a notch; the McDonalds, both in their sixties, our neighbors right up the street, their Ford F-150 packed to the gills and hitched to an overloaded trailer, were leaving.

Mr. McDonald sat behind the wheel and watched as his wife pulled shut the front door. She turned the key in the lock and then stood there for a minute on the stoop, staring down at the key in her hand as if she didn't know what to do with it. Then she bent down and tucked it under the mat.

Pete idled at the curb as they pulled away. Mr. McDonald rolled down his window and stuck out his hand in a kind of salute. Then they pulled out onto the highway, and we sat for a minute watching their rig shrink into the distance.

I'd known the McDonalds all my life. Mrs. McDonald was the one who had watched me the weekend James was born.

They were heading up to Washington State to be close to their oldest daughter, who'd made them grandparents the year before. Most likely I would never see them again.

It was like a tree that was sick, diseased, and losing its leaves. Just a few at first, one at a time, but soon the disease would grow too strong and all the leaves would turn brown and fall to the ground.

And then the tree would die.

"Fuck it," I said, louder than I meant to. Pete looked at me curiously. "Let's go see your hot piece of tail," I said, and when he pulled out onto the highway the roar of the road through the open windows was loud enough to keep me from thinking anymore.

So they say that Burning Man is a cultural experiment in radical self-expression. They say it functions as a gift economy, and that once you're inside it's not about money. No one is supposed to charge anyone else for anything, and you're not even supposed to barter. You're supposed to show up ready to give to others, just because, without expectations of getting paid back.

This is all bullshit, of course. Having grown up in the desert, I'm smart enough to understand that you don't survive a week on the playa without some pretty serious supplies—water, food, and shelter, to start. Add the cost of all these supplies to the $360 ticket and you figure out pretty quick that Burning Man isn't necessarily as inclusive as the people who run it would like the world to think it is. Not to mention the cost of getting to the middle of our desert. It all adds up.

It's sort of like the Weekend Warriors who spend Monday through Friday at their corporate white-collar jobs and then hop on their fifty-thousand-dollar Harleys to tool around in the foothills. Those guys aren't bikers.

And the Burning Man crowd isn't what they say they are, maybe even what they *think* they are. I'd like to see them survive for a year in Gypsum. Working in the mine, spending every waking moment with the same small group of people, putting up with the damning heat and the painful cold day after day, night after night—and dealing with the *boredom*, the never-ending *sameness* of the desert landscape, the small-town life, the inescapable insularity.

But I guess that wouldn't make for much of a party.

So instead they show up, they have their life-changing festival in the middle of our desert, and then they kick some dirt into the dozens of holes they've dug all across the playa to shit in and go back home to blog about how amazing, how transformative it all is.

Life in the desert *is* transformative. My dad doesn't look anything like the old pictures of him.

About a mile before the entrance to Burning Man, I saw an RV parked on the side of the highway along with a little tent and a big old canvas tent, too. A clothesline was strung up with a few cotton shirts hanging on it. A pretty strange place to set up camp, if you ask me.

Then I saw the sign, a plywood A-frame positioned so

you could read it coming to and going from Burning Man: FORTUNE-TELLING.

Pete slowed his truck and edged off the highway, his wheels sending up a dry cloud of dust.

And then the door of the RV opened, and a girl stepped out.

Pete was saying something, and Hog Boy was rapping his knuckles on the little glass window that separated the truck's bed from the cab, but these sounds didn't mean much to me. All I had room for in my head was the girl—the most beautiful girl I had ever seen.

CHAPTER FOUR

LALA

They came out of the dust of the desert, down the long, flat road that seemed to have no beginning and no end.

I was not watching for them, but their arrival did not surprise me. The three of them came out of the truck—rusted, old, but still straight—each in his own way.

First out was the fat one. He hopped down from his perch in the bed of the truck with a loud snort of a laugh. Later, when I heard the others call him Hog Boy, I wondered if perhaps they were more intuitive than they seemed.

Next came the driver of the truck. He was handsome, very much so . . . tall, with rather narrow shoulders and slim also through the hips. He wore his hair long around his ears and loose across his forehead, which gave him something to do with his hands—brush the hair back in a way that I suspected gathered quite a few female admirers.

His energy was different from that of the boy who rode like livestock in the back of the truck; his eyes held secrets, and pain. My first hope was that I would have the chance to hold his hand palm up between mine and ferret out the secrets he hid within those eyes.

And then I watched, amused by their childish antics, as they yanked open the passenger door and tried, one and then the other, to pull some third, unwilling visitor from his seat.

I could not see the face of this reluctant guest, but still I noticed much that interested me. Neither boy—not even the fat one—could force him from the truck. So he must be strong. And the faces of the other two, the handsome one and the one who resembled swine—they were by turns affable and persuasive, but neither looked angry—whoever was so stubbornly immovable in the cab of the truck was someone they respected, someone each of them loved deeply.

Finally, the handsome boy held his hands up, supplicating, and at last the third boy rose from his seat, closing the truck's door behind him.

Though I was not near them—I stood perhaps thirty feet away, near the door to our motor home, with Violeta beside me—I heard clearly the sound of the metal door slamming shut. It was a sound of finality, of the end of something—or perhaps this was just how I chose to hear it. Perhaps it was just a closing door.

His back was to me. His shoulders were broad and well muscled. An athlete—that was clear. His hair was a mixture of light brown and blond, lightened by the touch of the sun. So he was someone who spent his time out-of-doors, his head uncovered. No helmet, then, required for his sport. The back of his neck was brown from the sun.

When he walked around the front of the truck, flanked by his two companions, the difference between him and them was marked. Though I had thought the other boy handsome, this one, who was clearly full of reticence and did not want to be here, seemed to me like the answer to a question I had not known I'd asked.

Deep inside me, it was as if something was waking and stretching its limbs. Some secret dragon hibernating in my core had been stirred by the presence of this boy.

It was flames I felt, a fire as the dragon yawned. My body felt possessed, overtaken. I heard my words as I spoke to Violeta next to me as if someone else was speaking them—"I will take that one, the one in the center, if they are here for their fortunes."

Violeta laughed quietly, so only I could hear her. "Why not?" she said. "You are not yet Romeo's bride. Be young for a change. Have a little fun."

Always Violeta said to me that I acted much older than my age, teasing and chiding me about my "old soul," as she called it.

I did not look back at her as I stepped forward, smiling. I knew from the expressions on their faces that the way I looked was pleasing to them—why should it not be? I too was young, healthy, full of life.

The fat one ate me up with his eyes, his gaze fondling my breasts, probing my hips as I walked toward them. I paid him no mind. My focus was clear.

Even as I approached the boys, I did not stop watching. I saw the tanned limbs of the center boy, the way the golden hairs on them glistened. He wore a thin T-shirt that read GYPSUM HIGH across the chest in block letters and shorts that left half his thigh exposed along with the length of his calf. For my people the lower body is unclean, but I was glad that the athlete did not cover his legs. I could not help but admire the thick, masculine muscles of them. I noticed his shoes—runner's shoes, a good brand, much too expensive to belong in that rusty truck, in this arid desert. And they were well worn; my eyes did not miss that detail. He double-knotted the laces.

"Welcome," I said. "You come for a reading?"

"No," said the boy in the middle, and my heart saddened before the fat one contradicted him.

"Yeah," he said. "That's what you call telling the future, right? A reading?" He snorted his disbelief.

I raised an eyebrow. "You do not believe, and yet you are here. Why is that?"

"*You* tell *me*." He laughed, pleased with his simple, common joke.

My voice was smooth when I responded. "You bring your friend, the reluctant one. You wish a reading for him, as he is about to begin a journey."

At last, the fat one was out of words. His mouth hung open, his eyes were round and wide.

"How did you know that?" asked the boy with the shaggy hair.

I merely smiled again and gestured with my head for them to follow me into the tent. Violeta, to my annoyance, had preceded us into it and was sitting behind a folding screen, working on her mending. Of course she would not leave me alone with the *gazhè*; always before I had welcomed her presence, but today her company seemed an annoyance.

I sensed the boys behind me. I could tell from the weight of his step that the fat boy had been the first to follow. He was my most ardent believer now, and all I had done was state that which was obvious.

Of *course* his friend was about to embark on a journey. It was not a secret that their town was on the verge of closing; Romeo had told me all about it the day before, after he'd returned from shopping at their little store.

"They walk around like ghosts," he had said, sounding pleased with the predicament these *gazhè* found themselves in. "All of them hooked their wagons to the mine and factory. Now that there is no more money to be made, the rich men who own them are shutting everything down. And everyone must leave."

It did not surprise me that Romeo had seen the *gazhè*'s ill fortune as a testament to our luck, but the smug tone he had taken when he talked about them irritated me. His happiness about another's sadness seemed miserly, as if he believed there was only so much goodness in the world, and that seeing the lack of another's happiness meant there would be somehow more fortune for us to harvest. I understood his satisfaction at their failure, though I did not approve of it and did not echo it in my own heart. The *gazhè* I had encountered had never made my people's welfare a priority, and I know my people largely wanted it that way—separate, never commingling.

50

But these townspeople's exodus from their home saddened me nonetheless. It was true that they were losing a measure of security that we Gypsies had never had in the first place; our families did not reap the benefits of steady salaries and company-provided health care, but neither did we suck at the teat of an unfeeling corporation that might cut us off if the winds of fortune changed.

Our families made our own fortunes, together, and together we tightened our belts when necessary. If one in our family was ill or injured, of course that would not mean less food for him and his children. That is what brothers, sisters, fathers, mothers, cousins, and kin are for—to provide, to buoy one up when one is not strong on his own legs for a period of time.

The *gazhè* are not like us. Each of them feels the whole weight on his back, as if he alone carries the world. Each is alone.

Once inside the tent, I rearranged the chairs so that the three of them could cluster together on one side of the table and I could sit across from them.

Today I wore my favorite skirt: long panels of purple silk, all different hues, radiating out from my waist and pooling at my ankles. Around my waist I had belted a strap of leather and above this wore a cool white cotton blouse, its neckline showing off my throat and the rise of my breasts to their best advantage.

I sat first and watched the three of them in the tent's doorway. The fat one shot forward quickly, an eager student now that I had made a believer of him.

"Hog Boy!" The athlete spoke, angry and embarrassed.

"You do not wish to be here," I said. "But your friends have brought you for a reason. Sometimes to be a friend means to allow others to give to you." I gestured to the chair in the middle.

His eyes glanced at the chair and then darted back and forth between his companions. I could see it there, his desire to bolt conflicting with an urge to do this for his friends, to allow them the pleasure of watching him. And I knew that his sense of duty would outweigh his reluctance.

Still, it took longer than I might have guessed for him to resolve his inner struggle and submit to his friends' whim. At last he crossed the tent's floor and sat himself in the chair across from me.

I had not realized that I had been holding my breath until I released it once he sat. Behind the screen my sister laughed quietly.

"You have money?"

Hog Boy nodded.

"Hang on." The one I had thought was handsome—until I saw his friend—stepped forward, putting his hand on Hog Boy's shoulder. "How much do you charge?"

I shrugged disarmingly. "I request a donation. There is no set fee for a reading."

"Well, how much do people usually . . . donate?"

"It varies greatly," I demurred. "Usually between fifty and a hundred dollars."

Hog Boy whistled. "That's a lot of dough," he said. "We've got twenty-two bucks between us."

"I thought we agreed no more than fifteen," said the boy who was still standing. The athlete closed his eyes and slowly shook his head. I could tell he thought this was quickly going from bad to worse.

"Shut up, Pete," said Hog Boy. He smiled at me magnanimously. "This chick is the real deal. If we're going to give Ben a real send-off, we can't cheap out now."

Ben. His name was Ben.

"Dude," hissed Pete. "I got that money from Melissa."

"Easy come, easy go," said Hog Boy. It seemed to me that for this Hog Boy everything must be like that—easy, someone else's problem.

"You guys don't have to do this," said Ben. His voice was warm. Like honey.

That was when Pete dug into his pocket, retrieving a crumpled-up twenty and a couple of ones. He smoothed them flat before handing them across to me, then sitting down on Ben's left. "Will that be enough?"

I nodded and folded the bills before tucking them into one of the pockets of my skirt. Now I could look at the boy in the middle, Ben—now it was my job to do so.

"Your friends have brought you for a reason," I said. "They want to send you into the world armed with some measure of knowledge. I am here to provide it."

Ben's brows knitted together. Clearly he did not believe that I could provide any such thing; he was not as easily swayed as his fat friend.

"Do you wish the cards, or shall I read your palm?"

He shrugged. "It doesn't matter."

I was about to suggest that he let me read his palm—it would be an excuse to touch him—but Hog Boy said, "Do the cards."

More reason to dislike him. But they could not see my disappointment as I nodded and reached to the table's edge for my Tarot deck, sliding it from its velvet bag.

I began to shuffle the cards. All three boys watched as my fingers turned and splayed the cards, as they arched between my hands and fell one by one into a tight stack again.

"What are those?" asked Pete.

"These are Tarot cards," I answered, passing them back and forth between my hands.

"What do they do?"

"There are many answers to that question," I began. "I like to say that the Tarot allows the Questioner to come into contact with his own unconscious, higher self. The best information, the truest answers, are those we already know. The cards act simply as an aid in seeing oneself—one's past, present, and future—more clearly."

I placed the cards on the table and pushed them across to Ben. He sat still, but with the tightly wound energy of one who is happiest in motion. "Shuffle," I said. "Your own hand will choose your cards."

He looked at the cards and then up at me. Our gaze held for a moment that stretched longer and longer, neither of us looking away. His eyes were blue, but very dark, almost gray.

At last he looked down at the cards. His right hand rose

from his lap and hovered over the deck. Then he tapped the cards and pushed them back to me.

"Do you have a question you would like to address?"

Again, his brow furrowed. This boy was a stranger to me. I did not know him. And yet already there was something in that expression—intense, focused, disarmingly beautiful—that made me wish to know him, made me want to hear his stories.

He shook his head. "No question," he said. "Just—"

But then he stopped. "No question," he said again.

I took up the cards and began to place them, starting with the card on the top of the deck—the Tower—until I had laid out ten cards in all.

"Hey, Ben," said Hog Boy, tapping his thick white finger against one of the cards I had dealt. "That one must be your brother. Check him out—he's got a rainbow flag."

I thought then that there was going to be a fight in my tent. I felt the energy shift, as if all the air in our small, hot space had been sucked out. Ben's body stiffened and I could see even more clearly the athlete in him—a panther, poised to strike, quick and clean and deadly.

But Pete leaned in and muttered, "Take it easy, man," and Hog Boy said, "Jeez, can't take a joke, can you, Stanley?" and soon the boy across from me was a boy once more. It was interesting to watch him, and informative—the way he took measured breaths, in for several counts, then out for just as many, in a way that was forced and unnatural but seemed to calm him.

When peace was reestablished, Ben turned back to the cards. I could tell he wanted to say something, to show that he was in control of himself. What he asked wasn't important to him, but asking it calmly most certainly was.

"Why do you lay them out like that?"

"Do you know anything about Tarot?"

He shook his head. So did Hog Boy and Pete.

"The Tarot is an ancient form of divination. Each card has a meaning, and each place a card is laid has meaning, as well. The same card in two different places would mean two different things. Do you understand?"

All three boys nodded. I waited to see if they would ask a question, and then continued.

"There are seventy-eight cards in a deck." I should begin at the beginning, I decided. And though I usually did not do so much explaining, I felt content to fill extra minutes, extending the time I could sit with Ben across from me. "The deck is composed of two parts—the Major Arcana and the Minor Arcana."

Here Hog Boy cut in. "What's an arcana?"

"An arcana is a secret," I answered. "The Major Arcana—twenty-two cards—tells the story of a journey. The journey of the Fool."

"That's you, Ben," snorted Hog Boy. "The fool going on a journey."

"We are all fools," I corrected. "And each of us takes many journeys. In this reading, you are right, Ben is the Fool"—I tapped on the card in the seventh space, the one that Hog Boy had joked about—"and he is beginning a journey.

"You see," I continued, "each of us begins every journey as a fool—unknowing, stepping out into the void. The Major Arcana tells that story—of the Fool as he travels, developing as he learns and progresses. There are twenty-two cards in the Major Arcana. The final card is called the World."

Ben's reading did not include that card. I shuffled through the remainder of the deck and found it. "Look here," I said, showing the boys. They were all interested now, leaning forward to see the card. It depicted a woman, full of vitality and smiling, one breast bared as she leaped through space, encircled by a wreath of flowers and ribbons, a wand in each hand.

"Her tit's hanging out," said Hog Boy.

Ben elbowed him. I forced myself not to smile. "She has nothing to fear," I said. "She is everything."

I tucked the World back into the deck and set it to the side. "But you did not draw that card," I said. "To continue . . . besides the Major Arcana, there is the Minor Arcana. This will most likely seem familiar to you. It is similar to a traditional deck of cards—four suits, each numbered ace through ten, including its own set of face cards. The numbers are important. The ace represents newness—a new job, a new house, a new way of thinking about things, perhaps. The early numbers—two, three, sometimes four—are still concerned with the beginning stages. The most tumultuous numbers are the middle ones. Nines and tens correspond with endings, both happy and unhappy.

"Each suit also contains face cards. But with Tarot, instead of jacks, kings, and queens, there are Pages, Knights,

Queens, and Kings. When these cards are drawn, they may represent actual people in your life who in some way embody the qualities or characteristics of that suit. For example, the Pages are apprentices, the childlike versions of the energies they represent. Knights are the young, strong, sometimes virile form of the suits. Finally there is the adult female—the Queen—and the adult male—the King—for each of the four suits. Of course, a female card might not necessarily represent a female person. It could be that the person to whom the card refers has a female energy in some way. Nurturing, perhaps, or fiercely protective of those he loves."

Hog Boy looked poised to make another comment here, but he seemed to think better of it and instead opened and closed his mouth like a fish out of water.

I continued. "The suits of the Minor Arcana are not the same as those in a deck of playing cards. We do not see diamonds, spades, hearts, and clubs. The Tarot has its own symbology. In the place of diamonds, we have the Pentacles. These represent the material world—earth, money, shelter, food, work." I tapped on one of the cards in Ben's reading, the Eight of Pentacles.

Pete swallowed hard. "Isn't that symbol . . . ," he said, pointing toward the five-pointed star on the card, "isn't that . . . you know . . . satanic?"

I shook my head firmly. "You are wrong. This is something different. The star represents the four elements—earth, air, fire, and water—crowned by spirit, or, I like to think of it as the four limbs of man, with the highest point representing the head."

He didn't look convinced, but I moved on. "Then there are the Swords. These correspond to the spades, and they are associated with the element of air—those things that are more mental, more abstract than the physical world of the Pentacles, but no less important. Hopes, thoughts, fantasies . . . cunningness as well. The ability to plan and betray."

When I said the word "betray," it seemed that Ben flinched.

"Then there are the Cups. In a regular deck of cards these would be the hearts. And like hearts, the Cups represent emotions . . . feelings . . . romance. Relationships. The element connected to the Cups is water."

"How come?" asked Pete.

"You are in love, are you not?"

He nodded. Hog Boy snickered.

"Then you should know that love, like water, changes its form according to the vessel into which it is poured. Water," I said, "like love, flows into whatever holds it."

Pete seemed to think about this, and he winced a little. I suspected that his love—his Melissa—might be less than overflowing with love when she learned what had become of her twenty-two dollars.

"And finally there are Wands, representing spirit. These correspond to clubs in a deck of playing cards. These we can think of as fire." Here I faltered, thinking of the fire that had been lit in me by one look at this stranger, this fool Ben. I placed this thought to the side and pressed on. "The Wands, like fire, represent creative imagination. Like fire, the Wands act as a catalyst—they can transform others, as fire can turn a tree to ash without itself being changed."

I looked at the cards spread before me. "Ben," I said, "you have not drawn any Wands."

"Is that bad?"

"It is neither bad nor good. It simply is. Are you ready to begin?"

"Wait—" he said. His eyes were difficult for me to read. There was so much in their depths . . . nervousness, perhaps, still some irritation with his friends, and attraction, I thought. "What's your name?"

"My name? Lala. Lala White."

"Lala. That's pretty."

I liked the way my name sounded in his mouth. He said it slowly, like a caress.

"I'm Ben Stanley." He stretched his hand to me, across the cards I had dealt. "Pleased to meet you."

His grip was solid and warm. I looked down, suddenly bashful and unsure of myself. It was not a feeling I was accustomed to. I did not like it.

I took my hand back and placed it in my lap.

The flaps of our tent were not tied shut, and the sudden gust of hot wind that blew in set them to dancing wildly. My hair blew across my face in a tangle of curls, but I ignored it as I rushed to keep the cards in their places on the table. Ben leaned forward too and both our hands reached for the same card—the Lovers—to keep it from blowing away.

Again I looked into the blue-gray eyes of Ben Stanley, and this time the message in them was easy to interpret.

They were like a mirror now into my own secret heart, and I saw twinned in them the desire that grew within me. The wind died down and the tent was silent, and the other boys and my sister waited silently as Ben and I released the card, each of us slowly returning to our seats.

CHAPTER FIVE

I'm not the kind of guy who believes in things. Ask anyone—they'll tell you. It irritated the hell out of my mom when I was little, my unwillingness to believe that some fat fuck came down the chimney each December to drop off presents.

For one thing, our matchbox of a house didn't have a chimney. For another, if some magical guy was going to bring me presents, he sure as shit wouldn't have bought the same crap you can pick up at the Walmart in Reno.

Mom used to say wistfully that there had been a time when I believed, but I don't remember it. My first memories about all that—Santa Claus, the tooth fairy, the Easter bunny—are all about incredulity, about hammering my parents with questions until they were forced to admit that those magical incarnations were really just them.

And that was better, right? I mean, that I had actual, living parents who wanted to give me presents, who wanted to hide plastic eggs full of candy for me? The reality of them seemed to me clearly better than the fantasy of a magical crew of creatures that snuck into my house.

God, too—nope. Not for me. On Sundays most of the families in Gypsum filed into one of the two churches on First Street, but not the Stanleys. I guess my parents, as much as they wanted me to believe in Santa Claus, didn't themselves totally swallow the God thing, because the only time we ever went to church was for Pete's dad's funeral.

Things don't just happen. Things don't magically appear, or disappear, or transfigure. You make things happen through hard work. End of story.

I wasn't a good runner because God was more interested in me being fast than Hog Boy, and it wasn't because of the fancy sneakers Santa Claus put under the tree. I ran fast because of my lucky genetic makeup and I ran fast because I ran hard, and consistently, even when there was something better to do, even when it was too hot to run, even when I hated running.

And yet here I was, wedged between Pete and Hog Boy in a tent that hadn't been here last week on the side of Highway 447, across from a girl who seemed magical to me, who seemed able to look inside my soul.

I couldn't think straight. That was the problem. I couldn't think straight enough to figure out how she knew these things about me, how she seemed to *know* me. She was bewitching me.

I'd never seen anyone like her. As she straightened the cards that had been shifted by the gust of wind, I had a minute just to stare at her without her looking back. Her gaze was on the table and her lashes, long and dark, hid her eyes.

Her hair—a mess of dark curls—had settled since the

wind had stopped, but even so it made her seem like she could take flight at any time. It was wild, tumbling around her shoulders and down her back, and occasionally she tucked a strand of it behind her ear. It would spill forward again, as if even she couldn't control it.

I tried not to look at her chest, but her white shirt split at the neck and I could see the edge of her lace bra—white, like her shirt—and the rise and fall of her breasts as she breathed.

The cards all arranged to her satisfaction, Lala looked up at me. I pulled my gaze up away from her chest, but she smiled a little as if she could read my mind.

Maybe she could. That was why we were here, right? To have my fortune told? Of *course* the guys would bring me here—they knew how I felt about all that mumbo jumbo stuff, and they wanted to see me squirm.

And any other day, in any other situation, I would have refused to play their game. But this girl—she paralyzed me. As long as she wanted me there, across the table from her, there was no way I could move.

Her eyes were almost as dark as her hair. Maybe they were the darkest brown imaginable, or maybe they were black.

"We begin with this first card," she said, tapping a card in the center of the table, one that was half-covered by another. "Here is the situation you find yourself in."

She slid the card from the table and held it up for me to see.

THE TOWER. On it was a tall, spiraling tower jutting up out of a black sea, set against a raging storm. Lightning had struck the top of it and it was on fire. People were jumping from it to their deaths; the base of the tower was ringed with craggy, pointed black rocks. The tower itself was cracking.

"Does this have meaning for you?" Lala asked, and suddenly I felt angry. She couldn't make me say it out loud— that the Tower was our town, Gypsum, and that the people diving to their deaths were my friends and neighbors.

I shook my head, my mouth tight.

"It reminds me of the Twin Towers," Pete piped up. "You know, on 9/11? How all those people jumped out the windows after the terrorists crashed the planes into the buildings? It looks like that."

Yep. It did look like that. But come on. Didn't Pete see how it fit our situation, too—or *his*, anyway? Not mine. I wasn't on that card.

I looked up at Lala. She was watching me with those dark eyes. I was afraid of her for a second—afraid she would tell Pete that he and Hog Boy were the ones in the picture.

She chose her words carefully. "This card is Ben's situation . . . or perhaps more to the point, this card represents how Ben sees his situation, at this point in time. But it is complicated, you see, by this second card. . . ."

She laid the Tower card back on the table and replaced the card that had covered it.

"This is the Crossing Card. Here, Ben, is what is crossing you, what is holding you back, perhaps. The Five of Cups."

This card showed a hooded figure, with a face pale as death, staring down at the ground. Three gold cups lay spilled at his feet, a red liquid—wine or blood?—staining the ground. Behind him was a gray, cloudy sky, a cliff in the distance, a lone bird.

"This figure has lost something," Lala said. "Three cups are emptied into the earth."

My family. There were three of them—Pops, Mom, and James. And there I was, staring down at them, unable to pick them up, to siphon the liquid back into the cups. There was nothing I could do.

"But notice," said Lala, her long, slim finger caressing the card, "what he does not see." She touched two more cups, still standing. "Look," she said. "All is not lost, Ben Stanley. The danger in your situation is to focus too much on what you cannot repair without remembering to preserve that which you still have the power to save."

I hadn't noticed the other two cups until she pointed them out. But their presence didn't make me feel any better. . . . What about the three spilled cups? How could you be happy about what you still had when so much was lost?

Then Lala touched a third card, one that lay directly above the other two. "This is the Crowning Card," she said. "We can see this as an overview, the way your situation looks from a distance."

"Lucky dog," laughed Hog Boy. I laughed, too, and so did Pete. Lala smiled, too. Her smile—the white flash of her teeth—seemed dangerously beautiful. I imagined her teeth on my lips, my neck.

"The Three of Cups," Lala said.

The card showed three pretty girls—one blonde, one brunette, and one redhead—dancing in a meadow, each holding a cup. The sky was blue, and fruit trees bloomed in the background. At their feet were baskets of grapes and apples and plums.

"UCSD," said Pete.

"This is the atmosphere of your situation," said Lala. "Bountiful and joyous. On the surface it seems that you are heading to the land of milk and honey—see, the grass is soft and green, the maidens are happy. It appears that you are going where there is no pain, only good fortune and beauty."

The guys didn't say anything. All three of us were uncomfortable, I guess. We hadn't talked too much about the inequality of our situations, but this was pretty much how I figured they imagined my life in San Diego.

But the card didn't show the early morning runs, the late nights of studying I knew would make up my life if I intended to earn that scholarship for another year. And it didn't show all the work I'd done to earn it for *this* year, either.

"But it won't be like that," I said, almost apologizing. "It's not going to be all sorority girls and partying."

"Are you telling *me* this, or your friends?"

"Fuck you, Stanley," said Hog Boy. "Poor little scholarship boy's gonna have to work so hard. Not that hard, if you ask me, compared to what's in store for me and Petey."

A hot wave of shame washed over me, knocking the fight clear out of me. Hog Boy was right. I wouldn't trade places with them, not for a million dollars.

"It won't change anything." I felt the sting of the lie I spoke.

"Bullshit," said Hog Boy. "It already has." But there was no bitterness in his voice. Just a straight-up statement of fact.

On my other side, Pete shifted uncomfortably. "It's okay, man," he said. "You've earned it. We all know you have."

We sat there for a minute, the three of us with our dicks in our hands, not knowing what to say. Then Lala said, smooth as silk, "Shall we go on?"

I wanted to say, "Fuck you." I wanted to wipe the cards off the table and get out of the fucking tent, but I nodded miserably, as if I deserved this, like a bad boy taking his spanking.

"Next comes the Root of the Matter," she said, tapping a card underneath the first pair.

The Hanged Man, read the card. On it was a man, swinging from one knee upside down from a tree branch, his hands behind his back as if bound, his face corpse white. The same color as my dad's face after a day of work at the mine, coated with a fine layer of gypsum dust.

"Here we find what is really going on at the heart of your situation," said Lala. "Perhaps we see exposed here a secret you have been keeping."

"No secret," I said. "That's my dad."

Lala was still before she spoke. "Bound, helplessly hung, emasculated?"

"The chick doesn't pull any punches," chortled Hog Boy. I just nodded, miserable.

"You see your father as out of options, out of time. His livelihood is gone. His hands are not free to help his family, or even to help himself out of his predicament."

I remembered my father sitting at the breakfast table,

thumbing through the Help Wanted section of the *Reno Gazette*. Hopeless.

"But you see," said Lala, lifting the Hanged Man, "when we invert this card, we find the situation may not be as dire as it may seem."

I blinked. Flipped over, the Hanged Man didn't look imprisoned anymore. One leg crossed over the other, a serene expression on his face, he looked instead to be relaxed, perfectly at ease.

"Sometimes what looks like a hopeless situation to one man can be an escape route to another," Lala said. "It is just a matter of perspective."

I considered that. Could she be right? But no matter which way I tried to manipulate the situation in my mind, Pops was screwed. No, she was wrong with this one—Pops was the Hanged Man, all right.

"What's next?" I asked, wanting to get away from that card as soon as possible.

She gestured to a card to one side of the first pair. "This is the Recent Past," she said. "You have been a busy boy."

It was the Eight of Pentacles. This was clear enough; the number "8" was in a circle at the bottom of the card and it pictured a boy, ten or twelve, working at a table. He was carving a pentacle into a piece of wood. Shavings littered the table and you could tell he'd been working a while; seven other carved pentacles were hung on the wall behind him.

There was a doorway, too, behind him, but he didn't seem to notice the view. He was focused on what was in front of him, his work.

"You see," said Lala, pointing to the green hills, the blue sky and clear lake just outside of his workroom door. "Look at the pleasures of life that this boy—that *you*, Ben Stanley, have turned your back on. So much for a boy to enjoy out there. But not this boy. For this boy there is his work. But see! He wears a smile on his face. For him, his work is a pleasure, too."

I found myself arguing with her. "Even if he likes his work," I said, "look how much he's giving up."

"True," she acknowledged. "And those sunny days, once lost, will not come again. Still, his work will be preserved. And it can be shared with others."

Not like running. That was just for me. I was the only person who gained from it; I couldn't bring James or Hog Boy or Pete along with me to college.

There was movement behind the screen. I'd almost forgotten there was someone else in the tent with us. "Is that your sister?"

Lala looked displeased, as if I'd said something that upset her. "Let us keep our focus on *you*, Ben Stanley."

"Dissed," said Hog Boy. Sometimes I thought he'd look much better with a few missing teeth.

"Next comes your Immediate Future," said Lala, ignoring Hog Boy. She tapped a card on the other side of the first two crossed cards. "Ah, the Page of Cups. Remember, I said these face cards of each suit, along with the Major Arcana cards, could represent actual people in your life?"

The figure on the card she was pointing to wasn't anyone I knew. I shook my head.

"Try not to be so purely literal," Lala urged. "This card can represent a person . . . a child, perhaps, or someone with a childlike nature. Don't you have a sibling?"

How could she know that? "Yeah," I said, "But he's a *brother*. The Page of Cups"—I jabbed my finger at the image—"is a *girl*."

"The gender is not so important," she said.

I felt myself beginning to panic. I knew where this was going, and I didn't like it.

"The person represented by the Page of Cups may be an apprentice of sorts, someone who is just coming into his or her self-realization. Perhaps it is a child who enjoys the arts, someone who is in touch with his or her emotions and imagination. A creative person."

Next to me, Hog Boy was doing his best not to blurt out something stupid. I knew from experience that it was just a matter of time.

Pete picked up the card and looked at it. "What's that in the cup she's holding?"

"It is a bird," said Lala. "It can represent freedom, or joyful self-discovery. Do you see the rays shooting out from the cup, the hopeful colors of the sky? This is a hopeful card. A very happy one, indeed."

Not much happiness that I could figure. Everyone in Gypsum knew that James was a little funny. So he wasn't a cowboy—so what? He was still a *kid*—only twelve. It was too soon for everybody to be whispering about him, labeling him behind his back.

And I'd spent the last five years making sure no one did,

at least not when I was around. I'd been in fights with most of the guys in my high school, including those who graduated years ahead of me, all of them wanting to make smart remarks about James. Only a couple of them made those kinds of comments more than once.

So what if that had earned me a standing appointment with Mrs. Howell, the history teacher who had doubled as our school counselor? She could tell me all she wanted to about the power of positive thought and the benefits of mindful meditation. I'd keep kicking asses as long as it took to keep James safe.

But next fall, when James started up at Archie Clayton Middle School in Reno, I wouldn't be there to protect him. I'd be on the beach in Southern California, working on my tan.

I could feel Hog Boy itching with his comment. We'd better move on before he ran out of self-control, I knew. "So that's me, right?" I asked, tapping on the card closest to Lala's right hand. "The Fool?" This was the card Hog Boy had laughed about earlier; a rainbow of colored ribbons was attached to the backpack the figure carried.

"Yes," said Lala. "Our next card. The Fool. This space in the spread represents the Questioner—that's you, Ben. Remember how I said the cards of the Major Arcana tell the story of a journey? You've chosen the card that corresponds with the beginning of an adventure. See how he steps out, full of hope? There are snowcapped mountains, but they are far in the distance. In this moment all is spring. See the flowers at his feet? And he has a pack on his back and a song on his lips—see the flute? He is off on a grand adventure."

Pete peered closely at the card. "Hey—isn't that the edge of a cliff?"

I looked closer too. It was easy to miss at first—the banner with the card's name, THE FOOL, obscured it—but Pete was right. The guy was just about to dance off the edge of a cliff.

"There is danger in every journey," Lala said. "This card reminds us that even when things may seem rosy and the path appears easy, the road can drop out from beneath us at any time." She leveled me then with her eyes. "Things can change in an instant," she said. "Remember this."

This time she wasn't telling me anything I didn't already know. Things had changed the instant I'd seen her.

The road I had been on—packing my bags, seeing my family begin their new life without me, boarding a bus to UCSD—that road hadn't been complicated. Fraught, maybe, with well-earned guilt, but not complicated.

But the way I was feeling right now, on this uncomfortable little folding chair in this sweltering tent in the middle of the desert . . . *that* was complicated. And it didn't make any sense. How could I feel the way I was feeling right now—like it would be okay with me if I never stood up again, if I just sat here, across from this stranger, for the rest of my life? Hell, even Hog Boy didn't seem as annoying right now, though I would have loved it if somehow he and Pete—and the pregnant chick behind the divider, too—all disappeared.

I wasn't the romantic type. I didn't dance. I'd never given a girl flowers. But something about Lala White made me want to write a fucking sonnet.

"This is you, as well," she said, touching the card above the Fool. And there I was—even though the guy looked nothing like me, I recognized myself.

Seven of Swords. He wore a hooded cape, drawn up to hide his face, and he was clambering over a wall, his arms full of stolen swords. The look on his face mirrored exactly the way I felt about leaving town—sneaky, underhanded, despicable.

He was leaving behind him a cluster of tents. His town—temporary housing, like Gypsum—about to fold. He was out of there.

"He cannot carry it all," said Lala. "Two swords are left behind."

So they were. "But he'd take them if he could," I said. "He'd take it all if he had more hands."

Her gaze was appraising. "Do you think so?" she asked. "Others do, too; the position of this card reveals the Views of Others. Perhaps this card shows not what the man would actually do, but what others in his circle might think of him."

The air around me seemed charged now. Hog Boy kept his fat mouth shut, which told me that Lala had pretty much hit the nail on the head. That was how Hog Boy saw me, and Pete, too? A thief in the night, sneaking away?

Well, that wasn't so different from how I saw myself.

"Keep it moving," I said, miserable.

"Holy shit," said Hog Boy. "Check out the fur burger on that one!"

No inner monologue. That was Hog Boy's problem. One of them, anyway. He was looking at the card above the Seven of Swords; this one was labeled *The Lovers*. He was right; the pubic hair on the naked woman was something fierce.

The only naked girls I'd seen had been in magazines and on a couple of pornos that Hog Boy had downloaded. None of them looked like this chick. They were all waxed and shaved until they were practically bald down there, and all of them had big, hard, round boobs. The girl on this card looked healthy—her breasts were round but not huge, her thighs touched at the top, meeting at a dark triangle of hair.

With a start I realized she looked like Lala—dark eyes, full pink lips, superlong black hair. And a red flush climbed up my neck as I looked at the naked guy pictured next to her—he could have been me. Blond, muscled, taller than the girl beside him. They stood together under a tree. She held a moon in her outstretched hand, he held the sun. Their other arms were wrapped around each other.

When Lala spoke her voice was even, nothing like I felt inside. "This card represents your Hopes and Fears," she said. "It can refer to a decision you must make, one which may define who you ultimately become on this journey. This card tells you to look carefully at your options—to not be hasty in your decisions."

"But"—I couldn't stop myself from asking—"this is one of those major cards, right?"

She nodded. "Yes, the Major Arcana. . . ."

"And didn't you say that the Major Arcana . . . that the cards in it can, you know, represent actual *people*, too?"

Lala looked at me as if she was considering something. Her head was cocked slightly to the side. A wisp of hair was caught in the corner of her mouth. It took all my effort not to reach across the table and stroke that curl back away from her face.

"It can," she said, "if you wish it. You are the Questioner—as I said, you determine meaning. But"—her hand touched the final card. This one needed no interpretation. It was a heart, bloodred, stabbed through by three swords. Rain darkened the landscape behind it. "This card represents the Final Outcome. Your path—depending on the path you choose—may not end the way you would will it to."

And as I sat staring at that final card, that bloody, betrayed heart, I found myself questioning everything. Could it be true—might there be magic in this world, in this tent, in this girl across from me? Because it seemed that she knew things about me—about my life, my fears, my desires—that no one else should know. And I made a decision then, as I looked back and forth between the Lovers and the Three of Swords.

It didn't matter what I had thought before about fate, about God, about magic. Lala White had appeared in the desert for a reason. She was meant for me.

No matter what the cost.

CHAPTER SIX

LALA

It seemed to me that Ben Stanley did not want to leave the tent after his reading was complete. I gathered up the cards, tapping them into a neat stack and then sliding them into their small velvet bag. I cinched the cord tight and tied a knot. The table was cleared; the cards were put away; our time together was over.

Yet still he sat across from me, his blue-gray eyes stormy with some emotion, one I could clearly read yet hesitated to put into words, even in my own mind.

The other two—Pete and Hog Boy—slid back their chairs and rose, but they did not leave the tent. It was as if they were unsure what moves to make without first watching to see what Ben would do.

I saw this too among my own people, this looking to a leader to determine which course of action to take. In my family, and in my *kumpànya* as well, it was to my father, Mickey White, that people turned for guidance. My father was the *rom barò* of our *kumpànya*. Probably to the *gazhè* he would seem something of a king, but actually his was an elected position, decided upon by a council of elders.

And they did not choose him blindly, just as these boys in my tent did not look to Ben Stanley for leadership without good cause. A *rom barò*—literally, a "big man"—is chosen for a combination of qualities: He should be wise and experienced, and, of course, clever as well. My father was all of these things, and my people listened gladly to his counsel.

Hog Boy and Pete had chosen well to follow Ben Stanley, I thought. After all, which of the three of them had earned a way out of their failing town, which of these three had an open door in front of him? He was too young still to be considered truly wise, and I gauged by the way he looked at me—desire tinged with flustered embarrassment—that his experience, at least with girls, was not wide. But he seemed clever, and something else—perhaps something I would consider more important than any of these three qualities, though my father Mickey White would disagree, I knew— Ben Stanley was kind.

I knew this was the truth because of the way he tolerated his obnoxious friend. I could read his kindness in his dismay over leaving his family. His kindness infused his desire to be good, good enough for everybody.

Romeo Nicholas would never be *rom barò*. He had some qualities, too, that might recommend him for leadership . . . but he did not have the makings of a wise man, not even if he was blessed with a hundred years to add to his eighteen. Wisdom, as they say, was not in the cards for Romeo Nicholas.

And yet soon I would be expected to follow him. He

would be my husband, and I would be his wife. He would lead me first to the wedding bed, and when I rose from it after the consummation of our marriage, I would be bound to follow him.

And because I was the daughter of Mickey White, it was that much more necessary that my purity be unquestioned. Never before had that felt like a burden to me; I had been in no hurry to touch a boy before I laid my eyes on Ben Stanley, nor in a hurry to be touched by one. The sounds of lovemaking I could hear coming from Violeta and Marko's room seemed to me like something from another language, one I did not speak, one I was in no rush to learn.

But Ben Stanley's appearance in my tent—his gray-blue eyes, his muscular, golden thighs, his gaze upon my face, mingled lust and confusion—these had started a reaction inside me, and the fire I felt raged brighter and hotter with each second we sat across from each other.

More deeply than I ever had before, I understood the meaning of my people's word *marimè*. Not just dirty, but spiritually unclean—tainted.

I wanted now for the boys to leave. Yet still Ben sat in his chair, as if he waited for something more to happen.

At last I rose. "I wish you luck, Ben Stanley, and safe travels."

His brow furrowed. This was not what he wanted—a dismissal. He stood, though. "Thank you," he said. He seemed to consider his next move, and then he motioned with his chin to his friends. They seemed to understand his meaning, for they left the tent.

I heard Hog Boy clearly as he said to Pete, "Ben's gonna try to score with the Gypsy chick!" Apparently he suffered under the misconception that canvas acted as a sound barrier.

Ben managed to ignore his friend's comment. He took two steps toward me, around the table. Up close like this it was clear how much taller he was; I am not a big person, just a few inches more than five feet, and standing so close to me Ben looked almost larger than life, filling the tent with his presence.

I heard my sister behind the screen, shifting her weight and clearing her throat. My sister could be silent, when she wanted to be. Clearly, now she wanted me to hear her. I understood her meaning: Get rid of the *gazhò*.

"Lala," Ben said, and his voice seemed to ache with some of the same fire I felt inside of me. "Thank you for the reading—"

He was about to say more, and it did not take magic fortune-telling skills to see where he was heading. But I intercepted him, cutting him off. "Do not thank me," I said. "Thank your friends, who brought you here."

"Yeah," he said. "Them. I'll thank them later. But first—I wanted to ask you—is there any way I could see you again? Maybe we could go out . . . maybe I could drive you into Reno to see a movie, or get a cup of coffee?"

There were of course things I wanted from life. I wanted someday to hold a baby in my arms, to press him to my breast and smell the particular scent that marks a woman's baby as *her own,* and no one else's.

I wanted to see my little sister grow into a woman.

I wanted to read all the books in the world, tasting them one at a time like fine chocolates.

I wanted to make my parents proud.

There were other things I wanted, too, though I kept these hidden from my family and turned my own mind away from them as well, as best I could. These desires did not matter—they could never be acted upon.

But never once in all my years had I wanted to date a *gazhò*.

Why would I? They are not like us; they do not understand the bonds that tie my people together, unseen but potent bonds of tradition, story, and shared suffering. They do not know our hearts; I had always believed that they *could not* know our hearts, even if we tried to share them.

I had watched their movies, their silly romantic comedies in which each heroine found as if by magic the one true love that was out there, as if created especially just for her, as she struggled and suffered and ultimately triumphed, as their faces came together in a perfect kiss, his hand tangling in the hair at the nape of her neck, her eyes closing, her face tilting, trusting, up to his.

And I had always known that it was not for me. That life was not my life. I was the daughter of the *rom barò*. I was the intended bride of Romeo Nicholas, son of Harold Nicholas, younger brother to Marko Nicholas.

I was marked, and not for this.

So why did it feel like something inside me was breaking as I arranged my face into a cold mask, as I told Ben Stanley with my eyes, with the thrust of my chin and the set of my shoulders, that what he wanted would never be?

"I do not like movies," I lied smoothly. "And I do not drink coffee."

His smile slowly slipped away as my refusal sank in. It occurred to me that Ben Stanley was not used to hearing "no" from girls.

"Oh," he said. "I see."

"Good luck on your journey," I said again.

I thought that he might try again. But though he looked deeply into my eyes, so intimately that I felt my cheeks flush, he finally nodded and turned away.

I paid for my refusal, though Ben Stanley did not see the cost of it on my face. As always my features were smooth, unreadable. My job was twofold: to read every secret on the faces of my clients, and to hide all of mine deep within.

I knew everything about Ben Stanley. I knew about his guilt. I had seen his fear and confusion about his brother. I saw how he felt about his father—ashamed, angry, and yet at the same time full of love. I saw how he treated his friends, and how highly he valued those friendships. I felt that I knew him down to the roots of his soul, though we had spent less than thirty minutes inside my tent. If I knew him another thirty years, I doubted that he could surprise me. Yet still it pained me to watch him walk away, to see him duck his head through the canvas slit as he went back into the heat of the desert.

I forced myself to stand very, very still, and I practiced the same measured breaths that I had observed Ben taking.

I let my gaze soften and stared at nothing in particular. I heard the dual slams of truck doors closing; then I heard Pete's engine hiccup to a start, and then I heard them driving away from me. All of this took eight even breaths. By the eleventh I could no longer hear the rumble of the truck. They were gone.

"That was a lovely reading you gave," said Violeta. She stood now, from her place behind the screen, wincing a little as she shifted her weight to her feet, her hand massaging her lower back. "No wonder your bride price is so high. You truly are magic, my little sister."

I forced myself to smile and kept my voice light. "The *gazhò* made it easy," I said. "He showed so much."

Of course Violeta was not fooled by my tone. She too was an expert in reading signs. Even heavy with pregnancy she moved gracefully as she halved the distance between us. "You liked the *gazhò*."

She knew, yet still I lied. "Don't be silly," I said. "I hardly noticed him."

"Ha!" she laughed. "Like a mare in heat, you were."

Now I felt the anger rising in me and I welcomed it. Somewhere else to channel the fire Ben's presence had awakened inside of me. "You know nothing," I said, stepping toward her. "You are a fool."

Violeta's laugh was like bells. Despite my venom she was nothing but amused. "I know what I am," she answered. "And I know the smell of desire. You burn for that boy. I can see it plain as day, though you would hide it from me."

It was the way she said it—*"You burn for that boy"*—that

caused me to drop my guard. It was exactly right. Perfectly true. I did burn for him.

She saw the change on my face and she smiled, triumphant. "I knew it."

"How could you tell? Do you think he saw it, too?"

Violeta was dismissive. "No, of course not. You think a *gazhikanò* boy could know your secrets, unless you told them to him? But I know, because I have felt the same fire."

"Do you mean . . . you've felt an attraction to a *gazhò*?"

Her nose wrinkled with distaste. "Of course not, don't be ridiculous. My Marko is the only man who has moved me in that way."

She saw the disappointment on my face, for she rushed on. "You were right to stop the *gazhikanò* boy. It would maybe have been better if you had suggested he come back for another reading . . . perhaps with more money. . . ." But then Violeta shook her head. "No. I can see that would not have worked for you. The pull you feel to him, it is too strong. Better, then, not to see him again." She embraced me, the hard mound of her belly between us. "Do not worry, sister," she soothed. "Soon enough, Romeo will tend to your fire."

A shiver went through me, despite the heat, and I felt cold inside.

The evenings in the desert cooled nicely, so we spent them out-of-doors. In our family the division of labor was clear—the women cooked, cleaned, and looked after the children. The men did not.

I imagine for girls not raised among our people, this might be a source of frustration, this inequity of labor. For

84

me, it had never been an issue. It simply was the way things were. Is there reason to be frustrated because the sky is blue instead of green?

Perhaps it was the heat in the desert that made me irritated on this night. Perhaps it was that I had been reading many books lately, exploring worlds other than my own. Perhaps it was that my thoughts turned to the face of Ben Stanley, a place where they should not go.

My mother was giving Stefan a bath in the inflatable baby pool. He laughed and splashed, rolling onto his stomach and kicking to show off what a good swimmer he had become.

"Oh, my, what a strong man you are!" my mother crooned at him. Violeta stood nearby, watching our little brother with new eyes. All her life she had helped to care for children. Although I was just eighteen months younger than Violeta and she had never assisted in bathing or feeding me, both she and I had tended to the needs of Alek, Anelie, and Stefan. And at times Violeta had complained something fierce about our chores.

But now, with a baby of her own soon to arrive, she watched our mother and Stefan as if she was glimpsing her future. Marko stood behind her, his arms wound around her belly, fingers splayed across it. He too watched and chuckled as Stefan played in the water. And when he stood up in the shallow pool, arching his back so that he could pee outside the water onto the hard dirt ground, Marko threw back his head and laughed, delighted.

My father and Romeo were working on repairing a hubcap, Romeo holding it steady while my father hammered out the dents. They worked well together, Romeo anticipating my father's every move and adjusting the hubcap before my father even told him what to do.

We had told fewer fortunes since the weekend had ended; Marko assured us that it was worthwhile for us to wait the five days for the Burning Man festival to conclude up the road. Just as the revelers had wanted their fortunes read on their way into the encampment, so would many stop to visit upon exiting.

Ben Stanley's visit had been one of just a few readings that day, and truly it was all I could think about. I could not stop my mind from turning to the pattern of the cards he had drawn. It was my job to help my customers find connections in the cards that turned up on the table, but oftentimes I found myself stretching to make everything fit together. That, I think, is what makes me so good at what I do: I think quickly, I ferret out information from my customers that make sense of the cards. The *gazhè* pay well for being told what they want to hear.

But today's reading had been different. Or perhaps what had been different today was not the cards, but rather myself.

I finished drying the dishes and carried them into the motor home to put them away. Alek was sitting at the little table playing on his Nintendo DS. He did not look up as I came in. The tinny sound of his game grated on my nerves.

At last my work was done. I took from my pocket the twenty-two dollars that Pete and Hog Boy had paid me and added it to the billfold where my father kept the money.

It was bulging already; we would pay for the cars in Reno with cash, and our fortune-telling had added substantially to the money we had brought. I had told Ben Stanley and his friends that people usually pay fifty to a hundred dollars for a reading. This of course was not true, but I knew from long experience that they would feel the reading was more valuable if they thought they were getting a bargain. Somewhere in the back of my mind I wondered if Pete's Melissa was angry with him for spending all her money.

Then I unplugged my phone from where it had been charging near the dashboard.

"Nice talking with you, Alek," I said over my shoulder as I left.

He just grunted, eyes riveted to the tiny screen in his hands.

Even in the few minutes I'd been inside, the night had cooled significantly.

Mother held Stefan wrapped in a towel on her lap and Violeta sat beside her. My father and Marko were smoking. Romeo was just pulling his guitar from its case, tuning it.

"Lala," he called. "Come listen to this song I am working on. It is for our wedding."

"Later," I answered. "I want to rest alone for a little while. It quiets my mind."

He called after me but I pretended I could not hear him over the roar of a passing truck. I went around the side of our tent and sat cross-legged on the ground behind it. My phone was in my hands, but I did not look at it.

Instead I looked out at the flat expanse of the desert.

And my thoughts turned to my wedding, which grew closer with each passing day.

We were to be wed on the twenty-third of September, the day after my eighteenth birthday. Traditionally my people elected to marry their children even younger, but the state of Oregon requires that those under eighteen get their parents' written consent, and my parents preferred—like many Gypsy people—to avoid unnecessary interactions with the authorities.

Violeta too had been married within a week of her eighteenth birthday. Her wedding was beautiful. It had cost a small fortune and our people had traveled, some quite far, to attend. I was the maid of honor. Romeo was the best man. All through the reception everyone came up to us, kissing us and saying, "You two will be next!" It was no secret that Romeo and I had been promised to each other for years.

This had not bothered me before, when the date of the wedding had seemed so far off. It had seemed . . . comfortable, I suppose, to know that my future had been well planned by the people who loved me and knew me the best, my family. And to marry the brother of my sister's husband—this would guarantee that I could always be close with Violeta. But recently my feelings had changed, though I was loath to admit this even to myself. When my thoughts turned to the impending wedding, I felt my heart thrumming hard like a caged bird.

I did not want to think about it anymore. I tried not to listen as Romeo strummed the first notes of his song, but the sweet strains of his music were inescapable. Tears I could not explain filled my eyes.

I pressed the button on my phone, bringing up the book I was reading, *The Catcher in the Rye*. I had read it before, but sometimes I liked to reread books that touched me in a way I did not fully understand. It was like this with people, too; I was drawn to those who seemed complex, whose motivations were unclear, whose desires were complicated.

So why did I think again and again of Ben Stanley? He seemed no mystery to me. An average boy, more handsome than most, this was true, but not special in any way I could see. I understood his desires and motivations—for one thing, he desired the press of my flesh. That had been easy to read in his blue-gray eyes. I smiled to myself, remembering the way he had looked at me.

And he wanted to make his family proud. This I could understand as well. I too wanted to please my family. I worked hard to be good at the things that were of value to them— learning to cook and keep house, watching my mother as she told clients their fortunes. And I avoided showing them the parts of myself that they might not approve of; I did not discuss the books I read, assuming that it would bother them— especially my father—that I derived such pleasure from the *gazhikanò* writers.

Perhaps there was something more to Ben Stanley, something that was not so easy to see but that my subconscious recognized as interesting, complex. Maybe this was why my thoughts had returned to him, again and again, all through dinner, when I should have had my focus on my parents, my siblings, and my future husband.

Or perhaps I was fooling myself. Maybe there was nothing deep about the *gazhò*'s pull on me. Maybe it was simply lust that drew me to him. For the attraction I felt was undeniable.

I shook my head. Unable to really concentrate on the words, I thumbed through the familiar text. Perhaps I was as bad as Alek, filling my time with images on a screen. Was his video game really any worse than this story of a spoilt *gazhò*?

I came upon the quote that explained the novel's unusual name. Holden Caulfield was speaking with his sister, Phoebe, telling her what he wanted to become.

He says to her, "You know that song, 'If a body catch a body comin' through the rye'?"

And Phoebe tells him, "It's 'If a body *meet* a body coming through the rye'! It's a poem. By Robert Burns."

Then Holden Caulfield explains what he would like to do: Stand in a field of rye near the edge of a cliff and keep the children playing in the rye from falling over. It made a pretty picture, a boy standing near a cliff's edge, the wind swaying the tall rye grass, and laughing children protected by his spread arms.

This image in my mind made me recall Ben Stanley's reading. I thought of him—the Fool—dancing merrily along the path, about to tumble off the edge of the cliff. And I saw in my mind's eye, as if in a dream, myself, a catcher of fools, coming out from somewhere and saving him—pulling him back from the precipice, turning him away.

But in my daydream it was not just safety I turned him toward. Instead, I turned him toward myself. I imagined him realizing what I had done for him, looking down at me with grateful eyes and his arms encircling my waist and his mouth slanting across mine, and our lips meeting in a kiss, a first kiss that fed the fire inside me.

I played with this image for a while, lingering on the idea of Ben's kiss. It would be soft, I felt, tender and gentle.

An alarm went off in my brain. To imagine myself kissing the *gazhò*—what was wrong with me? Reluctantly, I forced myself away from the thought of Ben's kiss. Instead I focused on the thought of the cliff. What if *I* were the one about to step over the precipice? Only I would not be blind, unaware. In a way I was heading there, every day, as my wedding day drew closer. The difference was only that I knew what I was stepping toward, where my path was leading.

Who would be there for me? Who would be my catcher in the rye?

The answer was clear. No one. There was no catcher in the rye for me, no one waiting to pull me back from the precipice over which childhood inevitably falls. Only there were people pushing me, urging me forward over that steep drop—my parents, Violeta, Romeo—all of them were waiting, eagerly, to see me fall.

CHAPTER SEVEN

BEN

"That chick was fucking hot," said Hog Boy. "But she scared the shit out of me."

We were standing around in front of the Gypsum Store, waiting for Melissa to get off work. Pete wanted me there for moral support when he told her what he'd done with the money; Hog Boy stuck around to watch Pete squirm.

"What'd you think about the reading?" Pete looked eager, as if he was at least hoping Melissa's money wasn't pissed away on nothing.

"It was pretty weird," I admitted. "I mean, you know I'm a skeptic, but she seemed to know all kinds of stuff."

"Who cares what she *said?*" said Hog Boy. "It was worth the twenty-two bucks just to stare down her shirt for half an hour."

I fought down the urge to smack the side of his head. It didn't make any sense for me to feel protective of Lala; I'd barely met her, and she sure had shot me down when I asked her out. But I didn't like the thought of Hog Boy's sick mind lingering on her.

"Yeah," said Pete miserably. "Listen, Hog Boy, don't mention anything to Melissa about how hot she was, okay? She's going to be mad enough as it is. I don't want her to get all jealous, too." He started chewing on his lip, imaging Melissa's reaction if Hog Boy started describing the girl who had her money.

"Hey, Pete," said Hog Boy. "Lemme borrow your truck tonight."

"No way," Pete answered. Then, "What for?"

"I'm thinking maybe the reason the Gypsy chick turned down our boy Ben is that she was hoping—you know, maybe she's hungry for a big, thick pork sausage." He rolled his hips, thrusting them into the air.

"I don't think so, Hog Boy," laughed Pete. "You saw the way she kept eyeing Ben—even if she did turn him down."

I tried my best to sound casual. "What do you mean, eyeing me?"

Hog Boy guffawed. "No way, Pete. She was just doing her job. You know—like how a stripper flirts with all the guys in her place, and the more dollars you put on the table, the more into you she gets."

"Lala was nothing like a stripper."

Pete heard it—the tone in my voice. Hog Boy was either oblivious or baiting me, because he said, "Wish she *was* a stripper. I'd be willing to lay down some serious cash to see—"

I didn't know what he was going to say next. Nothing good. But I didn't wait to hear it. My hand shot out and connected with his nose—*pop*, just like that.

One thing about Hog Boy—he's an easy bleeder. Didn't take more than a tap to get the blood flowing.

"Fuck you, Ben," he said, tilting his head back to control the bleeding. He grabbed the hem of his shirt and pushed it against his nose. "This was a new shirt, too. I'm out of here."

He half stumbled down the street, not really watching where he was going. I smiled grimly at his retreating back.

"Don't you think that was a little harsh? I mean, not that Hog Boy doesn't deserve it. But over a girl you don't even know?"

I shrugged. "I don't know, man. I just couldn't stand it—hearing him talk about her like that. Knowing that he was *thinking* about her."

Pete's appraising gaze made me uncomfortable. After a minute he whistled. "Man, you've got it bad."

I didn't bother denying it. "Pretty lame, huh? Less than a week before I leave the state, and I fall for a girl who'll only talk to me if I'm paying her. Wrong place, wrong time, wrong girl."

"Can't you just, I don't know, channel some of that energy toward Cheyenne? I'm pretty sure she would take you back, even if you do have one foot out the door."

"Yeah, maybe," I said vaguely. I hadn't ever told him or Hog Boy what had happened with Cheyenne—how she'd wanted to sleep with me, how I'd balked and run.

"We could go on a double date this weekend before we all leave town," said Pete. He sounded hopeful now, making plans. "Maybe I could borrow my mom's Taurus and we could go into Reno for a pizza."

I considered saying yes. Not because I wanted to—an evening with Cheyenne, after the way things had gone down, sounded like torture—but because it would make Pete happy. It was something I could do for him, like a gift. Didn't I owe him that—a gift? It was something he wanted, something I had the power to give to him.

But then some inner part of me remembered the way Lala smelled—like cinnamon and ripe oranges—and I shook my head.

"Nah, man."

Pete looked disappointed, but he didn't put up a fight. He just nodded and kicked at the dust on the sidewalk.

I felt like I should explain. "Listen," I said. "You know how it is—with you and Melissa?"

He nodded. We all knew how crazy Pete was for her.

"Well, I don't know why, but it's like that. There's something . . . I don't know, something *great* about that girl. I want to find out what it is."

Pete laughed a little, but not in a mean way. He patted me on the back, friendly-like. "You've got it bad," he said again.

I stuck around just long enough to make sure that Melissa wasn't going to carve Pete a new one over the twenty-two dollars. Pete made it sound like a joke—getting my fortune read—and when Melissa asked what the fortune-teller looked like, Pete lied his ass off. I was a good enough friend not to bust him on it.

Then I wandered home, taking the long way around the town's perimeter, jogging real slow, barely faster than a walk, just to burn off some steam.

Lala, Lala, Lala. Each pace I took fell into the rhythm of her name.

Okay, sure, part of the attraction was the way she looked. Her eyes, edged with those thick black lashes, looking up at me like there was something more she wanted to say. Pete thought she had been eyeing me. I wondered what she saw when she looked at me.

I glanced down at the clothes I was wearing. A stupid Gypsum High T—that would mark me as a small-towner, nothing real sexy about that. And my running shorts. Great. Just what girls like.

But for a minute I indulged my fantasy. What if she *did* like the way I looked? Most girls did—that had never been my problem. But then why had she turned me down? Maybe I wasn't her type.

She wasn't *my* type, that was for sure. I guess I'd always liked the look of real athletic girls, tall ones with long, lean legs and small, tight breasts. The girls who caught my eye when we cruised the mall in Reno pulled their hair up in high ponytails and wore skinny little jeans and tank tops. They painted their nails the color of cotton candy, and their mouths, too.

Lala wasn't like any girl I'd ever met before. She was almost like a mirage, it was so clear that she didn't belong out here in the desert. I wondered where she was from. She didn't speak with an accent, but she seemed foreign somehow. And she was all curves and softness—her hair, the thick, dark ringlets of it, her breasts cresting out of that white lace bra, her little waist and then her hips, like a curvy vase.

But that wasn't all of it, the way she looked wasn't the whole attraction. It was some of it, undoubtedly, but it wasn't just that, how she looked, the way she smelled.

Her eyes—they weren't soft. Not even a little. They were hard, shiny onyx. They saw everything but showed nothing. Even though she looked about my age, she acted way older, and like she knew everything there was to know—about me, about everything. I wanted to know everything too, everything about *her*. I wanted to hear her story, and I wanted to be the guy to soften that steely gaze.

I was running hard now, even though I hadn't intended to. My arms were tight at my sides, slicing through the air, and I sprinted right past my house. I felt the familiar burning in my lungs and down the backs of my thighs as I pushed myself even faster, going an extra block and trying to forget about Lala for a minute, pouring everything into my running.

It worked—for half a block my mind was clear at last as I forced myself to go even faster. All my focus went to my feet hitting the ground, my breaths in and out. And then I crossed the imaginary finish line I'd set for myself, and I slowed back to a jog, then, at last, to a walk.

I felt good. Emptied out. Clear. Running did that for me.

It was the counselor, Mrs. Howell, who'd suggested it— channeling my anger into my running. During freshman year, after I'd sat with an ice pack against my swollen eye from a fight with Chad Harrison, a senior. I'd had my ass handed to me, but I did get in a couple of good hits.

"You've got a real talent, Ben, and a shot at something big," she'd chastised me. "But you're going to screw it all up if you can't learn to control your anger." I guess I sort of became her pet psychology project—not that I wasn't grateful for it. Probably, without her help, my school record would have been too riddled with fights and suspensions resulting from fights for UCSD to give a rat's ass about my running times.

When I rounded the corner back onto our block I heard James banging around back by the fort. It sounded like he was trying to take it apart single-handedly.

Guilt. I remembered that I'd promised to help him tear down the fort that afternoon. Now the sun was getting ready to set, and we hadn't even started. I imagined how the day had probably gone—my little brother waiting patiently for me at the kitchen table, his hands folded in that peculiar way of his, with the thumbs crossed, too. How long would he have sat there before he figured out that I'd forgotten about him?

I peeked over the fence and watched him for a minute. He was in his own little world, methodically swinging Dad's heaviest mallet again and again against the side of the fort. His swings weren't hard; it was more like he was measuring time than really trying to do any serious demolition.

In the desert, wood dries out pretty quick. Really, it was

sort of a miracle that the fort hadn't collapsed already, over the years.

James wasn't dressed for manual labor. Was he ever? His shorts were plaid cotton, neatly pleated down the front. He wore a T-shirt like any other twelve-year-old, but somehow he managed to make it look formal. And his shoes were these ridiculous leather Jesus sandals he had *needed* to have. They were the dumbest-looking shoes I had ever seen in my life. He'd found them online somewhere and had bullied Mom for three straight weeks until she finally ordered them.

"I don't know," she kept saying. "They look like *girls'* shoes."

Each time James would sigh and shake his head. "They're not *girls'* shoes, Mom. Look at the model. He's a *boy*."

Mom hadn't looked too convinced that the androgynous Asian kid in the pictures was really male, but at last she'd given in.

That was the problem. When I wasn't around to talk James out of these ridiculous ideas—which I only had about a fifty percent success rate at, anyway—who would clean up the inevitable messes he created?

And it wasn't like I hadn't had a choice, if I wanted to be completely honest. I'd applied to Reno's University of Nevada campus as a backup and I'd gotten in, of course. I could have enrolled there, stayed at home a couple more years, maybe transferred once James was out of junior high. But I couldn't hold his hand forever. And UCSD was my *dream* school. I'd only had the nerve to apply there because I'd read in one of those "How to Apply for College" books that you have to be rejected from at least one school or you'll always wonder if you didn't aim high enough. So UCSD was the school that was supposed to turn me down.

Only it didn't. And once I got the acceptance letter— along with an offer for full financial support—how was I going to say no to that?

James was excited too, I told myself. Now he'd have someone to visit in California.

I was lying, though. How would my parents ever be able to send him out for a visit? They'd barely have enough to pay their bills now that the mine was closed, now that Pops was out of work. Even when they'd both been working there had never been any extra money. There wouldn't be a travel fund set up anytime in the near future.

The way James swung the mallet made me laugh a little. It was the same as how he swung a bat, back when he used to play T-ball—terribly. He swung entirely from the arms. And he had pretty strong arms, but he didn't get any rotation in the hips. He'd never get a solid hit like that. I'd tried to teach him, so had my dad, but James was not interested in taking instruction.

That was something else he and I didn't have in common. I was perfectly happy learning from someone else's mistakes. It only took me watching Hog Boy puke himself silly after drinking an eighth of Jägermeister for me to decide that I would *never* get that drunk. But James—he wanted to figure everything out for himself.

I watched him swing the mallet a few more times, until it

just got too painful to watch. Then I unlatched the gate and let myself into the yard. "Give me that thing," I said.

James's face lit up like Christmas when he saw me. "Ben! You're home!"

This made me feel even more like shit. If someone had kept me waiting the whole afternoon, I wouldn't be all that happy when he finally turned up. But James just seemed glad that I'd decided to put in an appearance.

He handed me the mallet. It was totally the wrong tool for the job. Dad had a sledgehammer out in the garage; I wondered for a minute why James hadn't chosen it, but then I figured that it was probably too heavy for him.

"Watch and learn," I said, and James took a couple of steps back.

It took me a minute before I swung the mallet. I took one last look at the fort—this was where Pete and I had smoked our first joint. My last joint, too, it turned out—one round of coughing and hacking was enough to convince me that the munchies weren't fun enough to counterbalance the effect smoking would have on my running times.

This was where the three of us—Pete, Hog Boy, and I—used to sleep on the hottest nights of summer, shooting the shit until it was too black outside to even see each other's faces.

This was where I'd come with Becca Wilson during sophomore year. She was my first girlfriend, and this was where I'd kissed her for the first time. I hadn't admitted to Becca it was the first time I'd kissed a girl, but I'm pretty sure my nerves gave me away.

"Well?" asked James. "Aren't you going to swing that thing?"

I nodded, sort of miserable. It seemed like I should say something, some kind of a eulogy to the end of an era, but I didn't have the words. So I swung the mallet, pivoting on my hips, and I tore through the first wall.

I pulled the mallet free and backed up a couple of steps before having another whack at the fort. Most of my hits were solid, and pretty soon the fort was starting to tilt to one side. James stood back a little ways, watching.

But after seeing me get in a few more whacks, James stepped back up. "Hey," he said, "let me have another try."

I handed him the mallet and wiped the sweat from my forehead. "Give it a go."

And I'll be damned if my little brother didn't swing that mallet like a motherfucker. My eyes just about came out of my head.

I thought maybe it was just a lucky hit, so I gestured to him to have another go. The second swing was as solid as the first and one of the boards cracked apart. The fort tilted a little more.

I was dumbfounded. "Holy shit, James, where'd you learn to swing like that?"

He shrugged and swung again, taking out a chunk of the back wall.

"Just a second," I said, and I ran to the garage. I found Dad's sledgehammer and took it out to James. "Try this one."

He hefted the sledgehammer for a minute and looked at

me like I was crazy, but then he swung it up on his shoulder. It was hard for him, but he did it.

And then he slammed it into the wall, carried off balance by its swing, and the board he struck splintered into pieces.

His eyes got wide with surprise, and then he grinned. I grinned too.

The next twenty minutes were awesome. We took turns swinging the sledgehammer and the mallet, and between the two of us the fort was decimated pretty quick. Then we pulled the wood into a big pile, stacking it in the center of the yard.

The wood lit on the first try. A giant bonfire sprang up, crackling and sending up sparks as the flames devoured the wood.

The kid was practically hopping from foot to foot, he was so thrilled. I was happy, too. I felt great. I didn't care anymore about the fort—so what if it had to come down, so what if our town was gasping its last breaths? Things were changing, sure, but maybe that was all right. Maybe they would change for the better.

Look at the kid—look at him! His hair was mussed, his preppy shorts were torn across one knee, and he didn't even notice. I felt a giant upsurge of hope. Maybe things were going to be okay. Maybe everything was all right.

James hooted and hollered as the fire burned. Mom and Pops must have seen the flames from inside because they came running out. They stood there in the doorway, and their faces looked worried at first—"You'll burn the whole place down," Mom said, but then she must have realized how little that would matter at this point, because she started to laugh.

It felt good like that, the whole family in the yard. I realized it had been a long time—it felt like years, but it couldn't really have been that long—since the four of us had been like this. Close.

Pops leaned down and said something to Mom that I couldn't hear and they turned together back into the house. A minute later Pops reemerged holding a fire extinguisher. "Just in case," he said, handing it to James and ruffling his hair.

James didn't even smooth it.

After a while the fire started to die down. Pops had gone back inside, so James and I had the yard to ourselves. We sat on the back porch.

It was hopeful. That's what it was. And I remembered the reading Lala had done—I remembered the card, the Page of Cups. What was it she had said about James? That he was somehow coming into his self-realization. That he was creative, emotional, imaginative. Okay. All of those things were okay. Maybe James was a late bloomer. Maybe he was just now getting a sudden rush of testosterone. After all, look at the way he'd swung that sledgehammer—he was a solid hitter, it turned out, just as soon as he learned to really pivot, to throw his weight behind it.

"You know," I said, "moving on to junior high is a pretty big deal. And you'll be in a new town, too. It's a good chance for a fresh start. Maybe you should think about joining a team or something. You know . . . to make some friends."

James nodded, looking into the dying fire. It was down to embers now, not as grand as the fire had been, but still crazy hot. "I've been thinking about it," he said. "About joining a club, maybe."

"A club! Yeah. Or maybe a team. Your swing looked pretty solid tonight. . . . Maybe you could try out for the baseball team."

He seemed to think about that for a minute, and when he answered it was like maybe some of the air had gone out of him. "Nah," he said. "I don't think that's really my thing."

"Or whatever," I said. I was backpedaling. He knew it, I knew it.

James was quiet for a few minutes. I felt nervous. Jittery. Like I'd downed a few cups of coffee.

Then he spoke. There was something in his voice that I couldn't really place. Almost like he was joking, or testing me. "I was thinking maybe I'd try out for the cheer squad. You know, if they have one."

It was silent for a minute before I could come up with a response. "Yeah." I choked it out. "Not a bad idea. It's a good way to get to know all the hot girls."

James turned, slowly, and looked at me. The fire was almost dead now, and his face was mostly in shadow. "Ben, you know I'm gay, right?"

And it was like the ground opened up under me.

It shouldn't have been. Of course James wasn't telling me

anything I didn't already know, or at least mostly know. But until he said it out loud, I guess there had still been room for me to hope.

"Yeah," I said. My voice sounded flat. "I know."

James turned back to the fire. He nodded. "I know you worry about me, Ben." He was matter-of-fact, as if we were talking about plans for dinner or how many reps to do at the pull-up bar. "I'm not dumb, you know. I hear what people say about me sometimes. I see you getting into fights, and I know what they're about."

I didn't deny it. He should know the dangers of what he'd just said. He should know the risks.

It's not that I thought there was anything wrong with being gay. It's just that it's a big goddamn leap between being okay with *other* people being gay and being okay with my own brother announcing he was.

"I can't help who I am, Ben."

"I know," I said. "It's just—damn it, James, isn't there anything you can do about it?"

I felt stupid. I wasn't some closed-minded redneck. I knew that being gay is no more something you choose than the color of your eyes. But I also knew about the value of hard work. Sure, I was a natural runner. But I ran every day. I made myself into an athlete.

"Even if I could," James said, "I wouldn't."

I couldn't help my anger. "I won't be there to protect you in Reno, James. You're going to get your ass handed to you. Especially if you walk around asking for it—wearing the clothes you wear, joining the *cheer squad*." James flinched at the sound of venom in my voice. "A big school like the one you're headed to, and it's not like you're moving to L.A. or Seattle. You'll still be in Nevada."

James just shrugged. He wouldn't look at me at all, and his face was unreadable now that the fire was dead.

I was so angry I wanted to shake him. I wanted to hit him myself, just to give him a taste of what it would be like. I wanted to scare some sense into him.

"Maybe you're gay, James, and maybe you can't change it. Okay, maybe you wouldn't even *want* to change it. But damn it, can't you try a little harder not to *look* so goddamned gay?"

James still didn't answer. It seemed he closed his eyes, though I couldn't be sure. I couldn't see anything except the ghost of the fire that had been there but wasn't anymore.

He stood up then, and wiped his hands down the front of his shorts. He turned to walk inside, but before he did, he paused. Slowly, deliberately, he tucked his T-shirt into the waistband of his shorts. Neat as a motherfucking pin.

And then he went inside.

It was a good hour before I finally went in, and by then James had already showered—he left the bathroom steamy as always, forgetting to crack the window—and was in bed, his back to the door. The light was out.

I stood in the doorway and watched him breathe. "James," I said.

But he didn't answer.

CHAPTER EIGHT

My people tell many stories. Some of them tell of Gypsy kings and princesses, poor travelers, unhappy sorceresses, dealings with the devil.

One of our stories goes like this:

Once there was a Gypsy blacksmith who had three sons. The first two were strong and handsome, but the youngest was crippled. The left side of his body looked just fine—handsome, even—but the right was twisted, weak, and ugly.

One day the blacksmith learned that the Gypsy king was looking for a bridegroom for his daughter, who was said to be a great beauty. He wanted to marry her only to the strongest Gypsy lad in the land. Wealth didn't matter, and anyone was welcome to present himself for a test of strength.

Each of the blacksmith's two elder sons bragged that he would win the princess's hand and tried to lift their father's anvil to prove his strength. But each struggled with the weight of it, unable to swing it onto his shoulder.

At last the crippled boy—Jepas—wanted to try to lift the anvil. His brothers laughed at him, but their laughter stopped suddenly as Jepas swung the anvil up to his shoulder as if it were a sack of feathers.

And when he proved his strength again in front of the Gypsy king, he was granted the hand of the princess, even though the king did not like the thought of marrying his daughter to a cripple. Still, a promise was a promise, and the king did not like to be a man who did not keep his word.

The princess wept when she saw the man she was supposed to marry. She tried to refuse. But Jepas insisted on wedding her, in spite of her unhappiness with the union.

When his brothers saw Jepas's new bride they were overcome with jealousy, and it was easy to see that she was not happy; her beautiful face was twisted in anger and contempt as she rode alongside her crippled husband.

That night, as Jepas slept, his brothers tied him to a tree and told the princess that now she was free and she could choose either of them to be her husband.

As coy as she was lovely, the princess demurred, saying she would have to think for a while before she could choose one or the other of them, but she let the brothers lead her away from her husband, who still slept, tied to a tree, and toward the blacksmith's house.

When Jepas awoke and found himself tied up, he was angered by the treachery of his brothers and his bride. As if the tree were no more a burden than a pack tied to his back, Jepas stood and made his way to his father's house on foot, the tree still strapped to his back.

When his wife saw him coming down the path, the mighty oak upon him, she shivered with mingled fear and admiration. Her

husband was the strongest man she had ever seen! Immediately
she regretted her decision to abandon him and prostrated herself
at his feet, begging his forgiveness.

Jepas broke the straps that bound him to the tree and turned
away from his wife and his brothers, leaving them to each other.

But now that the Gypsy princess had seen Jepas's strength, the
other brothers were of no interest to her. She vowed to recapture
her husband's love, no matter what the cost.

This is not where the story ends. The Gypsy bride travels
far and wide searching for Jepas. She is captured by an evil
sorcerer, she finds solace in a song she sings about her lost
husband, and at last she is assisted by a helpful bird that sings
her song to Jepas, far away.

Finally Jepas forgives his wayward bride and rescues her
from the evil sorcerer. Together they live in happiness until
the end of their days.

As a young girl I had listened with rapt attention as my
mother told me this story, one of my favorites. I loved many
things about it—most especially, it sat well with my innate
sense of justice that the naughty princess was punished before she was forgiven for abandoning her husband. I liked to
imagine that I was the princess. Of course I would never be
as shallow as the girl in the story. I would see the crippled
Gypsy's hidden potential; I would be faithful from the start.

But it turned out that I would not have to see inner
beauty in spite of an ugly façade; the groom my father had
chosen for me would not have caused the king's daughter
any misgivings. He was fine and straight, darkly handsome
in just the ways Gypsy men are said to be.

The morning after I had done a reading for Ben Stanley, we had a little flutter of business. It was Wednesday, the middle of the *gazhè*'s Burning Man festival, and many busloads of people headed up and down the highway to get more supplies at the little store in the dying town. Some of them stopped and visited us.

Violeta was cranky and said her back was hurting. Mother was busy with the baby, and Anelie was still my apprentice, a watchful learner but unable to do readings on her own. So it fell to me to deal with the stream of visitors to our tent.

It was difficult for me to focus on the readings. The oppressive heat seemed to bear down on me, and I felt like a leaf or flower that was being pressed between the pages of a thick, heavy book—trapped, smothered.

I must have done a dozen readings all through the morning and early afternoon. It was nearly three o'clock when all the *gazhè* had gone away. The heat was the worst at this time, and no one in his right mind would be out in it now.

The perpetual dryness was perhaps just as bad as the heat. At home in Portland everything was damp, even when the rain ceased temporarily. Nothing ever dried out completely, not the lawns or the flowerbeds or even the pavement. This desert world was bone dry.

Almost all of my family was resting. Mother had quieted Stefan, laying a wet washcloth against his back to cool him down until he settled into sleep. She must have fallen asleep too, for the curtains were drawn in the motor home.

Violeta and Marko were in their tent. It was silent there. Romeo was sitting with Alek in the shade cast by the motor home, showing him how to strum chords on his guitar. Alek watched him with intense concentration. He loved Romeo and could not wait until we were married and he could rightly call Romeo his brother.

My father was crouched not far from the entrance to the tent, and as I showed out the final group of *gazhè* Questioners, three young women who all wanted to know if they would find love, he nodded to them cordially.

Anelie stood behind me and we watched as they drove away, waving to us.

"I will never be good like you and Violeta," she whined to me.

"Your problem is that you do not listen, and you do not really look, either. It is easy to know what someone wants if only you are aware."

"What do *I* want, then?" asked my father. He looked amused by the little lecture I was giving to Anelie.

"That is easy," I said. "You want a glass of iced tea."

"Exactly right." My father beamed. "Anelie, bring us each a glass. But be sure not to wake your mother."

I squatted down next to my father. It was perhaps slightly cooler closer to the ground.

When Anelie returned with the iced tea, handing a glass first to my father and then to me, she asked, "How did you know he wanted a drink?"

I took a sip of my tea before answering. "Anelie," I said, "it is well over one hundred degrees right here in the shade where Father is sitting. Who would not want a cold drink?"

"Hey!" she said. "That's cheating!"

"No, it is not," I said. "It is fortune-telling."

Father laughed. "You are my clever girl. Always you have had insight beyond your years."

I hid my smile against the rim of my glass as I sipped more tea.

"Well," said Anelie, with that particular tone of argument in her voice, "what about you? What do *you* want?"

"Become a better observer," I said. "Perhaps you will see for yourself."

We sat, the three of us, in companionable silence, enjoying the tea.

After a time, Father spoke to me again. "Soon," he said, "you will not be my girl anymore at all. You will be Romeo's."

There was nothing to say to this. It was not a question; it was a statement of fact.

"Your wedding will be even bigger than Violeta's," said my father. "Everyone loves coming to a fall wedding."

"I wish you hadn't chosen purple dresses for the bridesmaids," Anelie complained. "I look much better in blue."

"No one will be looking at you," Father said. "Everyone will have eyes only for Lala, the beautiful bride." He nodded.

My tea was gone. All that was left were two ice cubes, and as I watched they turned into water at the bottom of the glass. I drank this too, and stood. "I think I will take a little walk," I said.

"Can I come?" Anelie stood up, too.

I nodded.

"Just a moment," said Father. He motioned to Alek, who sat strumming Romeo's guitar, and called, "Alek. Go with your sisters."

I hid my displeasure the best I could. "I think it is too hot, Father, for any wild animals to bother us."

"It is not animals I am worried about," he said. "It is the local boys, and the *gazhè* at the festival."

Alek thrust the guitar back at Romeo and stood up, clearly disgusted. Romeo smiled at me with a mouth full of sharp wolf teeth and winked. Then he looked down to his guitar and began playing a new song.

I felt myself reddening and busied myself retying my sandals so that I would not have to respond. *Coward*, I said to myself.

Although he was close to thirteen, Alek was small for his age and not strong. Too much time spent playing his video games. The thought of him protecting me and Anelie out in the desert if any predator threatened us—animal *or* human—seemed laughable.

But I knew better than to argue. And I knew also from the way Alek seemed to puff up when Father, eyeing the boy, told him to stay close to us that Father had reasons for sending Alek along that had very little to do with predators and all the world to do with his son.

"Who would want to take a walk in the middle of the day out here in the desert?" Quickly enough, the thrill of guarding his sisters wore off as Alek trudged after us.

"Have you heard the term 'cabin fever'?"

He shook his head.

"It means I'm sick of seeing the side of our motor home," I said simply. "I need a change of scenery."

"Some change," snorted Alek.

I had to agree; we couldn't wander very far before the heat became too much to bear, and even from a hundred feet away I could still see the motor home and our tent. I could still hear the strains of music coming from Romeo's guitar.

I felt defeated. Trapped and defeated.

There were few plants dotting the hard, cracked earth. I made my way toward the largest one in the vicinity—a gnarled, stunted plant that looked like it wanted to be a tree but could not quite muster the energy to grow past a shrub.

Anelie and Alek followed behind. The three of us sat together, as if by unspoken agreement, in the little shade offered by the shrub. It felt no cooler, but at least the brightness of the sun was lessened.

"I'll bet it's raining right now in Portland," said Anelie wistfully.

"It is probably no warmer than seventy degrees," said Alek.

All three of us closed our eyes. I think we all imagined that we were back in Portland, hidden beneath its nearly omnipresent cloud cover.

"I will never complain again of being cold." Anelie twisted her dark, thick hair into a knot at the nape of her neck.

Looking at her felt like looking backward through time. So much about her—the way she held her head, how her hair parted just to the left of center, the particular darkness of her eyes—mirrored me.

But there were differences that time would correct. Where I was softness and curves, Anelie was still angles. Her arms and legs were just a bit too long, like a filly's, and she sometimes seemed as if she did not know where to place them. "Gangly"—that was the word for Anelie.

I had looked like that until just before I began my monthly bleeding. Then, about six months before my first cycle, I had plumped up. My breasts began to swell, of course, but so too did the rest of me. My cheeks, the tops of my arms, my belly—all over it was as if I took on a sheen of pudgy fat.

And then my cycle began. The fat melted away, and I emerged, a woman.

For my people the days of a woman's menstruation are a time when she is especially unclean. I was twelve when I first saw the flow of blood. I told my mother what had happened and at that moment my life shifted.

I was not allowed to help prepare the evening meal that night—not that this was such a punishment!—as a menstruating woman is unclean and cannot touch the food of the rest of the family. During the four days I bled, I could not leave the house or interact with the men in my family. And I had to wash all of my clothes separately from the rest of the family's clothes.

These things were tradition. I understood them; tradition was part of who I was. And in those first few months, I felt a sort of pride when I had my monthly blood, when I had to stay away from my father to avoid making him unclean, too.

It grew tiresome, though, the isolation and the rules. All the rules. And the more I read the *gazhè* books, the more frustrated I became. I began to have thoughts that I should not have.

For example—why should a woman be considered unclean just because she is menstruating? There is nothing dirty about the monthly flow of blood—it is a natural part of life! This was perhaps one of the most difficult ideas for me to truly accept, though I acted among my people as though I did.

Once you begin to question your people's beliefs, it is a slippery slope. Soon you can find yourself questioning everything.

Must we *really* wash clothes for the upper part of the body separately from clothes for the lower part of the body? *Must* we separate women's clothing from men's before we put them in the washing machine?

Could not my father cook a meal, especially on the days when Mother did so many readings and looked so tired by the evening?

And from there the questions became even more dangerous: Must our fathers choose for us the men we shall marry? Must *my* father? And . . . must I obey him?

That evening Marko and Romeo built a fire. Father had bought some meat in town. Mother arranged it on a spit over the flames and Violeta, Anelie, and I took turns rotating it. I did most of the turning; it was uncomfortable for Violeta to bend over the fire, and Anelie was afraid of the flames.

Mother sat nearby with Stefan on her lap. He chewed a biscuit and laughed happily at the fire.

Romeo was playing his guitar again, the same song he'd wanted to play for me the evening before. But his eyes were not on his instrument; he watched me as I turned the meat, and his slow smile seemed full of intention.

He looked very handsome this evening. He was experimenting with wearing his hair a new way, combed forward rather than back, and to the side. It suited him.

His body was straight and strong. He was young and came from a good family and his eyes told me that he desired me.

So why did I feel this way—like a cornered animal, prey?

Mother took Stefan inside to wash his hands and face. Somehow, suddenly, it was just me and Romeo by the fire.

This rarely happened—finding ourselves alone together.

Romeo did not waste the opportunity. The song ended abruptly and he placed his guitar back in its case. I stood up and turned to face him, arranging a smile on my lips.

"Lala," he said, and he put a hand on my hip, squeezing me there. "You look delicious."

I tried to speak, but before a word could come out Romeo's mouth was upon mine, his kiss aggressive, his hot tongue filling my mouth. I tried to step back but the fire was behind me and my skirt was long. There was nowhere to go, and so I stood perfectly still and waited for him to finish kissing me.

I remembered the story of the Gypsy princess. She had not welcomed her marriage; she had tried to flee from it. But she was wed nonetheless, and in time she came to desire her husband, and she begged him to embrace her.

How long would it be, I wondered, before I accepted what had been given to me?

Would acceptance come by our wedding night, when Romeo pushed apart my thighs and claimed me as his own?

Would it come later, when I bore him a child?

Might it be possible—might it never come? It filled me with terror, the taste of it metallic in my mouth. For the first time I allowed myself to think the truth—I might *always* feel as I felt just then—trapped in a wasteland with no way out.

The door of the motor home slammed open. Romeo stepped away from me, his face flushed from the heat of the fire, grinning.

It was Anelie. She stood framed in the motor home's doorway, holding a platter of fruit.

"The meat is burning," she said.

We ate our dinner, put away what was left, watched as Marko and Alek scooped dirt over the fire to make sure it was completely out. It was after ten o'clock when Anelie and I climbed into the tent.

We undressed in silence, hanging our skirts and slipping into our thin nightgowns. Then we took turns braiding each other's hair, a nightly ritual we shared.

The bedrolls were kept behind the screen, away from the eyes of the *gazhè* who visited during the day, and we spread them out after moving our table to one side. I had begun to wonder if Anelie was going to say anything at all when at last she spoke.

"By the fire—"

My eyes were heavy with sleep and I had to bring myself back to wakefulness to answer. "Yes?"

"When Romeo kissed you—it looked so beautiful, like something from a movie. The two of you look so well together."

"He is a handsome man," I said.

"But you do not want him."

It was not a question.

I hesitated before I responded. "Why do you say that?"

"Earlier, I complained to you that I would never be good at telling fortunes. Remember?"

I nodded.

Anelie could not see me in the darkened tent, but she went on. "You told me that my problem is that I do not listen, and also that I do not truly look. You told me that if I did so, I could easily see what people wanted."

"I remember the conversation."

"Well," she said, her voice dropping to almost a whisper. "I have been watching *you*."

I asked, "And what have you learned?"

"That you are not happy. That you do not want to be Romeo's bride. That you are afraid."

"Afraid?" I scoffed. "What could I possibly fear?"

"I don't know," Anelie answered. "But I saw it in your

eyes—twice. Once out in the desert, when you sat under the tree. And again, right before Romeo kissed you."

I did not know how to respond. At last I said, "You will be a fine fortune-teller, Anelie."

"I knew it!" Her voice had the happy triumph of one who has won a game. But then she grew more sober. "But *why* are you not happy, Lala?"

If I answered too quickly, the tremor of the tears she could not see would echo in my voice. I took measured breaths. Breaths like those Ben Stanley had taken. It seemed a lifetime ago that he had sat with me in this same tent. Now my bedroll was spread on the ground where his chair had been.

"I will *learn* to be happy, Anelie." By the time I spoke, my voice did not betray me.

"But what if you do not? Then what?"

"Anelie," I said, "do you remember the story of Jepas?"

"The half man? The one who was lame down one side of his body?"

"Yes. You remember it?"

"Of course I do. You used to tell it to me at night before I fell asleep. It sometimes gave me nightmares."

I was surprised. I had not known the story frightened her. "Anelie! You should have said something. I would have told you a different story. Which part frightened you? The evil sorcerer?"

"No," she said. "The half-man. I thought the gypsy princess was crazy to want him, no matter how strong he was."

"That is strange," I said. "It was the princess I did not

like. She judged Jepas solely on the way he looked. She did not deserve such a man, I used to think."

"The princess was right not to want him. He was ugly."

Anelie was still a child. I realized with a sinking feeling that I agreed with her, though the reasons behind her conclusions were faulty. She thought that Jepas was not a worthy suitor because of his deformity.

Jepas had married the princess without knowing her at all. He wanted her for her beauty and because she was a princess. In this way, he was no better in his desire for her than she was in her disgust over his deformity. They were two sides of a coin.

And worse, he married her in spite of her fear—because he wanted her.

He forced himself upon her, and no one spoke up to stop him. Her own father gave her away.

Perhaps he *was* twisted; and if this was true, then maybe it reflected too on the story's audience. We were supposed to identify with Jepas; we were supposed to boo the princess when she defies him and cheer later when she grovels for his touch.

We were supposed to agree with the rules that allowed Jepas to take his hard-won prize, even if that prize was a human being.

My father Mickey White was *rom barò*; that made me a Gypsy princess. And Romeo—Romeo was just a boy. He was not a cripple, not a villain, and not a great hero, either.

But he didn't know me, any more than Jepas had known

his bride. He knew who my father was; he knew my face. But our souls? We were strangers.

"I am scared," I whispered to Anelie.

"What frightens you?"

It took me so long to answer that I didn't know if Anelie was still awake to hear my answer.

"Being the Gypsy princess."

In my dreams, Romeo was chasing me through the desert. He limped as he ran, the left side of his body a deadweight that slowed him down. He would never catch me, not like that. I ran faster and faster until my feet no longer touched the ground.

Until I flew.

CHAPTER NINE

BEN

Thursday morning, James left early to go up the street to say goodbye to his pal Shane. He and his family were on their way to Northern California, where some friends of theirs lived. It was as good a place as any to go, considering that neither of his parents had found work yet.

Every day that passed meant more cars pulling out of town for the last time. Everywhere I looked was another overloaded pickup truck, another closed-up house, another goodbye.

I felt bad about the way my talk with James had gone the night before. It seemed like nothing I'd said had come out right. I wanted to be a good brother to James. I'd lain awake for a long time, just listening to him breathing. If I was really honest with myself, a big chunk of what bothered me about James had nothing to do with *James* at all. It had to do with me.

It occurred to me that maybe I owed James an apology. For the things I'd said the night before, sure, but maybe for some other things, too. Things I *hadn't* said but should have.

When I went into the kitchen Mom was just sitting at the empty table, staring out the front window. She had a cup in her hand; it was empty.

"Hey, Mom." I tried my best to sound cheerful.

It took her a minute before she looked over at me. When she did, she kind of blinked her eyes as if she was bringing herself back from someplace far away. She smiled at me, but her whole face looked distracted.

"Good morning, Ben."

I sat down next to her. When I did, she leaned across and kissed my forehead.

"You want me to get you some more coffee, Mom?"

She looked into her cup. "Look at that. It's empty." But she didn't answer my question.

She was starting to worry me a little, actually. She wasn't usually like this—sitting, for one thing. Unless she was working on a project, Mom was nearly always on her feet. "What's up, Mom?"

"Your father's out in the garage, screwing around with that old dirt bike again."

I laughed. Dad had been struggling to get that piece of shit running for the past three years, off and on. Mostly off—whole months would go by without him so much as looking at it. "It's too bad we couldn't have just thrown it onto the fire last night along with the fort. One less thing to pack."

Mom shook her head. "Your father seems determined to see that thing running before we move. I don't understand why. But he's been at it since five, and about half an hour ago I actually heard the engine for a couple of minutes before it cut out."

"No shit!"

"Why don't you take your dad a cup of coffee, give him a hand."

I shrugged. "Sure. Where are the cups?"

Mom looked around at the piles of half-packed boxes. Then she held out her cup to me. "Here," she said. "Take mine."

Pops was working at his bench, putting the pieces of the carburetor back together. The rest of the dirt bike looked pretty good. All the pieces, which for the last three years had been taken apart and reassembled about a dozen times, seemed to be in the right places. It was a junky old bike; the red leather seat was torn and layers of decals and touch-up paint made it look like a mechanical version of Frankenstein's monster.

Over the last few years Pops had either replaced or repaired pretty much all the major systems and most of the minor ones—the engine, the transmission, the exhaust manifold, the brakes, the clutch, the gas tank, the suspension. Even though he'd gotten the bike for free from one of his buddies down at the mine, I'd guess he'd put close to a thousand dollars into it, along with dozens of hours of his time.

Part of the problem was that Pops knew next to nothing about motorcycles. When he'd gotten the bike I think his plan had been to give it to me when it was all fixed up, and

126

I'd been pretty excited about that three years ago, when I was fifteen.

Fast-forward to now, though, and I kind of hated the bike. It'd sat out there taunting me, always seemingly close to running but never complete. I'd given up on it ever working about nine months ago, when we'd gotten the news that the mine was closing and all of Pops's extra energy had started going into looking for a new job. He hadn't really touched the bike since.

I suppose I could have tried to work on the bike myself, but between school and running there never seemed to be time.

Now that it was too late to do me any good, Pops looked to be on the brink of getting the damned thing working at last.

"Hey, Ben, give me a hand with this."

I put his coffee on the workbench and watched as he replaced a couple of rubber gaskets, and then I helped him lift the carburetor back into place on the bike.

He moved with a lot more assurance now when he worked on the bike than he used to; all those hours had finally amounted to some degree of confidence. He reconnected the fuel line to the carb. "I had it running pretty good earlier," he said, "but the engine was bogging when I cracked the throttle, so I figured I'd just give the carburetor a cleaning, for good measure. It should be good to go."

He wiped his hands on a red rag he had tucked into his back pocket. "Wanna take it for a spin?"

"You're kidding, right?" Four days before we left town, a

hundred hours before I was going to get on a bus and leave the goddamn *state*, and the bike was finally finished.

Pops gave me one of his sideways grins and I could tell he knew what I was thinking. "Better late than never, right?"

I switched into jeans and laced up my shoes, then pulled on the dusty helmet I'd been waiting three years to wear.

While I was inside changing, Pops had rolled the dirt bike out of the garage to the driveway. He flicked the bike's starter switch to RUN and flipped the fuel switch to ON. Then he gestured to the bike. "It's all yours, Ben."

I'd had some fun riding dirt bikes off and on over the years, mainly when we would visit Mom's brother's family out by Tahoe. They had a couple of acres and a bike I could tool around on, so I knew how to ride.

I straddled the bike and turned the choke on. Then I found the kick-start peg with my right foot, pushing it down as hard as I could.

It took a few tries, but finally the engine roared to life. It was loud, but it sounded smooth and strong. I looked up at Pops and we grinned at each other like a couple of idiots.

"Be careful," he called after me as I pulled the bike into the street.

I rode around town for a few minutes, cruising up and down the streets I'd run so many times over the years. The bike seemed pretty stable; not perfect, the tread on the tires was kind of worn and they slipped to the side a little when I took corners, but considering that Pops had been the one putting it together, I was pretty impressed. I toyed with the idea of suggesting that he look for a job helping out at a bike shop when they got to Reno. But realistically, there were probably a hundred younger guys hungry for work who knew more about bikes lined up for any job that might open up. What were my dad's chances of finding a job anywhere?

I reached the end of town, where First Street widened into 447. Probably Pops wouldn't like the idea of me taking it out onto the highway, and it wasn't street legal, so if I got pulled over by a cop I'd be looking at a pretty hefty ticket. But the idea of seeing if I could get it up over fifty was a pretty strong draw—I'd always loved speed—so instead of turning down Freesia I pulled in the clutch lever and rolled the throttle forward, using the tip of my left shoe to lift the shift lever into third gear. Releasing the clutch, I rolled the throttle back to give the engine more gas.

The bike responded, surging forward strongly. Inside the helmet I grinned ear to ear. I leaned forward, closer to the handlebar.

I hadn't really thought about which way I was heading on the highway. Well, shit, maybe that isn't entirely true—I knew where the road headed.

And I felt nervous—not because of the speed of the bike, but because what if the whole thing wasn't there anymore? What if all of it—the encampment, the tent, Lala herself—really had been some kind of complicated and beautiful mirage?

And then there it was—shabbier-looking than I remembered it, just up the road. Of course it had been real. I knew that. But I felt myself relaxing as the tent grew larger the closer I got. She was still there.

I could see why her family had chosen this place to camp. It wasn't too far from the entrance to Burning Man, but it was far enough out of Gypsum that no one would bother them. And there was a nice flat pull-out where they'd parked the motor home, so they hadn't had to drive it far off the asphalt. The tent was a little farther away, off to the side and on the dirt.

The sign was there, too, the plywood A-frame that read FORTUNE-TELLING on each side. I downshifted, pulling my bike to the side of the road, rolling to a stop, and cutting the engine.

It took a minute for the engine's roar to fade away after I'd turned it off. After being surrounded by the bike's noise and vibration, the desert's stillness seemed even quieter than usual. The sky was this intense blue, and the air was crackling dry and so hot. I felt rivulets of sweat going down my back under my T.

The entrance to the tent parted and Lala ducked her head out. She was wearing a skirt like the one from the other day, but this one was red. Her dark hair was pulled back today and lay across her shoulder, across her breast, and down her side. As she emerged from the tent she tossed it behind her.

"Here for a reading?" she called, a polite smile on her lips. She didn't come too close, staying back about a dozen steps.

"Hey," I said, and realized I was still wearing my helmet. I flicked open the chin strap and pulled it off, pushing my sweaty hair back from my forehead. "Lala," I said. "Hi."

The smile she was wearing stiffened as she seemed to realize who I was—that guy who'd asked her out. I felt like an idiot.

But I was already here, so I shoved my heel down on the kickstand to balance the bike and swung off it, putting my helmet on the bike's torn red seat.

"Ben Stanley," she said.

She remembered my name. Why did that make me so ridiculously happy?

"Yeah," I said. "How are you doing?"

With relief, I watched as her expression shifted to an authentic smile. "How do you think I am doing? It is miserably hot and I am in the middle of the desert. I suffer like a dog."

But she didn't look like a dog; she looked great, like a cool drink that I was so thirsty for. I took a step forward. "It's good to see you again."

Her eyes narrowed. "Why *are* you here, Ben Stanley? Did you forget something when you were here last?"

For a second I toyed with the idea of saying, "Yeah . . . I forgot *this* . . . ," and sweeping her into my arms for a big, dramatic kiss.

Instead I said, "Uh . . . not really . . . but I was hoping I could get you to reconsider my offer."

This time it was Lala who stepped forward, just a little. She looked amused. "Your offer of a movie? Or a cup of coffee?"

"Of a date," I said. "You don't like movies, and you don't drink coffee. I remember. But maybe dinner? I'll bet you eat dinner."

"I have been known to eat dinner," she admitted. "But . . . still, I must decline. Though I thank you."

The way she talked killed me. It was kind of formal, like she'd picked it up from an old book instead of from real conversation. Still, even though she was turning me down, I got the feeling she didn't really want to. She looked, in those hard onyx eyes, like she wanted to say yes to me.

I've never been a real aggressive guy. I've always figured, if a chick isn't into me, well, there are other girls. No reason to get all worked up. Some guys are really into the chase; they like girls who play hard to get, but when they finally catch them the thrill kind of wears off.

I guess I've always just been too busy for any of those games. And kind of shy, too, in a way. So I don't know what came over me out there in the middle of the desert with Lala.

Maybe it was the heat.

But I couldn't just quit and ride away. It seemed like too much to give up. So I tried again. "Don't you feel it too, Lala?"

She tilted her head a little to the side. I would have paid a million bucks, if I'd had it, to know what she was thinking. To me, her face was a mystery—unreadable, beautiful, totally *other*.

"Ben," she said, "I think it would be best if you did not visit me here again."

It was a kick in the stomach. But she hadn't said no—that she *didn't* feel what I felt. So I hung on to that and closed the distance between us, until my track shoes were up real close to her sandals.

I towered over her up close like that, and she seemed nervous, like she didn't know whether to look up into my face or down at the ground. But she didn't step back.

"You think it would be best if I didn't visit you again," I said. "But do you want me to leave?"

Now she looked up at me, those thick, dark lashes fanning up, revealing her bright dark eyes. "What one wants does not always matter."

I could have stood there all day arguing just to draw out the pleasure of being so close to her. She smelled the way she had the other day—like citrus and cinnamon. I wondered if it was her hair or her skin that smelled so good, and I wanted to lower my face to her, to bury my nose in her hair and breathe her in, to run my face along her neck and smell there, too.

"What *you* want matters," I said. "At least, it does to me."

She seemed to consider this. At last she asked, "Why?"

I answered honestly. "I don't know."

"It is because you find me beautiful and exotic," she said. It didn't sound like she was bragging; she didn't even really seem happy about the idea that I thought she was pretty. She said it like she was disgusted.

But it wasn't the whole truth. "Of course I think you're pretty," I said. "Who wouldn't? But that's not everything." I struggled to put it in words, the draw she had on me. "It's more than that. I want to know who you are. I want to hear about you—you know, where you come from, what you like to do—stuff like that," I finished lamely.

Lala smiled. "My stories are not for you."

"Why not?"

"You are a *gazhò*," she said.

I didn't have the slightest clue what that meant, but I could tell from the way she said it that it wasn't a good thing.

"Maybe we can work that out," I said.

Her laugh was infectious. It was loud and sudden, and I smiled too at the sound of it. It seemed like finally maybe we were getting somewhere, but just then someone called out her name.

"Lala?" From around the back of the tent came a guy. He was about my age, and he was holding a guitar by its neck. "Do you need help?"

He was dark like Lala, and he seemed like the kind of guy who spent a lot of time on his hair. He walked toward us.

Lala dropped her gaze and shifted away from me. I felt the space between us and I didn't like it.

"Is that your brother?" I asked.

The guy ruffled like an angry peacock. He walked up to Lala's side and put his arm around her waist. "Her brother? No. I don't think so."

Lala's voice was back to being formal again, distant. "Ben Stanley," she said, "this is Romeo Nicholas. He is traveling with my family. He is my . . ." Here her voice trailed off, like she didn't want to finish.

"Lala will be my wife in three weeks' time," said Romeo.

This was too much to believe. Who *were* these people?

134

"You're joking, right?"

The guy didn't look like he was joking. He looked pretty pissed, actually.

"And—Romeo? Is that your real name?"

He took half a step in front of Lala so he and I were practically chest to chest. I had him by a few solid inches at least, but he was the scrappy kind. I had no doubt he'd be happy to make our discussion more physical.

"Ben—Stanley?" He said my name like it was a question. "Are you here for a reading?"

I wished suddenly that I had money in my useless, empty wallet so I could pay for a reading—it would be a way to get Lala alone, at least. But I didn't. I shook my head.

"Then I think it is time for you to leave. That is . . . if you can get your bike to start?"

I looked at Lala. Her face was blank again, her eyes flinty cold. But she met my gaze, and she nodded.

"All right," I said. I took my helmet and put it on, straddling my bike. If Lala wanted me gone, I'd leave. I didn't want to cause trouble for her. But I felt like I'd stepped through a portal into an alternate universe. I didn't understand these people—who the hell tells fortunes for a living and gets married so young? Hell, who the fuck names their kid *Romeo*?

It was bad enough that I had to leave like this. But when the bike wouldn't start, that was even worse. Romeo just stood there, that piece of shit, with a grin on his face as I kicked the starter again and again. I flooded the engine and had to wait for it to settle. At least my helmet was on so they couldn't see my embarrassed blush creeping up my neck.

135

At last the engine caught.

I looked up and saw that Lala was watching me, her gaze intense and focused, as if she was trying to tell me something without words. But I didn't know what the hell it was.

I revved the engine a couple of times and squealed out onto the highway. I felt them watching me all the way down the road, but of course I didn't look back.

At home Pops was helping Mom dismantle her crafting station. She liked to make baby blankets when women in town were pregnant, and every year the school auctioned off one of her quilts to raise extra money for first-aid supplies.

So she had a whole dresser full of scraps of fabric and different-colored thread, and she and Pops were loading all of it into boxes. She'd already packed away her two sewing machines, wrapping them carefully in old blankets before sealing them into boxes labeled FRAGILE.

"Hey, Benny Boy," said Pops. "How was the ride?"

"It was fine."

My dad didn't look like he thought my tone was enthusiastic enough, so I said, "The bike ran great, Pops. A little hard to get started once I cut the engine, but it flies on the highway."

"You took that piece of shit on the highway!" My mother sounded horrified. "Honestly, Ben, it's like you don't even want to make it to college alive."

"The boy knows how to ride a bike, Sarah. And he's not

even a boy. High school graduate, eighteen years old, off to college—he's a man."

"Some man," I scoffed. I was thinking about how things had gone down with Lala, how I'd backed down and ridden away. I was already sorry—so *what* if she was engaged? The guy was a tool. He didn't deserve her.

"Where'd you ride to?"

"Just up the highway toward Burning Man." I paused. "There are some people out there, camping not far from the entrance. Fortune-tellers."

"Oh yeah," said Pops. "The Gypsies. Harry told me about them."

"I don't know . . . I guess maybe they're Gypsies." I paused, thinking. "They're different, that's for sure. I got to talking with some of them. . . ." No need to go into details, I figured. "A couple of them are engaged. I don't think they could be any older than I am."

"Maybe the girl is pregnant," suggested Pops.

"No, I don't think so," said Mom. "I read about Gypsies once. Interesting people. That's just their way—they marry young. And their parents pick their spouses for them."

"You mean like arranged marriages?" This was getting weirder and weirder. I had that feeling again, like I'd run up against another world, one that looked a lot like this one and operated under very similar principles, but was different in a few essential ways.

"Just be glad we didn't choose a bride for you," Pops teased. "The pickings in Gypsum were pretty slim."

I shook my head and thought about it. So an arranged marriage—maybe that explained the way Lala seemed. Restrained. Unhappy, even?

I wandered into my room and flopped down on my bed, crossing my hands behind my head and thinking.

It was none of my business. That was clear.

And there was nothing I could do about it. That was obvious, too. Hell, I couldn't even help my own family with its problems. Dad's unemployment, the family's relocation, James's . . . whatever you wanted to call it. . . . Every way I turned I was stymied.

Lala White—her problems, her *engagement*—none of that involved me. It would be better for everyone if I just put her out of my mind and forgot we'd ever met.

Even if I *could* convince her to go out with me, no good could possibly come of it. I was counting down my last few days in town, and she was clearly just passing through. Any interference from me would probably just make trouble for her with her . . . fiancé, I guess.

Better just to mind my own business and pack my bags. Spend the little time I had left with my family and friends here in Gypsum.

And that was what I did for the rest of the day. When James came home from Shane's house I took him out to the garage and showed him his new dirt bike. I strapped the helmet on his head, showed him how the kick start worked, and explained about the throttle, how you had to be careful to turn it easy so you didn't jolt ahead too sudden.

I watched as he rode around on our street, up and down the block experimenting with the hand brake and shifting up and down through the gears. He picked it up pretty quick. It made me happy to see how good he was on the bike. That was a skill—dirt bike riding—that would help him out in Reno. Other kids would want to take rides on the bike. It might be a key for him, something that would open doors to friendships, something that might help him fit in a little better. As long as he didn't go spray-painting the damned thing pink.

CHAPTER TEN

LALA

I woke Friday morning thinking about my mother's sister Ana. It had been a long time since I had thought about her, but I woke in the hot tent startled from sleep by the sound of her name loud in my head—*Ana*.

I had not seen Ana in several years, since I was thirteen. And in that time I had not spoken her name aloud, not a single time. No one in my family had. Stefan, who had been born after Ana left our family, was not even aware that Mother had a sister.

No one ever told me exactly what Ana had done, but it was not difficult to guess. Every picture of Ana was removed from our house; Mother threw away the few articles of clothing that Ana had loaned to her. It was, very suddenly, as if Ana had never been born.

She was my mother's younger sister by a handful of years, and in some ways she seemed more like an older sister or a friend to me than an aunt. She had been married since the age of fifteen to Jackie Lee. He was well liked and respected in our community.

After she left him, Jackie Lee left as well. He went to visit family in Seattle, but he did not return. We had word last spring that he had married a widow with four sons and a daughter. Even then no one mentioned Ana's name.

If a wife is unfaithful to her husband, she is *marimè*. Even worse, a *kris-Romanì*—a panel of elders that makes decisions about such things—can declare that in addition to the woman, her family is also *marimè*. Not only the woman who has betrayed her husband, but also all her relations— her parents, her siblings, her children—by extension, all of them can be declared *marimè*, and all of them can be cast out. This word—*marimè*—is almost taboo among my people. Rarely is it spoken, though its threat is always present, a silent reminder, a warning.

Friday promised to be the hottest day we had so far experienced in this wasteland. The long, straight road of the highway shimmered like a river. I thought about the book of Greek mythology I had read a year ago. I remembered the river Styx, the waterway that separates the land of the living from the land of the dead.

It would look like this, I imagined, if there were such a place. The river Styx would be like this desert highway.

Stefan was fussy and irritable. A heat rash covered much of his body. Mother did her best to soothe him, offering him cup after cup of water with sugar.

Violeta was no longer bragging about how clever her Marko had been to conceive of this plan. There was a bright flush in her cheeks, and though she was tired she could not sit still in one position, so much did the weight of her baby add to her discomfort. She would sit for a few minutes, but then she would shift to another position. Inevitably she would rise and pace for long minutes before sitting again.

And all morning no one stopped at our tent, and only a handful of cars even traveled down the road.

Once a motorcycle went by, and a surge in my heart told me that I hoped it was Ben Stanley. But this motorcycle was sleek and shiny and black, and its rider wore full leathers.

The three of us—Mother, Violeta, and I—had already placed close to four thousand dollars in the billfold we kept inside the motor home. Marko promised that the road would be swollen again with travelers leaving the Burning Man festival, that carloads of them would stop as they headed back toward their homes and that they would pay us well for our services.

So we had nothing to do but wait all that long day for the weekend to pass and the travelers to come to us.

Nothing to do but think. Over and over again I remembered the way Ben Stanley had looked at me—yesterday, when he had visited me on his motorbike, and the time before that, after his reading in the tent.

The truth was, I was not sure exactly what Ben Stanley wanted from me. For me, this was most unusual. That had always been my skill—seeing what someone wanted from me, and accommodating them by re-creating myself in the particular image they desired.

Sometimes this was easy for me; the person might want me to be something I already was or something I wanted to be. An obedient daughter. A loving sister. A seer.

Being what my family wanted me to be had never been a hardship, at least until these last few days. And the little I wanted for myself—time to read my books, to spend occasional hours all alone, away from my people—though these were not usual among my family, they seemed not too much to take for myself.

True, among the Gypsies a solitary life was frowned upon. Always our houses were full of voices, of laughter, of the aroma of coffee poured out and shared. Doors opening and slamming, sometimes heated arguments among the men, the near-constant drone of the television left on to amuse the children—ours was a life full of noise and company.

My parents had indulged my whim for solitude, though they did not understand it. Now perhaps it was simply out of habit that they accepted my preference to sit alone at the edge of the tent rather than join in with the others. Romeo did not like this about me. I could see it in the tightening muscle of his jaw when he invited me to sit beside him and I refused.

But he allowed it—most likely because we were still in my father's *vìtsa*. After our wedding we would live with his parents in their home, and then there would be no time—and no space—for me to be alone.

Fifteen thousand dollars was a heavy bride price. In a way, I suppose, Romeo and his family liked that they had paid so much. It showed that they were a family of great wealth, able to afford a bride for Romeo who had such a future before her, such money-earning potential.

But the reality of the situation was that I would be entering a family fifteen thousand dollars in debt. Doubtless, my new mother-in-law would expect me to earn it back.

In many ways I would belong to Romeo's *vìtsa* as soon as the wedding feast was finished. I would be expected to serve his family, to answer to and obey his mother unquestioningly.

I had never really considered whether or not I was a particularly obedient person. I worked in my family as a valuable part of the machine of our household. We all worked, in one capacity or another, to provide for and maintain our way of life. It was not a question of obedience. I gave with a glad heart.

But in Romeo's family, I knew that obedience would be expected—demanded, even—by his mother, Clara Nicholas. Violeta had managed to convince her Marko to stay with our family instead of his, but I knew I would have no such sway over Romeo.

Romeo was his mother's dearest son. The most beautiful boy, she crooned, and always with a kiss for her, always her closest and best. Under no circumstances would she allow Romeo to leave her home until we had enough children— three or four at least—that it would become necessary for us to have our own space.

And I knew, too, that Clara Nicholas did not think I was good enough for her son, regardless of the bride price I had fetched. No girl was.

I do not think I truly recognized how precious solitude was to me until it became clear that I would not have it much longer. And growing in me like ivy, strengthening each day and choking out everything else, was the resentment I felt at the impending loss of it.

"Everyone, come," boomed my father. "We will go into town. It is too hot to sit here like this. We will go to the little store. We will buy ice cream and cold drinks."

Father came slamming through the door of the motor home, slanting his wide-brimmed cowboy hat over his eyes to cut the glare of the sun. He wore that expression that won him so many admirers among our *kumpànya*: steely determination, the look of a man who has chosen a path and will follow it.

Today that path would lead us to ice cream. About this I would not complain. I was fond of ice cream, but more than that, I knew it would do me good to feel the air whip against my face as we rode into town, windows rolled down.

There were too many of us to fit at once into the Jeep, so it was decided that Father would make two trips. First he took Mother with the baby along with Violeta and Marko. Romeo, Alek, Anelie, and I waited for him to take them into town and then return for the rest of us.

Marko helped first my mother and then Violeta into the backseat of the Jeep. Then he handed Stefan to my mother before climbing into the front beside my father. As they drove away we waved, and Alek even ran alongside the road as the car gained speed, jumping and calling goodbye with the energy of a child.

Then they were gone, and we settled in the tent's shade to wait for my father to return for the rest of us.

Alek took up Romeo's guitar. He had learned a few chords; that, I suppose, is one of the advantages of a trip like this, one where there are so few distractions.

"Show me how you do that," begged Anelie, and Alek passed her the guitar.

"Put your fingers here and here," he showed her. "Then go like this with your other hand."

Romeo and I watched as Alek taught Anelie the basics of strumming the guitar. Alek looked very serious, as if he had been playing all his life.

"So the student becomes the teacher." Romeo laughed. He sat cross-legged with his hands across his knees. He dressed in the fashion of the *gazhè*, something our boys could get away with but the girls often could not. He was wearing light-colored slacks and a white shirt unbuttoned partway down so that a flash of his chest was revealed. His skin was a beautiful color—a brownish-gold, young and taut and full of beautiful health.

He was a nice boy. He would make a fine husband. I had nothing to complain about; Romeo had never threatened me, he had never spoken harshly to me; he was handsome and clever and from a good family.

I saw it then, our life together: long, like the road in front of us, long and flat.

When Romeo reached to take my hand, I pulled away.

His eyes showed that this hurt him, but he said nothing. We stared together out at the desert highway, the heat making it waver like water, waiting for my father to return.

Though we had been in the desert for seven days, this was the first time I had left the campsite. I sat in the back of the Jeep with my brother and sister. We had the windows open all the way. Hot, dry air, like a dragon's breath, blew my curls and Anelie's every which way. Alek sat between us covering his face with his hands, doing his best to avoid being whipped by the tendrils of our hair.

There was so much of it, though—her hair and mine. Ropes of it caught up in the draft of the air, tangling together like entwined fingers and lashing poor Alek until at last the car began to slow, pulling into the town's limits, past a sign that read *Gypsum, Population 489. Welcome to Nowhere.*

The town itself was a sad shell of a place. I could see that the small main street had been home to fewer than a dozen stores at the height of its inhabitancy. Now, though, every shop was closed and dark save for one—a double-wide storefront marked GYPSUM STORE.

I knew him right away, even before we reached the store. He was bent over his motorbike with the one they called Hog Boy, looking together at the engine. His helmet rested on the sidewalk behind him. The third boy—Pete—stood not far away. He seemed to be looking through the store's window, at someone or something he could see inside. His face was wistful, dreamy.

My father parked his Jeep just behind the motorbike. When he turned off the engine, Ben Stanley looked up, away from his motorbike and directly into my eyes.

All around me my family talked—Alek whined about our hair, Anelie laughed at his complaints—and in front of us Father and Romeo were discussing the mileage the Jeep had been getting lately, deciding whether it would be better to tow it into Reno after we left this place or have Marko drive it.

At the same time, the distance dividing us—me and Ben Stanley—seemed to collapse as if the fabric of space could fold and wrinkle in upon itself, as if even though we were twenty feet apart, separated by the bodies of my family and the glass and metal of the Jeep, we were at the same time as close together as we had been out in the desert when he called on me.

Then Anelie opened the car door and she and Alek tumbled out, bickering all the way into the store. Romeo got out of the car as well. He did not open my door; he did not look back for me. The set of his back was rigid. When he walked past Ben Stanley, his foot brushed the helmet into the gutter.

I would have liked to believe it was an accident, but I knew too much about Romeo—as surefooted as a goat—and about human nature. I understood the intention behind his movement.

Before I could get out of the car, my father stopped me. My hand was on the back of the seat in front of me, and Father covered it with his.

"Stay," he said.

The car, now that it was not in motion, felt hot like an oven's mouth.

I did not speak. Ben Stanley had retrieved his helmet from where it had landed. He was holding it and watching me.

"Is there something you would like to talk about with me?" Father asked.

I looked at Ben Stanley. I looked beyond him, at the door to the shop where my family waited. I looked at my father's hand atop my own. It was deeply tanned. One of his fingernails—the one on his index finger—was smaller than the others. Before I had been born, he had injured that finger with an electric saw while working on a table he was building for our home. Since then the nail had not grown back the same.

I looked in my father's eyes. They were dark like mine, bright and dark and sharp with sight.

It was not my father's fault.

"No, *Dadro*, nothing. There is nothing to say."

One can learn so much, if only one looks carefully. I saw many things even before I entered the Gypsum Store: I learned from Ben Stanley's face and the way he took half a step toward me before thinking better of it and staying where he was that he would still very much like to take me on a "date," in spite of having met Romeo and learning of our engagement.

I learned from the way his friend Hog Boy leered at me that he too would like to find himself alone with me, and I saw that he was all bluster; when I met his gaze his ears turned pink and he looked sideways at the curb.

I saw that Pete was anxious and that I was the source of his anxiety; he looked quickly back and forth, back and forth, between me and the entrance to the Gypsum Store.

When I pulled open the door to the store and stepped inside, I understood his discomfort. Behind the cash register was a plain girl with shoulder-length brown hair in braids and a name tag that read MELISSA.

So this was Pete's Melissa. The two of them were well matched, I could see that as well. She, like Pete, was clearly earnest; her hair was neatly arranged, and though her nose was pierced she wore just the tiniest sparkle of jewelry, appropriately discreet for work. Her apron appeared freshly laundered. Her nails were clipped short and unpolished.

I saw my family over in the refrigerated section of the store. Apart from my people, the store was nearly empty.

My younger sister and brother were staring down into the glass-topped case of Popsicles. They pressed their hands flat against the case, soaking up its coldness.

Marko stood near Violeta and my mother, who held Stefan in her arms, by the display of soda pops.

"Gimme root beer," pleaded Stefan, while my mother tried to get him to accept apple juice instead.

Romeo was near the counter. A small display of sunglasses was set up there and he tried on one pair after another. I felt him markedly ignoring me. Perhaps this should have hurt my feelings or made me uncomfortable, but it did neither of these things. His attitude seemed childish and impotent, and I felt no desire to help soothe his wounded ego.

Behind me, I heard the bell above the door announce another customer's entrance. Before the door closed, Hog Boy's loud squeal of laughter permeated the store. Then the door shut and thankfully muffled the sound.

It was Pete who had entered the store, and he sidled up beside Melissa. He wore a miserable expression and he pulled his bottom lip in between his teeth. Melissa slowly crossed her arms over her chest. She smiled a tight line. Pete started to say something to her but she ignored him. Her gaze was on me, appraising, and one eyebrow rose in a feline arch.

"A real dog, huh?" she hissed at him.

I could have heard his response if I cared to, but I took several steps away, doing my best to allow them privacy.

I had only one aim: to extend my time in the store as much as possible. Now that I was finally away from our camp, the thought of returning to it was torturous. The store was not air-conditioned, but several box fans whirred loudly, stirring up the hot, still air.

I wandered the aisles of the store though I needed nothing in particular, browsing just for the pleasure of looking at things.

The store stocked all the same basic supplies as any small-town store: boxes of cereal, canned beans, toilet paper, a row of chewing gum.

From the front of the store one would never guess that it was doing its last few days of business. But if you looked more closely, it became clear: most items were labeled *Two for One* or *Half Off,* and a whole section in the back read *Clearance: 75% Off.*

"What do you want, Lala?"

It was Anelie who asked. Her face looked up at me from the ice cream case, eyes wide with the pleasure of choosing, and I felt like one of the Questioners at a card reading.

What did I want? This, I did not know. Perhaps, though, I knew—all at once, and with a great certainty that I had not felt before—what I did *not* want.

"Why don't you choose for me," I said to Anelie.

"You have to choose for yourself," she said. "I might pick the wrong thing."

I nodded dumbly and bent my head over the ice cream case, though I did not clearly see the packages inside. I heard behind me my father's voice as he asked who was ready to return to camp; Marko and Violeta said they would go, and Romeo, who had chosen nothing, said he also was ready to leave.

The four of them left without a word to me. I kept my head bent over the ice cream case until I heard the Jeep pull away.

It would take my father ten minutes to get to our camp. And then another ten to return to the store to fetch the rest of us.

I had twenty minutes.

"Anelie," I said.

This is what I thought, while staring without seeing into the case of ice cream: Before Ben Stanley's reading, he had not shuffled the cards. Tapping them, he had passed them back across to me. What if the reading I had done for Ben Stanley was, in some way, my reading, as well? What if, when Ben Stanley drew the Fool, truly the Fool was me?

Could I be the Fool? Could I find an unexpected bend in the road? Could I step to the edge of a cliff, a steep and treacherous cliff from which there might not be any recovering?

And if I found the courage to do these things, could I take one step farther—deliberately, and understanding the cost of such a move—off the cliff's edge? All on my own—by my own choice, of my own will?

My feet moved beneath my skirt. My hand pushed open the door. I stepped outside.

He stood beside his bike, his back to me. I saw the tight bunching of the muscles of his shoulders as he faced his friend Hog Boy. I wanted to reach out to him, to lay my hand against the tension there, to smooth it out.

I did not.

Hog Boy said something that sounded like "the scary Gypsy girl," and it made my mouth turn up at the corners, the way Ben Stanley's shoulders lifted slightly higher before he turned to me.

"It's you," he said.

"None other."

He smiled slow and warm, and there was no mystery in his eyes. It was all there, simple for me to read, and so beautiful—his easy gladness that I had come to him, the eagerness that propelled him to reach out and touch my arm, the kindness I had first seen in him, as well.

"Wanna go for a ride?"

There was only one correct answer to that question: No.

But I could not bring myself to shake my head or step away. I had come this far—out the door, across the sidewalk, to Ben Stanley's side—and I would not stop now.

Later, perhaps I would blame it on the heat of the desert—that oppressive, hellish heat that beat down upon us day after day out there in the wasteland.

Or I could blame it on the pressure of my impending wedding, crashing on me with a weight I could not bear.

I think, though, that it was not either of these things. I think it was simply the way Ben Stanley looked, smiling at me, his face full of hope and promise.

Whatever it was—the heat or the wedding, or Ben Stanley himself—I took the helmet he offered me. I pushed it over my curls, and after Ben Stanley swung his leg over the bike and pounded the kick start with his heel, I bunched up my skirt around my thighs and straddled the seat behind him, wrapping my arms around his chest and turning my face into his back as we roared down the street and through the town, the sound of Hog Boy's cheer almost as loud as the pounding of my heart.

CHAPTER ELEVEN

I headed through town and out onto 447. Lala hung on to my waist, her arms clenching me tight and her thighs, too, tight around my hips. I felt the press of her against the back of me and I tried not to get hard.

As soon as we passed Freesia I opened up a little, picking up speed. I'd given my helmet to Lala and so I took the blast of hot air straight in my face, my hair puffing up like a Brillo pad. The bike had a little shimmy to it once I really got going. The road stretched out in front of us so straight and flat, I imagined for a minute that we'd never stop, that we'd just ride like that, Lala tucked behind me, forever.

I had hardly believed it when they'd all pulled up in front of the store. When the first load of them got there I'd been just hanging out, watching Pete fool around on the bike. He pretty much sucked on it; even James handled it better than Pete, and Hog Boy was getting a kick out of pointing out every time Pete screwed up.

Then a car pulled up in front of the store, blocking my view of Pete, and people started climbing out of it. Even if I hadn't recognized the Jeep from when I'd been out at their camp, I'd have known these people were Lala's family. They were unmistakable.

This thrill of excitement had zinged through me when I first saw the dark-haired girl in the back of the Jeep next to an older lady who must have been her mother. I thought it was Lala, and that maybe I'd get another chance after all.

But when she turned to climb out I saw that even though she had Lala's same wild mane of hair, she wasn't Lala. Her hard, round belly was a clue, but even more than that, it was the way she looked at the guy who gave her his hand to help her down.

Adoring. That was the look. She stared up at him with big doe eyes, not even watching where she put her feet, as if she knew he would never let her fall.

I hadn't seen Lala look at Romeo that way, engaged to be married or not. I hadn't glimpsed even a fraction of that intense . . . I don't know, *connection*, I guess, between her and Romeo.

I wanted her to look at *me* that way.

So when the Jeep pulled up again a little while later and I saw that this time it really *was* Lala in the backseat, with a couple of younger kids, I wanted to do something. Something . . . *big*, some gesture that she would be able to interpret.

Then that fucker Romeo kicked my helmet into the gutter, and I guess I got distracted.

I spent the next couple of minutes just breathing, calming myself down.

"Let's rush the fucker," said Hog Boy. I wasn't the only one who appreciated a good fight, and I guess Hog Boy saw this as an opportunity for a little fun.

"No," I said. "I don't want to make things hard for her."

And that was when I knew I wouldn't be making any grand romantic speech outside the Gypsum Store that afternoon. But I'd stay there, right where she could see me, and all she'd have to do was say the word.

I was already hers.

When she finally got out of the Jeep and walked by me, it hit me again like a wall—her scent. I would have given anything just then—hell, even my golden ticket to college—just to be alone with her, to fill myself with the smell of her.

Then she opened the door to the store and went inside.

"Knock, knock," said Hog Boy.

I heard my voice as if from far away. "Who's there?"

"Ben Hur."

"Ben Hur who?"

"Ben Hur over your motor bike and give it to her from behind."

Basically Hog Boy has one joke with occasional variations. I tried not to let myself channel my frustration into pounding Hog Boy, but it wasn't easy.

Pete groaned. "Goddamn it. Now Melissa's gonna take a good look at your Gypsy chick, Ben, and then I'm in a world of shit."

He yanked open the door to the store and slumped inside.

My Gypsy chick. Yeah, sure, that would be the day. She'd barely looked at me when she walked by. I kicked at the sidewalk, angry with myself for feeling so lame, so totally helpless.

A few minutes later a group of them headed back out to the Jeep and drove away. Lala wasn't one of them. But Romeo was.

After the others had climbed into the Jeep he turned to me before getting in.

He narrowed his eyes at me and carefully brushed his hair back from his face. Jesus, if the girls at our high school thought *Pete's* eyes were smoldering, they'd go into heat if they took one look at this guy.

"Lala knows her place," he said. "Remember yours."

I didn't need Hog Boy's two cents, that was for sure, but he stepped up anyway, puffing out his chest and pointing his finger in Romeo's face. "My boy Ben's place is wherever the fuck he wants to be."

"All right, Hog Boy, step off," I said. So much for not causing Lala any trouble.

Romeo hesitated for a minute like he was going to say something else or maybe stick a shiv in Hog Boy's flank, but then he spat at our feet and hopped into the Jeep.

"What the fuck was up with that guy?" asked Hog Boy as we watched them drive away. "You been holding out on us, Stanley? Have you been dippin' your stick in his candy?"

"Fuck you, Hog Boy."

He squealed his laugh and thumped me on the back. "Way to go out with a bang, big man!"

I didn't bother straightening him out. He wouldn't believe me anyway. He sees the world through swine-colored glasses, that's for sure.

But then there she was—Lala. Her eyes looked wild when she came out of the store, and she looked over her shoulder as if she expected someone to follow her. She looked scared, that was what it was, but defiant, too—and when I handed her my helmet, before her face disappeared behind its mask, she smiled at me. It was brilliant and beautiful and looked more sure just for that second than I've ever felt in my entire life, outside of running a race—when I know I'm leading the pack, when I can tell my feet will cross the finish line first.

And now here we were, at last, as if it was the way we were meant to be. That was how right it felt—having her pushed up behind me like that. Like we were a lock and a key, and just by pressing our bodies together in this way we'd managed to swing wide open a door that neither of us could open on our own.

But we couldn't ride forever on the old 150, so when I saw the turnoff for the mine I downshifted to second and pulled off the highway onto the dirt road. We passed the plant where the gypsum was crushed into dust and formed into sheets, and I saw our half-pipe on the empty shipping dock. I drove past it, farther down the road, all the way into the pit mine, down the road's long, curved decline, until we were fifty feet below street level, where men had dynamited a hole in the earth.

This was where our entire town's livelihood had come from—this mine. I used to think it was pretty cool—how in this time of technological advances, when so many people were building their fortunes on *ideas* rather than *actualities*, we in Gypsum still dealt in the basic stuff of the earth.

Rock. Big white hunks of it, torn from the ground, excavated, crushed and then manufactured into something else. You could get your head around it. There it was—a rock. A saleable commodity. It used to feel secure, I guess, and as a kid I thought it was neat how my dad and the other men in the town could just go dig up some rocks and trade them for money.

Of course that was a kid's oversimplification of a giant industry, and it failed to take into account the possibility of a collapse in the housing market.

I wasn't the only one who hadn't considered that possibility. No one in our town had seen it coming, back when our orders kept doubling and then doubling again, when it seemed that our country would just keep growing and building.

Newton said it best: What goes up must come down. That's why they call it a crash.

So our town was folding, and the mining operations were closed, and in a matter of years the desert would reclaim our houses, our whole town. The good people of Gypsum, Nevada? It would be like we'd never even lived here.

But the scar blasted into the earth out here at the mine? The violent, torn-apart landscape we'd created to get to the gypsum? That wouldn't heal.

I killed the engine at the bottom of the pit mine. We were hidden from view from the road, and the ledge of the pit cast a long shadow. I'd spent my share of days out here during school breaks and summer vacations, mostly as an errand boy for the guys who ran the big equipment. Every now and then they'd let me operate the excavator.

I was seeing the mine through new eyes, I guess, wondering how it looked to Lala. It was sort of awesome—half in shadow, half in sunlight, the pit was enormous. Above me the walls of the pit rose in a series of steps, designed to slow any dislodged boulders and prevent the quarry workers from being struck. The walls were stratified: bright white down at the base where the gypsum was, then a lighter orange in the middle layers, and a dusty brown where the topsoil was. It was cavernous, really, the enormity of the pit mine. Close to one of the walls the pit had been dug out even deeper so that all the runoff could gather in one place, forming a pond.

We came here to swim sometimes on the hottest days of summer, but even though it had been killer hot, not many of us had felt like hanging out at the mine this summer . . . too many ghosts, I guess.

But the mustangs were there—about a dozen in this herd, all different colors, black and brown and dun, drinking from the pond and lazily flicking their tails at flies. Protected by congressional law, the horses were free to roam pretty much wherever they liked in Nevada. It was illegal to harass them, and we weren't supposed to feed them, either. They lived off the sagebrush and wild grasses.

For a minute after we stopped, neither of us moved. Lala's arms stayed tight around my waist. I felt the press of the helmet between my shoulder blades.

I wondered what she was thinking. Was she regretting that she'd come with me? How much trouble would this get her in later, when she went home?

Probably this meant that things were off between her and Romeo. I didn't think that could be a bad thing, but I wondered how pissed off her parents would be that she'd disappeared with me.

There would be plenty of time to think about that later, I decided. We'd deal with all of them when the time came. But right now—alone, finally, with this girl, I wasn't about to waste any time talking about her maybe-ex-boyfriend or her parents.

I think Lala came to the same conclusion because when she loosened her arms from around my chest and swung off the bike, her skirt billowing down to the ground, and when she pulled the helmet off her head, she wore the same smile I'd seen in front of the store.

"The die is cast," she said, holding the helmet out to me. I took it.

We walked together to the coolest spot we could find, up against the rocky wall of the mine past the edge of the pond, a little extra-deep divot that was created when workers had pulled a larger-than-usual rock out of the earth. It wasn't a cave or anything like that, more like an inlet.

I wished I had a blanket to spread on the ground or something, but of course I hadn't exactly planned this whole thing.

I guess all my daydreams about Lala had led up to this instant in time, being alone with her. Now that we were here . . . I didn't really know what to do.

But Lala didn't seem unsure, not in the slightest. She found a flat spot on the ground and lowered herself Indian-style to the dirt. Then she looked up at me and offered me her hand.

Our fingers laced together easily, and I settled on the ground next to her. It was way cooler in the shade, and being close to the water helped, too. Once I was sitting I didn't want to let go of Lala's hand. I kind of felt like now that I had ahold of her, I'd better hang on tight.

It occurred to me that we hadn't gone through any of the small talk—the introductory, warm-up conversation that people go through when they first meet. You know, where are you from, what are you into, what kind of music do you like, shit like that.

But considering what had just happened—Lala ditching her family at the Gypsum Store to ride out here with me—it seemed kind of dumb to start playing twenty questions now.

Luckily I didn't have to be the one to get the ball rolling. Lala spoke.

"How can you tolerate this heat?" she asked, and she took her hand away from me to push her hair back and out of her face, her fingers twisting it up into a knot at the nape of her neck.

For a second I worried that maybe the hair thing was just an excuse to get her hand out of my sweaty palm. But then, sort of shyly, she slid her hand back into mine. Our fingers laced together again.

"It's pretty hot," I admitted. I managed to sound casual, I thought. "You get used to it, though. I guess you can get used to pretty much anything."

Lala arched an eyebrow. Just one. "Out of necessity, perhaps," she agreed. "But with a cost."

"Where are you from?" There—I'd done it.

"Portland."

Her answer kind of took me by surprise. Portland—such a normal place to be from. I guess I don't know what I had expected her to say. Something more exotic, I guess. Like somewhere in Europe.

"Lots of rain, huh?" I could have kicked myself, I sounded so lame.

She smiled, though, like she thought I was mildly amusing. "Constantly," she said. "Everything is green and damp. It is often cold."

The weather. We were talking about the weather.

"Look," I said. "I'm really glad you came here with me."

Lala's thick lashes lay against her cheeks and a pink flush colored her face. "I came because I wanted to," she said.

It seemed like a simple enough answer, but I think I understood what she meant. Seriously, how many of us do the things we really want to do? I've said it before—I don't always run because I *feel* like it. I'm pretty sure Mom and Pops moved out here to Gypsum not because it sounded like so much *fun* but because they thought it would be their best chance at the kind of life they thought they should give their kids.

Hog Boy—maybe *he* made all his choices based on what he felt like doing at that particular moment in time. But we can't have a world full of Hog Boys.

"There is something else I would like to do." And then Lala leaned over toward me.

She hesitated before she kissed me, and I forced myself to be perfectly still—not to lean forward like I wanted to and smash my mouth against hers, but to wait for her. She stayed like that, her lips so close to mine and the citrus-sweet scent of her surrounding me. Her lips were parted. They looked full and soft, so tempting I could hardly control myself. Mrs. Howell's breathing technique came in handy again, and I just waited, wound tight and so wanting her, until finally she leaned forward that last half inch, and she kissed me.

I closed my eyes. It seemed like I'd lost all sense of direction—it didn't matter which way was up or down, whether I was standing or sitting. All that mattered was that Lala was kissing me.

It was different from when Cheyenne and I kissed. Cheyenne was all eager pressing tongue, and kissing her had always felt like kind of a competition. Lala's kiss—it was sweeter than honey, and soft, too, like velvet. And it was as if time went away when her mouth was against mine. I didn't feel that urgency to push forward, to see how far I could get. It was like I had everything I wanted.

Too soon, though, she pulled away, just a little, and I opened my eyes. She was still right there, so close to me, and I tilted my chin forward a little, hoping she'd kiss me again.

Lala laughed. "I like you, Ben Stanley." She sat back, widening the distance between us. "I am pleased to be here with you."

I cleared my throat and grinned. "Not half as happy as I am."

"I want to hear about you, Ben Stanley." Lala's voice sounded different, now that we had kissed—full of confidence, I guess, like she'd sounded back in her tent with the cards.

"Don't you already know everything there is to know?"

"Most likely," she said. "But I would like to hear it in your voice."

I chuckled a little. She sounded so sure of herself. "So is it magic?" I asked. "What else can you do? Can you pull a rabbit out of a hat?"

"No magic. None at all. I am sorry if this disappoints you. The truth is, you *gazhè* give away so much. You make my job very easy."

I felt a little offended. Maybe she hadn't meant to, but she had said that word—"*gazhè*"—like it was something bad.

"I'll bet you don't know as much about me as you think," I said.

"You are an athlete, and the older of two sons. You feel

terrible guilt about leaving your brother on his own because you fear what will become of him without you there to offer him protection. Your friends are faithful, and look to you as a leader. Here, too, you feel you are shirking a responsibility by leaving them. You will leave in a matter of days to go to college. And even though you know you shouldn't, you feel an attraction to me, a desire to be close to me, to touch my flesh."

I didn't know what to say. Part of me felt embarrassed, to have it laid out there so plain, and part of me felt kind of angry. I guess I felt . . . I don't know, invaded.

She must have seen that, too, on my face because she said, "I do not mind these things. I do not mind that you desire me."

I wasn't used to it—this kind of naked honesty. Chicks aren't like that. Most of the time it's like they're trying to be mysterious, to make things difficult.

It's usually all smoke and mirrors, as if they want to complicate matters to distract us guys from the truth—that they're as lost and confused as we are.

But Lala didn't seem like she was trying to hide anything, and still she was a mystery to me.

"Tell me how you know all that stuff."

"I pay attention," she answered. "That is all."

I tried to quiet my mind, to think back to the reading she had done. If I really thought about it, I guessed that some of it made sense—she could see the way Hog Boy and Pete sort of looked up to me, and I kind of remembered Hog Boy making one of his comments about James, so that must have been when she found out I had a brother. College—that must have come up in conversation, too. I hadn't really been trying to hide anything; maybe I did give an awful lot away. And the way I felt about her—I guess that was pretty plain to see.

"Okay, but how did you know that I'm an athlete?" I was pretty sure I hadn't mentioned anything about that.

"You have a beautiful body," she said. "Strong muscles and sun-kissed hair. This does not happen without work, and time out-of-doors."

I tried not to show it, but I was sort of embarrassed when she called me beautiful.

"Let me try it," I said.

"All right," she answered, and she sat very still.

I tried to look really carefully at her face, and at the clothes she was wearing, the way she sat.

She had a little half smile on those fabulous lips, like she thought I was amusing or something. I saw that she wasn't wearing any makeup. Even though her eyelashes were long and dark, they weren't clumpy at all, like Cheyenne's used to get when we'd go out on a date. And the color on her lips hadn't rubbed off when she'd kissed me; it was hers, naturally.

Her hair was starting to unwind from the knot she'd pulled it into and I let myself reach across to her, wind a tendril of it around my finger. I saw as I brushed the back of my hand against her cheek that she sort of caught her breath.

"You're not one of those fancy girls who's hung up on how

she looks," I said. "I'll bet you don't spend too much time looking in the mirror."

Then I let my gaze trace over the rest of her, hoping it wouldn't make her uncomfortable for me to look at her like this. I saw that she was wearing the same white shirt she'd been wearing the first time I'd seen her, and that like then, it was tucked into her skirt, belted with a thin piece of leather.

"You're not really into the latest fashions," I guessed. "You have your own style, and you don't care if it's not what other girls are wearing."

I wanted to look into her face to see how I was doing, but I pressed on. I saw that she had a thin gold bracelet around her right wrist. It didn't have a clasp, and it wasn't really loose or jangly. "You're left-handed," I guessed. I figured she'd put the bracelet on whatever hand she used the least, kind of the way I did on the rare occasions when I wore a watch.

"Well?" I asked. "How am I doing?"

"Not terribly, for a beginner. I am left-handed, that is true. And I do not care for makeup. You are right there also. But the fashion . . ." She shrugged. "I do like fashion," she said. "But for my people—and especially in my family—it is not common for the women to show their legs."

"Really? Why not?"

"It is complicated."

"Try me."

She looked conflicted then, and I got the feeling she wanted to tell me more but wasn't sure how much to say.

"Lala," I said, "I want to know everything about you."

She thought before she spoke. "Have you heard of *marimè*?"

I shook my head.

"It means . . . unclean. Not dirty—worse. Like a darkening of the soul."

"And fashion—that's *marimè*?"

"Not fashion," she said. "The body, from the waist down, is unclean. Especially the lower body of a woman. At best it is unclean. At worst, a source of *marimè*."

I could tell she was embarrassed. And she took her hand back from me then, and wrapped both of her arms around her knees like she was cold, which I knew she couldn't be, not out here in the desert midafternoon.

It made me angry. That Lala should feel that way about her body—any part of it—that there was something shameful or wrong about it. I didn't want to insult her or be disrespectful to her culture, but from where I sat it just didn't make any sense at all.

"Well," I said finally, "I don't know about that. If it weren't for these babies"—I thumped my hands against my thighs—"I'd be heading to Reno instead of San Diego next week. And I don't want to be . . . I don't know, insensitive, I guess, to your culture . . . but I got a quick look at your legs when you were getting on my bike back in town. There's not a thing wrong with them."

She flushed a deep crimson red then, and I think tears came to her eyes, but she blinked them back pretty fast.

I didn't say anything for a minute, I just kind of looked

away to give her a chance to sort of compose herself. But then I put my hands on her arms, wrapped tight around her legs. "Can I do something?" I asked.

For a second she held on even tighter. Her eyes looked around kind of panicked, like maybe she would run. Then her gaze landed on my motorbike and I guess she remembered the hugeness of what she had already done, coming way out here with me, away from her family.

And she nodded, and she let go.

CHAPTER TWELVE

LALA

Ben Stanley knelt near my feet and his hands touched the hem of my skirt. I was in a place I had never been in before. This landscape, first of all, with its husked-out rawness, bare dirt and rock all around me, and, as if a miracle, this other thing I never would have guessed could be here—a body of water, white tinged by gypsum dust but a real oasis, one you could not see from the road, a beautiful surprise.

And horses. To me horses had always been something special. They seemed to embody my own secret heart, what I often wished to be but did not always feel—wild and free, proud and strong.

There used to be a saying, back when my people traveled in caravans: A Gypsy without a horse is not a Gypsy.

Of course, the days of traveling by horse-drawn caravans ended long before I was born. In these modern days my people kept permanent homes more often than not, and when we did head out on the road we traveled like everybody else, in motor-driven vehicles.

Still, it seemed somehow just right to see these horses in Ben Stanley's quarry. As if our two worlds were in some way more linked than I could have guessed.

I think it was because of the horses that I allowed Ben Stanley to slowly raise the hem of my skirt. He pushed the fabric up above my knees and looked at my bare legs. No one before had looked at me like this. I had not known that it was possible for anyone to do so, and I felt shame wash over me. To allow him to touch the hem of my skirt, to gaze as he was at the skin of my lower limbs—it felt unclean, more than that—*marimè*.

But I had made a choice when I left the store and climbed on Ben Stanley's motorbike. This was where that choice had led me. So I asked my body to stay still, and I waited to see what would happen next.

He took my right leg in his hands. His blond head lowered over it and I felt his hot breath against my bare skin. And then his lips touched the inside of my ankle, feather soft, the lightest of kisses.

I had never before known true hunger. When his lips connected with my leg, kissing me first on my ankle and then in a line, kiss after kiss, up the inside of my leg to my knee, it burst like a flame in my core—urgent, pressing hunger, a desire I could not refuse, one I would not want to refuse even if I knew how.

I heard a little sound like a whimper, and as if from far away I recognized that it had come from my own body. Eyes closed, head back, I allowed myself the pleasure of receiving his kisses without thinking about what they meant, what taboos they were breaking, one after the other, each kiss severing one of the many ties that bound me.

He untied the laces of my sandals and slipped them off. His hands, so strong and warm, caressed my feet. I opened my eyes and looked at him. Still his head was bent, worshipful.

And then came a wave of something that at first I did not have a word for. I liked the sensation, and I considered carefully how to name it. Ah. It was power. I felt *powerful*, with my feet in Ben Stanley's hands. I felt powerful, and beautiful too—but perhaps what was even more wonderfully surprising was what I *did not* feel. . . . After that first instant of fear and the rush of pleasure that had followed, I did not feel shame. No—this was not entirely true. The shame was still there, less now than before but with me still, as if drawn behind a curtain of something much, much better.

"You see?" said Ben Stanley, smiling up at me.

"I do." I smiled, as well.

He rested my feet in his lap, his fingers playing lightly on my calves, drawing invisible patterns across them. I saw in his eyes that he felt it, too, the hunger that nearly consumed me, but I saw, too, that he intended to control it.

He did not want to frighten me. He did not want to push me farther than I might want to go. I liked this. Ben Stanley, *gazhò* or not, was kind.

This I had known all along.

"Tell me more about you," he asked.

"What do you wish to know?"

He shrugged. "Whatever you want to say."

Down by the water, one of the horses laid back his ears and nipped at the horse next to him. The other horse took several steps away.

"When I first came here, I hated the desert," I told him. "It seemed to me that there was not much to see, and what little there was held no mystery. But today you are showing me places I could not have guessed existed."

Most likely he thought I meant this quarry, which was true enough, but I spoke also of the way I felt. It had been like a desert—barren, flat, scorched dry—but it seemed to me now that there could be secret, hidden places anywhere, unexpected oases just beyond the horizon.

"The desert is pretty much all I've ever known," Ben said.

"Soon you will leave it."

He nodded. My feet he held still in his lap, and his hands felt warm and wonderful.

"Your family will be pretty pissed about your coming out here, huh?"

Of course he could not possibly comprehend the enormity of what I had done, coming as he did from his *gazhikanò* world. For him it would be like a game, to disobey his parents, to go where he was not supposed to be. Perhaps he would be put "on restriction," or his parents might "ground" him. Child's play.

I did not wish to tell him what it would mean for me. He would feel responsible, but he was not. I had made my own path.

So instead of answering his question, I asked my own. "What will you miss the most when you leave this place?"

He answered right away without having to consider. "The feeling that I totally belong. Here, everyone knows everything about everyone. It sucks a lot of the time, but it's nice, too. To not have to explain myself or introduce myself or anything. Even the things that aren't so great about me—and there are lots of them, probably—everybody knows what they are and accepts me anyway. I guess they don't really have a choice, in a town this size."

His answer resonated deeply. Already I felt my family stretching far away from me. Where were they now? What were they doing?

They had of course discovered what I had done. My father would have returned to collect the rest of us. My mother would have told him that I was missing. Ben Stanley's friends—Hog Boy and Pete—perhaps my parents would press them for information. Or perhaps my parents had turned their backs on me already. Like Ana's, it could be that my name already was *marimè*.

My mother and father, they would recover. They had other children. And Violeta, much as she loved me, had Marko and her baby to consider. Stefan was still too little to comprehend what had happened, and it seemed doubtful if Alek would really care—he and I had not been close. But Anelie—her heart would break and break and break for me. She would have to muffle the sound of her tears.

I wanted to talk about them. I wanted to pretend just for a little while that they would be waiting for me to return. "I have two sisters and two brothers," I told Ben Stanley. "A big family, most likely it seems to you."

"I've just got the one brother. But you knew that." His smile, endearing and so open.

"Yes. My older sister—you have seen her."

"The one who's pregnant?"

I nodded. "Violeta. She is not so much older than I am. We were children together." I did not say the rest of it—that we had planned to be wives together, and mothers.

"But also," I continued, "I have younger siblings—one a brother, almost thirteen."

"Not much older than James."

"And a younger sister, too, and a baby brother as well. Not so much a baby anymore—he is three years old—but he is my mother's last, and so he will be the baby always."

"With James, I feel like I'm doing this terrible thing, you know, by going off to college." He did not say it as if he expected or hoped I would contradict him. He was not looking for me to assuage his guilt. He was sharing his fears with me, that was all.

Still, I felt the argument well up inside me. "You do well to leave your brother," I said. "He is not your child, he is your sibling. He will miss you, of course, but he will learn from example—that it is all right for him to leave also, when he is of age, that he has the right to lead a life of his choice. Perhaps it is your leaving that will give him courage to follow his own path, wherever it may lead."

There was real passion in my voice, and it was not lost on me that I was making an argument in favor of my own betrayal.

"I'm not so sure I want James to follow his own path.

Sometimes it's safer to stick with the herd. Like those horses," he said, raising his chin at the mustangs. "They know there's safety in numbers. In blending in."

"Ben Stanley, are you a hypocrite? *You* did not win any races by staying with the pack. In order to win, you had to forge ahead."

He grinned. "Yeah. I guess so. But I'm stronger than James."

"What makes you so certain?"

He opened his mouth to speak, but then he seemed to realize that he did not have an answer. Finally he said, "I don't know."

I nodded, satisfied. "No," I said. "You do not."

We watched the horses. They seemed to be enjoying the pond; several of them stood ankle-deep in it, eyes half-closed.

"Why were you going to marry that guy?" Ben's question came out suddenly, as if he had finally built up the courage to ask something he had been wondering for a long time.

"My people are very different from yours." I did not know how much to reveal; I wanted to share myself with Ben Stanley, but at the same time I did not wish to hear him scorn our traditions, our beliefs. Even as I questioned many of them myself, I was not inclined to listen to others' reactions.

"My mom said something—about arranged marriages? Is that true?"

I listened to the way he spoke, searching for any sign of mocking or disgust. But all I could hear was curiosity, and in his face I saw his eager desire to know me—nothing more.

"It is true," I said. "Our parents choose our spouses, often when we are very young."

"And do you—have a choice in the matter? Do you *have* to marry the person they choose?"

"My people recognize that these are modern times," I began. "If I were to refuse, most likely my parents would support my decision. Now, however, it will probably not be an issue anymore."

"You mean because you came here—with me?"

I nodded. And then I went on. I told him more than I had meant to share—about the way I had known for many years that I would marry Romeo Nicholas, about helping Violeta prepare for her wedding to Marko, about my life at home in Portland, how it had revolved always around the family, and also about how things had shifted—grown less certain in my own mind—as my eighteenth birthday and the day of my wedding grew closer.

He was a good listener. Truly he seemed interested in what I had to say; he asked questions occasionally, like why I had not attended high school and what kind of work my family did, but mostly he was quiet. His eyes did not leave my face, and when I tried to pull back my feet, to tuck them beneath my skirt, he squeezed them, began to massage them, so luxurious to me that I could not draw them away.

"But it's all off now, huh?" It was sweet the way he could not disguise the pleasure he felt because my engagement to Romeo had been broken.

"Unfortunately, it is not so simple as that," I said. "There is the matter of the bride price, already paid. It will cause my family embarrassment . . . embarrassment and shame to have to return the money."

"Bride price?" His forehead wrinkled. "Do you mean that Romeo—he *paid* for you?"

There it was. It had taken longer than I thought it might, but at last it emerged—his incredulity, his disgust at my people's practice. This time when I shifted and pulled my feet from his lap, he let them go.

"Fifteen thousand dollars," I said, knowing the amount would shock him.

"I don't care if it's fifteen *million*," he said. "Money shouldn't have anything to do with love."

"Often," I said, "love does not have anything to do with marriage. This is true of your people, too. We are just more honest about it."

I saw the fight in him, and I saw, too, how he restrained it, willing himself to listen to me. So I went on.

"It is not ideal," I admitted, "but very little of life really is. And it is not as if I was to be sold into slavery. I could have refused. My father would have listened."

"So why would you agree to it?"

"You think you see things clearly, but you do not see *deeply*, Ben. The same is with the way you think about your brother, and your parents' situation also. You see only how things appear to be from where you are sitting. But rarely is an answer so easy, so one-sided. Perhaps there is more than one truth."

He ignored my philosophical interpretation. "Did you *want* to marry him?"

180

"I wanted to stay close to my sister Violeta. I wanted to please my parents. I wanted to make my family proud."

"So why are you here? With me?"

I looked out onto the pond, imagining how wonderful it would feel to shed my clothes and wade into the water, walking farther and farther until my head was completely submerged.

"Have you ever read a book called *The Catcher in the Rye*?"

"Sure. It was required reading last year."

"What do you think of Holden Caulfield?"

Ben shrugged. "I don't think too much of him. He's kind of a pitiful character, I guess. Closed-minded."

"Do you know the scene—when he sits with his sister Phoebe and tells her that he wants to be a catcher in the rye—that he wants to stand in a rye field near the edge of a cliff, and keep kids from falling from it?"

"Sure," he said. "I wrote a paper about that scene. My teacher was crazy about that book. She loved to talk about Holden Caulfield, about how he based his whole fantasy around something that wasn't even real."

"I do not understand," I said.

"He thought that the poem said 'If a body catch a body,' but really it said 'If a body *meet* a body.'"

"Yes," I said. "I read that. His sister corrects him."

"Yeah, but my teacher made us read the actual poem. It was written by this guy Burns. Mrs. Clark—my teacher—said the word 'meet' doesn't just mean . . . you know, meet. It means . . . hook up with."

I felt confused now, a feeling I did not enjoy. "Explain this to me," I said. "I do not know the poem."

"Well, Burns meant—you know, he meant that if a man and a woman met in a field of rye—where no one was looking, where no one would know that they had met at all—would it be so wrong if they, you know, enjoyed each other. If they made love." He looked embarrassed. "I know the poem, actually," he said. "I had to memorize it for class. For extra credit."

"Tell it to me."

"Well, it's different. It doesn't sound like regular English." He must have seen on my face that I very much wanted to hear the poem, for he cleared his throat and said, "Okay. Here goes . . . 'Comin thro' the rye, poor body, / Comin thro' the rye, / She draigl't a' her petticoatie, / Comin thro' the rye! / O, Jenny's a' weet, poor body, / Jenny's seldom dry; / She draigl't a' her petticoatie, / Comin thro' the rye! / Gin a body meet a body / Comin thro' the rye, / Gin a body kiss a body, / Need a body cry? / Gin a body meet a body, / Comin thro' the glen, / Gin a body kiss a body, / Need the warl' ken?'" He stopped.

"I do not understand."

"Well, you've kind of got to translate it. Basically he's saying, this girl Jenny was coming through the rye field, dragging her petticoats. She wore a long skirt, like you. And it's all damp, you know, from brushing against the grasses. And she met somebody. A man. And the poet asks—can two people meet, and kiss, and go on their separate ways?

Does that have to be a tragedy? Does the rest of the world need to know about it?"

We were not in a field of rye. And I was not a girl named Jenny. I was Lala White, daughter of Mickey White, *rom barò*, and in my life privacy and secrecy were not allowed.

I was here, with Ben Stanley—this other body. I had kissed him once. I yearned to kiss him again. But I suffered no delusions that this was without a cost.

"Thank you for telling me the poem," I said. "I feel I understand the book more clearly now."

"Do you like to read?"

"Very much. It is—it has been—a way for me to see the world."

"I'm not much of a reader," Ben confessed. "I read all the books required in my English classes, but it's not really my thing."

"You prefer action."

He nodded.

"What is it like," I asked him, "to compete as you do?"

He smiled, showing his white, even teeth. "It's the best feeling there is. It's like nothing else. You train so hard, you know, to prepare for a race, but when it comes down to it, what really matters, aside from all the practice, is if you can find it right then, when you need it. If you can bring it up to the surface. And when I'm running like that, flat out, there's nothing like it. The guy breathing down my neck, whether or not the people are cheering, all of that sort of goes away. It's just me. And if I don't win, that's all me, too. Some guys don't like the pressure of racing. But I love it. Because it means that no matter what, win or lose, it's all on me."

This I understood. The desire to feel that kind of control, that kind of responsibility. It was what had brought me here.

The sky above us was the brightest blue I could imagine, shot across with streaks of white. The air was perfectly still, as if the world was holding its breath.

"My people tell many stories," I said to Ben Stanley. "I would like to tell you one of them."

"Okay."

"It goes like this: Once there was a rich Gypsy magician who lived alongside a magical river. His one sadness was that he and his wife did not have a child. But one day while he was washing his face in the river, an eagle flying by dropped a mouse from its talons and it landed right in front of the magician. He picked up the mouse and dipped it in the river, transforming it into a little girl. He took the little girl home to his wife, who cried with joy, and they raised her as their own daughter.

"But the time came, as it always does, for the man to marry off his daughter. He loved her dearly, and wished to marry her to the most powerful man in the world, so he summoned the Sun God and asked his daughter if she would like to be married to him.

"But she said, 'No, Father, he would burn me with his rays.'

"So the magician asked the Sun God if he knew of someone even more powerful to whom he could marry his daughter.

"The Sun God said, 'Yes—the Cloud is stronger than I, for it can hide my face.'

"But the daughter did not wish to marry the Cloud, either. She found him too dark for her liking.

"And when the magician asked the Cloud if he knew of someone even more powerful to whom he could marry his daughter, the Cloud suggested the Wind.

"Unfortunately, the girl was not happy with this choice, either. 'He is too changeable and cold,' she said. 'He will freeze me.'

"So the magician asked the Wind for a suggestion—who was more powerful than the Wind?

"'The Mountain,' suggested the Wind.

"The girl found fault here, as well: 'Too big,' she said.

"Frustrated now, the magician asked the Mountain, 'Does there exist one more powerful than you?'

"'Yes,' replied the Mountain. 'The mouse, for given enough time, it can destroy even me.'

"And so the magician asked his daughter, 'Do you want to marry the mouse?'

"To this she answered, 'Yes. But you will have to transform me into a mouse again.'

"And so he did, and the two mice were married, and they lived together happily for all of their days."

Ben Stanley was quiet for a long time after I finished telling him the story. At last he said, "I don't get it."

This made me laugh. "It is meant to teach a lesson."

"What lesson?"

"Ah, that is the question. Some of my people say that it

shows that people should stay with their own kind—that Gypsies should stay with Gypsies and *gazhè* should stay with *gazhè*. Nothing but trouble comes from trying to become something you are not."

"And the others? What do they say?"

"They say that it is a lesson about why we should let people make their own choices. Without freedom, the girl would have been married to the wrong man. Given freedom, she chose correctly."

"What about you, Lala? What do you think?"

Now I was the one who was quiet. At last I said, "I am not a mouse. And I am not convinced that the girl in the story was anymore, either, not truly. She may have once been a mouse, but then something changed and she was not. The mouse girl was wrong to think she could return to what she had once been, and the storytellers are naïve to teach that happiness can come in this way. It is possible that I am not yet who I will become. It is possible that none of it is for me. I may not yet know what I want—but I am coming to understand what it is I do not want. If I stay where I am—with my family, with my people, I know what lies ahead for me. I have seen my future on that path. I have seen it in the face of my mother, in the belly of my sister. That is not what I want. Not now. Perhaps not ever."

CHAPTER THIRTEEN

BEN

I'd said that I didn't want to cause Lala any trouble. That was a lie I'd told myself, I think, so I'd have the nerve to get her here alone with me. If not causing her trouble had been more important to me than finding a way to be close to her, I never would have offered her my helmet.

So here was proof—as if I needed any—that I was a selfish fuck. I guess it was pretty easy for me, with a full ride waiting for me at UCSD like a fucking leprechaun's pot of gold at the end of a rainbow, to go screwing with other people's lives. If I were a better person—a stronger person—I would have ignored her at the store.

She didn't look worried about it, though. She looked . . . peaceful. The expression on her face reminded me of something. But I couldn't remember what.

The heat was killing me. Maybe it was worse because I felt like I was burning up on the inside, too, thinking about what I had done to Lala. The brightness was overwhelming, the way the sun hit all that white and reflected off of it. It was sort of like living in a mirror, being out here at the quarry. The water looked cool, half-shaded by the wall of the pit mine. I knew from experience that the far side of the pond had a dangerous drop-off and some really sharp rocks, but this side was mellow if you knew where to step.

"Do you want to put your feet in the water?" The question didn't come out nearly as nonchalantly as I'd intended.

Lala looked out at the pond. I watched her face change from that peacefulness as her eyebrows pulled together and her mouth kind of twisted to the side. She glanced behind her, up to where the road led down into the quarry. She stared off that way for a minute, almost as if she was expecting to see someone driving down it.

I'm not as good at reading people as Lala is, that's for sure, but her expression didn't seem that hard to interpret. She looked thoughtful, and then she looked a little scared, maybe insecure.

But when she stood up and spoke, her voice didn't show any of that. "I would like to swim," she said.

Of course my mind went immediately to what this could mean—that she might take her clothes off.

Okay, what I felt about Lala, I didn't have any experience in feeling. There was this vibration between us, a connection, a closeness that I hadn't felt with anyone else. I felt closest to Pete, and when I was a kid I'd been tight with my parents, but this was different than either of those relationships, of course.

Still, none of these sweet, romantic thoughts were pure enough to keep me from wanting to see her naked.

Conflicted. That was what it was. Part of me wanted to

protect her virtue and talk her out of swimming with me out here in the middle of nowhere—something I was damn sure her family wouldn't approve of, not in a million years—but the other half of me was crazy giddy at the thought of Lala dripping wet.

So even though I offered her my hand—like a gentleman would—I didn't feel entirely good about what I was helping her toward.

We walked to the edge of the pond. Lala looked into the milky depths of the water.

"Is it safe?"

I shrugged. "It'd better be. I've been swimming here every summer since I was a kid."

I guess we were lucky that our town mined gypsum. All pit mines end up with ponds, but most of them are toxic because of heavy metals in them. Gypsum isn't toxic and left the pond safe for swimming, though I wouldn't drink the water. Didn't seem to bother the horses.

Silver lining, again; while it was nice that our pond was safe for swimming, if we'd mined something else, even something toxic as shit, my dad would probably still have a job.

I watched as Lala's hands went to the leather belt at her waist. She began to uncinch it.

So she was going to take her clothes off. I felt my face flush, and Lala looked at me with a smile. "Is this all right with you?"

"Sure! I mean, if you want to. I mean, you know. . . . Do you want me to look the other way?"

"If you would like to."

Come on. What kind of answer was that? Of course I didn't *want* to look away, but if I didn't, what kind of a guy did that make me?

I settled for sort of turning and facing out toward the water. Even though I couldn't exactly see her like this, I felt her movements next to me and I saw a flash of white as she untwisted her wrap shirt. There was a hesitation between her undoing her shirt and taking it off, as if she wasn't quite sure about what she was doing, as if she might change her mind. I'm not proud to admit that I was practically praying that she'd keep undressing, and I felt myself let out a breath I hadn't realized I'd been holding as she made up her mind and tossed it aside. Then she unfastened her skirt. I heard a quiet whisper of cloth as it pooled at her feet.

When she walked forward into the water I could see her clearly.

Her hair was like a cape, cascading across her shoulders and down her back, all the way to her hips. I saw a flash of her white panties—real panties, not butt floss like Cheyenne wore—and then her curvy legs—paler than her arms and face, probably because she always wore those long skirts—as she walked waist deep into the pond.

She turned and looked at me over her shoulder. I could see that she was wearing a bra—also white—and even though these two items of underclothing covered way more of her skin than the bikinis most other girls wore, I still felt like I was seeing her more naked than anyone I'd ever seen.

Her face was flushed, too, and it seemed like maybe she

was acting tougher than she felt. Still, she asked, "Will you join me?"

I was still dressed. Fuck. That made me a voyeur, right? I fumbled out of my jeans, kicking off my sneakers and socks and almost tripping in the tangled mess of fabric, and pulled my T-shirt up over my head.

For a quick second of panic, I couldn't remember if I'd put on underwear that morning. I peeked down—yeah. There they were, a pair of the boxer briefs my mom had bought for me.

It was pretty clear from the bulge in the front of them that Lala had made quite an impression on me, and I could see from the angle of her eyes that she noticed.

And she took her time looking me over—I could practically feel the heat of her gaze as she looked at my legs, my groin, my stomach and chest—and for a minute I felt . . . I don't know, on display, I guess, but I just stood there anyway, at the edge of the water, and let Lala take her sweet time.

The ends of her hair were wet now, dipped into the water, and strands of it clung to her body, across her belly, over her hips. She was such a pretty shape—all soft curves and slopes—and against the craggy, angular backdrop of the pit mine, the desperately hot and blank blue sky, she looked like a delicate, beautiful vase.

"You're beautiful," I said.

She didn't look like my compliment made her really happy. I think maybe she would have preferred if I hadn't commented on her body at all, but she looked so fragile, so unsure, standing there in the water, it was almost as if I could see her invisible battle between the urge to cover herself with her hands and her desire to let herself be seen.

Still, she said, "Thank you." And then she scooped her hand full of water, tossing it at me. The cool drops splashed across my chest. "Come in," she said.

She didn't have to ask me twice. I ducked under, closing my eyes tight until I resurfaced. Then I shook my head like a dog, and I could tell from her squeal of laughter that I'd gotten her.

I caught her hand in mine and we waded deeper. I knew where to put my feet, negotiating the uneven pond bed easily from years of practice. Lala kind of clung to my arm and she did her best to step where I'd stepped. A couple of times she stepped on a rock funny and lost her balance and I held her upright. We stopped when she was about chest deep and had found a level standing place about a dozen feet in from the edge of the pond.

Lala loosened her grip on my arm when her footing was secure and we stood there together, quietly, just enjoying not being hot for a change. That wasn't all I was enjoying, I guess—standing next to Lala like that, alone except for the horses, who'd only taken a few steps away when we'd gone into the water before they went back to ignoring us—that was worth enjoying, too.

My arm wrapped around Lala's waist. Almost weightless in the water, she floated up against my side. Slowly she shifted until we were face to face, chest to chest, and she wound her arms around my neck. I felt all of her—her breasts, her belly, her hips and thighs—float up against me, though it seemed that she didn't want to let her legs touch mine. All her slopes and curves fit against my hard angles and I thought again of what I'd first felt on the bike—that pressing our flesh together just right created something magical, turned some lock that released us both.

Her kiss felt shy at first, but I wasn't in any hurry to push her into anything, so we just kissed like that for a while, our lips brushing against each other's, and I did my best not to do anything she didn't seem to want. But after a little while it was like she melted a little, her mouth softening to me, and I couldn't help but hold her tighter, and she didn't pull away, and it seemed to me that her kiss grew eager and open, and even though her body was cool now in the water her mouth was hot. I felt a need that made me squeeze her tighter, lifting her off her toes.

One of my hands held her waist and my other moved into her hair, lost in her wet curls, and I let myself kiss her this time like I'd wanted to before—hungrily.

She was breathing harder now and her hands clutched at my shoulders. I felt the hard, steady drum of her heartbeat. Mine felt wild, frenetic.

I pulled her hair away from her neck and kissed her there, and across her collarbone.

I couldn't think anymore; my mind was full of the smell of her, the taste of her, the feel of her flesh in my hands. If I thought at all, it was about how glad I was that I hadn't slept with Cheyenne when I had had the chance. I didn't want anything else to compare this to—anyone else to muddle my thoughts, my feelings. All I wanted was Lala.

For a long time the only sounds were of us breathing, the occasional splash of the water around us. The stillness in the air, the quiet of the late afternoon . . . I could almost imagine that we'd stepped through that doorway we'd created and out of the boundary of time. Maybe we were floating—in the water, sure, but in space, too, beyond the reach of clocks and schedules, calendars and deadlines. Maybe where we were there wasn't anyone waiting to wrap up my town in chain link and barbed wire like some kind of demented Christmas present. Maybe we were in a place where there weren't any angry, disapproving parents and maybe-ex-fiancés watching the minutes tick past. Maybe we had slipped into the picture I had seen on one of Lala's Tarot cards—the Lovers—and maybe they held the sun and the moon in their hands because together they could make time stop—keep day from turning into night, keep my bus from pulling away three days from now.

It was nice to think so, just for a minute, and with Lala in my arms and the cool water all around us, right then I had everything. But then I heard wheels turning onto the dirt road at the top of the pit mine, and I knew someone was coming for us.

Lala knew it too. I felt her stiffen in my arms, and even though I still held her tight she was already moving away from me. I kissed her again, one more time on her mouth, and then I had to let her go. The front of my body where she had been pressed against me felt cold now as water filled in the space. I didn't want to move, but when she started back to shore, I followed her.

Before I looked up to see what car was coming down the hill, I sort of prayed that it was someone from town—anyone, even Hog Boy with his smarmy comments, would have been okay. I just didn't want to see the Jeep that I knew would bring Lala's people to take her away from me. I didn't even want to look up at the vehicle that made its way down the winding road.

But I'm no coward, so I forced my eyes up.

There it was—the faded black Jeep.

It was still too far up the hill for the passengers to see us clearly, but with a little imagination they could have figured out that we'd been in the water together. Anyway, I thought as I shoved my wet legs through my jeans, our wet hair would give us away for sure.

Not that I regretted it—not one bit. But I could see in Lala's face, though she set it in a steely expression, that this would cost her.

She wrapped her white shirt back around her chest and immediately her wet bra dampened two ovals over her breasts. This would have been funny in some other situation, and I could hear Hog Boy's abrasive laugh in my head, the comment he would have made if he could have seen her.

She pulled her skirt on, too, and I noticed with admiration that her hands were steady as she tightened her belt.

I managed to fasten my jeans and yank on my shirt, but there was no time to deal with my shoes before the Jeep pulled into the bottom of the quarry, sending up plumes of dust. I could see there were three men in it—her father, her sister's husband, and Romeo, of course.

Lala was dripping wet, her hair hanging in ropes around her face. Just before the Jeep's engine cut out, Lala turned to me and said, "Stay behind me."

Her father remained behind the wheel of the Jeep. I didn't know him well enough to read the expression on his face, but if I had to guess I would have said he was furious. Not that he looked mad; it was just that it didn't make any sense for that tight-lipped smile he was wearing to mean he was actually happy.

Romeo was easy to read. His face was beet red and he slammed out of the car just ripe for a fight. His brother stayed a step behind him, hanging back a little to let Romeo take the lead.

"*Curva*," Romeo spat at Lala. "Your mother and sisters are sick with worry, thinking maybe you were kidnapped, and here you are with the *gazhò* like one of their whores."

"Hey," I said, and I stepped up next to Lala. I didn't care that she'd told me to stay behind her. There was no way I was going to just stand around and listen to this piece of shit talk to her like that.

Her hand reached out and took mine, squeezing my fingers. "Wait," she said.

That was the last thing I wanted to do. Romeo didn't seem to feel much like chitchatting either. He marched right up to us, his brother on his heels.

And then he pushed her—hard. His hand shot out right

to her chest, up on her collarbone, and he shoved her to the ground. She landed on her butt, letting out a little sound like he'd knocked the air out of her. And that pretty much ended any chance for rational discussion as far as I was concerned.

When I stepped up, Romeo's brother sort of nodded at him as if he was saying, "Go for it." He didn't move toward me, so I figured that he was going to let Romeo try to take me on his own, but I wasn't suffering under any delusions. His energy was all fighter, and I knew that he was ready to step in anytime things looked like they were getting out of hand. There was no way I was going to get the best of this situation. Maybe I could take Romeo—maybe not—but they were brothers, and if things started looking grim for Romeo, I knew his brother would be right there to back him up.

It didn't matter. I was going to get my ass handed to me one way or the other, but okay. I'd do some damage first.

I didn't wait around for Romeo to decide to hit me. I cocked back my right fist like I was going to clock him in the jaw, and when he feinted to the left I kicked him hard in the knee.

He didn't see it coming. It wasn't fair fighting, maybe, but neither was two against one. He went down hard and made a sound like the one Lala had made when he knocked her down.

It was grimly satisfying—an eye for an eye. He rolled onto his side and clutched at his knee. Lala backed up and stumbled to her feet, looking surprised for the first time since we'd met.

Kicking Romeo sure woke his brother up. I could see from

the set of his mouth that he wouldn't be as easy to throw off as Romeo had been. He was thicker through the middle than Romeo and a scar bisected one of his eyebrows, a thin white line that he could have gotten anywhere but that I bet he'd earned in a fight.

He came at me with a roar. I felt a sick rush of adrenaline that made everything seem to happen a little slower and a little more sharply than normal. I heard the pounding of hooves on the packed dirt road as the horses galloped away.

I was ready for his first swing and got mostly out of the way, his punch glancing off my shoulder instead of landing in my face like he'd intended. Then I managed to connect a couple of quick jabs, one on the sharp edge of his cheekbone, the next on his midsection.

I was faster than he was and my reach was longer, but I was fighting barefoot at the bottom of a mine, and it wasn't much of a surprise when I stepped wrong on a loose piece of rock. I stumbled and tried to catch my balance, but Romeo's brother wasn't about to miss a chance like this.

He hit me solid in the jaw; my head swung to the side hard and I spun off center. I knew he was going to throw a left hook now, I could see him rotating for it, but I couldn't get my arms to do what I wanted them to.

I remember thinking that I didn't want Lala to see me like this—losing.

Sometimes wanting something—or not wanting it—isn't enough. It happens anyway, or it doesn't. Some things are stronger than we are. Some things are faster. In that moment, Romeo's brother was both.

There's nothing romantic or pretty about a fight. His second hit was just as solid as the first one and there was nothing I could do about it. I was on the ground and reeling, blood trickling into my eye from a cut on my temple.

I scrambled to my hands and knees, trying to figure out which way was up so I could stumble to my feet but having a hard time of it.

Lala was screaming, maybe in English, maybe in some other language, I couldn't tell, but I heard panic in her voice, and it scared me.

Romeo got up, inspired I guess by seeing me on the ground, and I did my best to pull my arms up over my face before he landed his first kick, his shoe connecting with the side of my head.

Lala's voice turned pleading. I could hear that she was crying, and I wanted to get up, I wanted to tell her it was going to be okay, but I couldn't. I got kicked again, this time in the gut, and I felt myself starting to pass out, sick and dizzy from the blows to my head. The next kick would do it, no doubt.

I don't know why it didn't come.

Two things happened then—I heard the rattle of Pete's piece-of-shit truck, and I heard Lala's voice get closer as she rushed toward me. I didn't know why, but even though Romeo had already knocked her down once before, all of a sudden he backed away from her—both of them did, Romeo and his brother—as if they were *scared* of her.

"*Curva*," Romeo said. I didn't know what the hell it meant, but it wasn't good, and it made me want to punch him in the face, if only I hadn't been so dizzy, if only I could have seen clearly.

Pete's truck came barreling down the hill. He turned hard and I heard him and Hog Boy slamming out of the truck, the engine still running. The smell of his truck's exhaust made me nauseated, but it was okay. My boys were there—it felt good knowing they had come. They'd take care of Lala now.

For a little while, then, all the pain went away. I went away, too.

CHAPTER FOURTEEN

LALA

It was like a nightmare to me. There they were—Romeo, Marko, and my father—and their eyes were angry and cold. Of course I had known what would come of my climbing behind Ben Stanley on his motorbike. It would mean that I would become like my aunt Ana, *marimè*, and I would lose everything. It would mean that I would no longer be Romeo's fiancée, or even my father's daughter. But I had left in the manner I had chosen for a reason—I had wanted to disappear; I had wanted to avoid causing a confrontation.

Even if they had wanted to find me—which I could not imagine they would have wanted to do—I would not have thought that they would track me here, to this remote place hidden from view of the main road. How they could have found us was a mystery to me; and that they had found us *here*, where we were so vulnerable, seemed like the very worst hand fate could have dealt.

Bad enough that they should come for me. But Ben Stanley, who had been nothing but kind to me, it was not right that he should bear the brunt of their anger. I had wanted to say this to Romeo—*"Leave him out of this"*—but he had not given me the chance, pushing me hard to the ground as he did.

And then I felt my heart cheering against my own people, hoping that Ben Stanley would be strong enough, quick enough to best them both, even as I knew this would not be the outcome.

And my father—he stood unmoving, refusing to make eye contact with me, staring past me as if I were a ghost.

Ben had managed to kick Romeo to the ground, but then Marko came after him. It was terrible, watching them fight, and more terrible still when Ben lost his footing and Marko began to pummel him in earnest.

"Please, Marko," I begged him, "stop it, leave him alone!" But he too ignored me, not even flinching at the sound of my voice. Romeo got to his feet and now it was the two of them together against my Ben Stanley.

I was a ghost to them. Perhaps they had come here to give me a chance to explain myself, but when they found me in his embrace in the water, when they saw me half-clothed and dripping wet, I had died.

Among my people it is men who hold most of the power. Why not? They are larger, and stronger, and they head our households, our *familìyas* and our *vìtsas* and our *kumpànyas*. But ghosts have powers, too, and if they want to be heard, then they cannot be ignored.

Women can have power, as well, if they choose to take it. Most women do not, for the cost of taking this power is very high. Since I was a ghost already, and since I could not stand to watch Ben Stanley, flat on the ground, his arms covering his face, take another kick as if he were a mangy dog, I seized the power that was rightfully mine.

A proper woman keeps her legs covered. She does not cross in front of a man, for to do so on purpose would make him *marimè* by association. She would never step over a man's resting body, for doing this also transfers her shame to him. And for a woman to wave her skirt at a man—this is unforgivable as it cannot be excused as a mistake, it cannot be undone unless the woman herself publicly proclaims that it never happened.

I knew all this. I had known it as long as I could remember. Therefore, I could never claim that I did not understand what I was doing.

A ghost has skirts, too, of sorts—long wispy transparencies it trails behind itself. So it was not difficult to imagine that the fistfuls of fabric I took between my hands as I rushed between them, between Ben and Romeo, were further proof of what I had become.

I waved my skirt as I screamed at them, Romeo and Marko, I cursed them in all the ways I could imagine, and I felt the deep satisfaction of the dead that have managed to communicate at last as their faces registered their shock and then their fear.

They backed away, hands up in front of them. Another vehicle came racing down the hill and Ben's friends slammed out of it and raced toward us—Pete dropping to his knees beside Ben, Hog Boy rushing to my side as if we had been lifelong friends.

"You have disgraced your family," said Romeo to me. "We came here to find you because your mother and sisters were sick with worry, certain you would never have left on your own, sure that you had been taken against your will. But we find you here—with him, naked together like the whore you are—" Romeo spat in the dirt as if no words could describe his disgust.

"Our wedding is off," he said. "We will tell your mother that you have made other plans."

Marko said nothing, just stood next to Romeo, his gaze locked on Hog Boy, ready to attack if Hog Boy moved an inch toward them.

"What the fuck is up with you guys?" said Hog Boy, aggressively angry, chest puffed out. "Which of you fuckers laid out my boy Ben?"

They didn't answer. Instead they turned and walked together to my father's Jeep, not even reacting as Hog Boy followed them, shoving Marko's back. I watched them go, my skirt still bunched in my hands, wrinkled and damp and dirty.

"Yeah, that's right. Run, you little bastards, run like bitches!" Hog Boy called after them.

Even as he started his Jeep and drove it up out of the mine, my father did not look at me. This hurt the most, much more deeply than Romeo's words. My own father would not gaze into my eyes. This was not a surprise. It was exactly as I had known it would be. But to imagine something this final, this terminal, and to actually *experience* it are two very different things.

And then they were gone, and I was alone with Ben Stanley, who bled now because of me, and his friends, who looked at me almost as if I had myself struck him.

"Jesus, chick, what the *fuck?*"

"Later, Hog Boy," said Pete. "Right now let's just get Ben home."

Together they managed to carry him to the truck. I picked up his shoes and socks and my sandals as well and placed them in the bed of the truck.

"Help us get him in," Pete said to me. Together the three of us maneuvered him into the truck's cab. Hog Boy reached across him and fastened the seat belt, moving carefully so as to avoid jostling him. Then he gently closed the passenger-side door and Ben's head lolled against it. He was half-conscious, incoherent, but all three of us heard him clearly as he said my name; then he slipped away again.

"After all that, he's still got the hots for her," marveled Hog Boy.

Pete did not respond to this. "Listen," he said, "I'd better drive the motorcycle back. Ben would be pissed as hell if I let you drive it, Hog Boy. You think you can manage to drive my truck back to town without crashing it?"

"Crashing it would probably improve its looks," said Hog Boy, but his voice did not have its usual jocularity. He was worried about his friend.

"You wanna ride on the bike with me?" asked Pete.

"No," I said. "I will stay with Ben."

I slid into the cab of the truck; I had to position my legs around the stick shift and did not relish the thought of Hog

Boy maneuvering it while I sat in this way, but I had already crossed so many boundaries today, my way home disappearing behind me like rope bridges cut and fallen, that this seemed by comparison just a modest inconvenience. I would not leave Ben; the wound on his forehead was bleeding still. I found a napkin in the glove box and tried to staunch it.

Hog Boy crushed in to my left behind the steering wheel, and he slammed the door shut. We were pressed up together in a tight row with no room to spare.

"I'll see you back at Ben's place." Pete fastened the helmet and rode up the dirt road.

Hog Boy shifted the truck into first gear, mercifully silent about the spread of my legs around the stick shift, and followed him.

"So," he said, "you wanna tell me what happened?"

"I might ask the same question," I said. "How did Romeo and Marko know where to look for us?"

Hog Boy's face tinged red with shame. "Yeah," he said. "That might have been my fault."

I did not respond, but waited for him to continue.

"I'd never rat out Ben. I'm not that kind of a guy. But it was crazy—after you and Ben took off on his bike, not two minutes later the rest of your family came running out of the store—your mom and the little guy and that other girl. Your sister?"

I nodded.

He went on. "At first they just looked confused— you know, looking around for you. Honestly, I was kind of shocked that you did that—gave them the slip. You all seemed pretty close."

He had not asked a question, so I did not answer him.

"Anyway," he said, "after a few minutes I guess they figured out you weren't gonna just come back around the corner, because the lady—your mother?—she started kind of freaking out. And that got the little guy crying—boy, can he scream—and your little sister, she looked all upset, too.

"Probably I should have just left, but I was waiting for Petey to get through inside with Melissa, so I stuck around."

More likely, I thought, Hog Boy enjoyed watching the dramatics.

"So then your mom pulls her cell phone out of her *bra*"—here Hog Boy stopped and shook his head. "Anyway, I guess she called your dad, because not too much later that Jeep pulled up again. There were three of them in it—your dad and the two pieces of shit that beat up Ben. I guess they'd dropped the pregnant chick and the other boy back off at your place—and all three of them looked meaner than cat shit. Your dad, he started asking your mom all these questions, like when she last saw you, if you'd been talking to anyone, stuff like that, and I tried to do my best to look like I didn't know a damned thing. Which, you know, technically I didn't. I didn't really know where you and Ben had headed off to."

Ben, as if he had heard his name, shifted his weight and his head fell over onto my shoulder. I found his hand, fingers splayed limply, and pulled it into my lap as he had done with mine back by the pond.

"Of course, that one dude, the short one—"

"Romeo," I said.

Hog Boy snorted. "Is that his name? For real? Huh. Okay, *Romeo*, then, he's not dumb, not by a long shot. He sort of started looking around and then he asked, 'What happened to the boy with the motorbike? Ben Stanley?'

"And the way he said Ben's name—like he'd heard it before, and didn't like it—kind of made me prick my ears up. I guess he noticed that I was listening to him, and he marched up to me all hero-like and started pointing his finger into my chest.

"'Where'd your friend go?' he asked me, and I was like, 'What friend?' and he was like, 'The one with the motorcycle,' and I was like, 'Hey, I barely know the guy.'

"I don't think he totally bought it, but he couldn't *prove* I knew Ben. I mean, the only person who'd ever seen us together except for you was that pregnant chick, and she wasn't there. Your father decided to take your mom and the kids back to your camp and see if maybe you were there, and he told Romeo and the other guy that he'd be back to pick them up and that they should ask around, see if anyone had seen you or knew where you might have gone."

We were nearing Ben's town now, and Hog Boy slowed down. Next to me Ben groaned and lolled his head up to center. "My head hurts," he said. It sounded to me as if his speech was slightly slurred. I thought perhaps he had a concussion.

"Is there a doctor we can take him to see?"

"Nah, his mom is a nurse," Hog Boy said. "She'll know

what to do." He turned onto a street marked Bluebell. Ahead of us I saw Pete on the motorbike steering into a driveway.

Hog Boy parked the truck on the street in front of the house. "Shit," he said, "Ben's parents aren't home. Their car is missing."

Ben's eyes fluttered open. "Hey, Hog Boy," he said. Then, "Lala, you're here. That's good."

He groaned and brought his hand up to his temple. "My head hurts," he said again.

"We need to take him to a doctor," I repeated, and this time Hog Boy looked concerned, as well.

Pete opened the passenger door carefully and put a hand on Ben's shoulder to prevent him from tipping out.

"His folks aren't here," he said.

"No shit, Sherlock," said Hog Boy. "Now what?"

I sat trapped in the middle of the truck's cab, and now that we were still it was heating up quickly.

"Where is the closest doctor?"

"Reno," said Pete. "Dr. Evans, he was retired but still sewed people up once in a while if they got hurt, he left town three days ago."

Looking up and down the street, I saw that more houses appeared vacant than occupied. The entire place was closing in on itself, crumbling.

"Then we should take him inside, where it is cool," I said.

The boys nodded, seeming glad that someone else was making the decisions for them. When they parted ways with Ben, they were going to have quite an adjustment to make.

That was their problem, for later. Now, we needed to take Ben inside and lay him down.

I left Hog Boy and Pete to carry him and I strode up the front walk to see if the front door had been left unlocked. It was, and it pushed open into a small, dark hallway. A tower of boxes labeled *Kitchen* kept the door from opening completely.

"Who are you?"

I blinked, allowing my eyes to adjust after coming in from the bright sun. A boy stood in a doorway down the hall, light from the window behind him making him look like a shadow.

"I am Lala White," I said. "I have brought you your brother."

Then Hog Boy and Pete stumbled in behind me, crashing into the boxes and toppling the two highest ones. I heard the sound of glass breaking.

"Oh, shit," moaned Hog Boy, still struggling under Ben's weight. "Now Mrs. Stanley's gonna be pissed at me, too."

"Put him on the couch," said James. Hog Boy and Pete moved to obey immediately; there was something compelling about the boy's voice. He, like his brother, was a leader, this much I could clearly see.

They carried him awkwardly into the family room, a brown-carpeted box of a room that had been stripped of all but the essentials in preparation for the move. All that was left was the couch, a reclining armchair, a rectangular coffee table, and an old television on a stand in the corner.

They tried to put him down gently, that much I will say. He landed with something of a thud and swore.

"What the fuck—"

"Hey!" said Hog Boy, cheerfully. "You're sounding like yourself again!"

"My head hurts."

"Yeah, you keep saying that," said Pete.

James left the room without a word and reappeared quickly with some pills and a glass of water, as well as a towel full of ice cubes. He thrust the pills into his brother's hand.

Ben tossed the pills in his mouth without looking to see what they were and then drank the entire glass of water.

He leaned his head back and lay very still.

James watched his brother swallow the pills before pressing the ice against his temple. I watched James. He was attentive, and seemed older than the twelve years I knew him to be. His body had the same look of athleticism as his brother's, though less muscled; he was a fine-looking boy and would surely grow into a handsome man. Neatly dressed in pants and a shirt of light fabric, clearly he cared about how he looked. His hair, much like his brother's in coloring and texture, was neatly combed and freshly trimmed.

"Do you want some water or something?"

James was polite, as well. He looked expectantly at me, waiting for an answer. I realized how very thirsty I was.

"Yes, please."

He nodded and left again, returning with three glasses of water balanced in a triangle in his hands. While he was gone Hog Boy threw himself into the reclining chair and pushed up his feet. Pete leaned his back against the wall and slid to sitting on the carpet, his arms around his knees. I perched on the end of the couch, near Ben's head, and laid my hand on his hair. Slowly, I brushed my fingers through it. He sighed as if it felt good.

When each of us had a glass of water James asked, "So what happened?"

"There was a fight," I began, unsure how much to reveal. I did not want to frighten the boy. "When will your mother return?"

"She and Dad won't be back until late. They drove into Reno to give our new landlord the deposit on our new place. We're moving into an *apartment*," he told Pete. I noticed then that aside from handing Hog Boy a glass of water, he had avoided that boy completely.

"Yeah, I think Mom and I probably are, too," said Pete. "Maybe we'll be neighbors."

"So you and your mom decided to go to Reno? For sure?" Hog Boy looked thrilled.

Pete nodded. "Yeah, I didn't really—you know—want to move too far away from Melissa. . . ." He pulled his lower lip between his teeth, clearly uncomfortable.

Hog Boy looked as if he was preparing to say something terrible, but I had no desire to hear what it might be. I spoke first. "If your mother is gone and there is no doctor in town, what do you suggest we do with your brother?"

"I'll be fine," Ben groaned. He struggled up to a sitting position as if to prove that he did not need medical care. "James, you'll take care of me, right?"

"Sure! Of course. But . . . what happened?"

I felt that I should press them to take Ben to a doctor, but he did look better now that he had drunk some water, and neither Hog Boy nor Pete seemed terribly anxious to take him anywhere.

"Good question," said Ben. "Why'd they stop kicking me?"

"They were *kicking* you? Who was kicking you?" James looked indignant, as if he couldn't believe anyone would kick his brother. He adored Ben, that was obvious.

"And how did you guys know where we were?"

Hog Boy shrugged, looking guilty. "Lucky guess?"

"You were telling me earlier how my family found us," I prodded Hog Boy.

"Your *family* did this to my brother?"

"Hard to believe, huh?" said Pete. "It's like the Montagues and the Capulets."

"Yeah," snorted Hog Boy, "except Romeo is one mean little motherfucker."

My instinct was to defend him, and of course nothing is ever as simple as Hog Boy seemed to want it to be. Romeo was many things—a talented musician, a dedicated brother and friend, a fiercely loyal protector of his family. Nothing had changed . . . except that he no longer saw me as inside that circle. By his logic, once I had betrayed them I was an outsider, no longer deserving of protection.

But a dark purple bruise was forming around Ben's right eye, and I could not summon words to speak in Romeo's defense.

It felt so strange, in my heart, to feel the final snipping of ties that had been fraying for many years, some of them—

like my tie to Romeo—probably never properly strong to begin with. That tie I let go gladly, feeling that there was more room to breathe without it wound about my heart. Letting go of the constraints of shame and insularity . . . I wanted to let those snap, but they were made of tougher stuff and would take more time to break. But others—the ties to my sisters especially—these were made of thin gold wire and they felt as if rather than loosening they were tightening, cutting into the meat of my heart.

Pete and Hog Boy were telling James about how they'd appeared at the mine just in time to rescue Ben from Romeo and Marko's assault—and I could see how it must have looked that way to them, as they did not understand the implications of what I had done.

"You mean they backed off just because the two of you showed up?" James sounded doubtful.

I cleared my throat. "They left because I shamed them. I made them *marimè.*"

Of course, this brought about more questions than it answered. And it did not sit right with me to explain all this to these *gazhè.* Ben deserved a full explanation; I would see that he got it. Later, when we were alone.

A good way to deflect attention from yourself is to ask a question of another. So I turned to Hog Boy. "You said before that it was your fault Romeo and Marko knew where we were. Would you explain that?"

"Jesus, Hog Boy, you never do know how to keep your mouth shut." Pete spoke with real anger, unusual for him.

"Fuck you, Pete," answered Hog Boy.

"What happened, Hog Boy?" Ben spoke.

"It was like this. All of them had left the store to go looking around town for Lala, and so I went inside to tell Pete and Melissa about what had gone down."

Pete nodded. "He came rushing in all wild eyed and practically hopping from foot to foot. Melissa and I were . . . hanging out . . . in the back room, and Hog Boy just came bursting in without knocking. I'd just told Melissa that my mom and I decided we'd be moving for sure to Reno. Anyway, he said that you were missing, Lala, and that your folks were looking for you, and that he'd seen you riding off with Ben on the motorbike. And then he and Melissa and I started talking about where you might have gone off to."

"And I guess that's when I fucked up," said Hog Boy apologetically, "but I never would have guessed that the little rat bastard was listening."

"Romeo?" I asked.

He nodded. "I didn't know it then, but I guess he followed me back into the store. He must have heard everything I said—about how I'd bet that Ben took you down to the old mine. You know, because it's private . . . and it has the pond. . . ."

I kept my face carefully neutral.

"But then Melissa decided to go back up to the register," Pete explained, "and when she opened the storeroom door, we caught sight of him leaving the store, and we put two and two together."

"Your dad drove up just then and Romeo flagged him down. They must have found the other guy, too, somewhere in town, and then they split." Hog Boy was quiet. "I'm really sorry, man. You know I'd never have said anything if I'd known anyone was listening."

"I know, Hog Boy," Ben said, half smiling. "You're a lot of things, but you're no rat."

Hog Boy nodded, as if satisfied. "And we would have gotten to the mine right on their heels, too, if Petey's piece of shit wasn't such a piece of shit. The engine kept flooding and it took him like ten minutes to get it started."

"Sorry, bro," said Pete rather sheepishly.

"Not your fault." Ben closed his eyes again and lay back, his head in my lap.

I felt a shock of mingled pleasure and shame. His head on my lap—as if he found it comforting. And I remembered the expression on Romeo's face when he had last looked at me—disgust. I had disgusted him.

Ben's head grew heavier in my lap. He was asleep again. James had gone into the kitchen to dispose of the melting ice cubes and returned with a damp washcloth. He laid it across Ben's forehead; it dripped cold water onto my skirt.

It was pleasant here, with Ben and his brother. Even the others, Hog Boy and Pete, did not bother me. They were all gathered around Ben, watching over him. This was a family of sorts.

But it was not mine.

I felt again the tightening of those golden threads around my heart, and I could have gasped from the pain.

"Hog Boy," I said, "Pete. Which of you can offer me a ride?"

CHAPTER FIFTEEN

It was all foggy, everything that had happened since Romeo and his brother had kicked my ass out at the mine. I remembered that part only vaguely, which was probably a good thing. I remembered knowing that I would lose. I remembered my foot making contact with Romeo's knee, and a warm feeling of satisfaction filled me as I thought about it.

And there was a hazy memory of Hog Boy and Pete showing up, the relief of knowing that even if I passed out Lala wouldn't be alone.

More clearly I remembered Lala and being in the water with her. The feeling of holding her, of kissing her, the look on her face as she let me look at her body—I remembered everything about that. And what it had cost her. I remembered that, too.

I woke more than once to the worst headache of my life. I felt like puking but couldn't seem to muster the energy to actually do it, so I just lay there—wherever "there" was—with the bitter taste of bile in my mouth.

I heard voices, but I wasn't sure if they were real or just

in my head. More than once I heard the snort of Hog Boy's laugh.

There was a sound in my head all the time, a high-pitched ringing that wouldn't go away. It got louder and softer but it never went away entirely. And there was something else—this sensation of an enormous orb of light, bigger and brighter than the sun. It was there behind my eyes, but at the same time immeasurably far away and just outside my reach. The orb seemed to come closer, closer, as if it would consume me in its giantness and brightness, and then it would spin away until it almost disappeared.

It was the scariest thing I had ever experienced in my life. On the one hand, the thought of being swallowed by the light was terrifying. Once inside it, I knew I would be lost forever. On the other hand, the prospect of *it* disappearing seemed intolerable. Even though I had just found the orb, the thought of existing without it made me feel panicky and sick to my stomach.

I lay paralyzed, half recognizing the voices of the people I loved all around me, unable to communicate with them, completely mesmerized by the glowing orb.

When I woke up all the pain was gone. I felt great. Better than I'd ever felt in my life, I guess. It didn't feel like I'd been in a fight at all. I rotated my head, raised and lowered my shoulders, and jogged in place. With each step I bounced a little higher until I could have just floated away if I'd wanted to. But I didn't want to. Because I saw someone—I saw *her*—just a little ways away, under a tree that confused me.

It wasn't a tree that grew anywhere around Gypsum. It was a giant, easily fifty feet high, with a great big canopy that must have spanned more than a hundred feet. The shade it threw was amazing, black as night and thick like syrup, and Lala was underneath it. I couldn't really see her because the shade was so dark, but I knew it was her. Don't ask me how, but I knew.

The tree's trunk was massive. The leaves were bright, waxy green, and there were millions of them. I knew that if I spent the rest of my life trying to count them, I still wouldn't come close to the total number.

The leaves rustled in the breeze. Ahh. There was a breeze. And it felt cool, and damp, as if blowing in from the ocean. And as soon as I thought the word "ocean," I could smell the salt in the air. If I listened, I could hear them—great, rolling waves, crashing on some far-off beach.

I walked toward Lala. Immediately I felt the luxurious sensation of thick grass beneath my bare feet. It was cool, a little damp, perfect. And as I walked toward the tree, the grass sprang up after each step I took as if it didn't mind a bit that I had stepped on it.

Bare feet. I looked down at my feet—and realized shoes weren't all I wasn't wearing. My legs were bare, too. Shit—I wasn't wearing *anything*. No pants, no shirt—I was totally naked.

I paused for a minute, contemplating how I felt about this. I wasn't cold. I wasn't hot. I felt just right.

And yeah, I was naked, but after the initial shock had passed I was okay with that. The breeze blew over my body like a caress, and I liked the way it felt. It ruffled the hair on my legs, and higher up, too, between them. I felt myself stirring there and looked down. I wasn't hard, but I wasn't soft either.

I started walking again toward the tree. Lala was there—waiting for me. She had sat down in the shade. When I got close enough, she stood up.

I thought for a minute about trying to cover myself. But then I stepped into the shade and I saw she was naked, too.

Her hair was down. It fell in long curls across her shoulders, covering her breasts. I could see the curve of them, soft and round.

Between her thighs was a triangle of dark hair. I pulled my eyes up to her face. Her dark eyes were shining and she smiled at me. And then she held her hand out. I stepped forward and took it. We turned together, side by side, our hands clasped, the tree solid behind us.

My other hand I held loose at my side, and I breathed in deeply. Lala breathed in, too, with me.

And then there was something in my hand, something round and warm, something that grew hotter and hotter until it almost burned me up, but I couldn't let go. I looked down to see what I was holding—it was the same glowing orb, and as I stared at it, it grew and grew.

I looked over at Lala and saw that she was holding something, too, in her free hand—it was round and white like ice, shiny and hard. At first I thought it was a lump of gypsum, but then it started to grow, too, just like the fiery globe in my hand. It was the moon.

And then it happened, that weird thing that happens sometimes in dreams—was this a dream?—a shifting of perspective, and all of a sudden I wasn't standing with Lala under the tree. Instead I was someone else, and I was looking at two figures, a blond male and a dark-haired female, standing, hands clasped, under a tree. She held the moon; he palmed the sun.

"Do you want another Tylenol?"

My head was killing me. It felt like it might split into two halves, like a cleaved melon. I groaned and struggled to sit up.

"Stay there," said a voice. I knew that voice—it was James's.

"Water," I croaked.

It was quiet for a minute, and then James said, "Here."

He pressed a cold glass into my hand. I took three deep gulps, choking on the third and coughing most of it up.

"Gimme the pills."

I swallowed the two pills he gave me and then drank some more water, carefully this time so I wouldn't choke again.

There was a light on, bright and piercing even through my closed lids. "Turn off the light."

I heard a click as he switched off a table lamp near my head. So I was in the family room, then, on the couch.

"Where is everyone?"

"It's just us," he said. "You and me."

"Where's—"

"Mom and Dad drove into Reno," he said. "They should be home in a while."

I hadn't been asking about our folks. It was Lala I was worried about, Lala I wanted beside me.

"Lala," I managed to say at last. It felt like my mouth wouldn't do what I wanted it to do. Her name came out slurred. I couldn't tell if James understood what I was saying.

"You're okay," he said. "Just go back to sleep. I'm here. I'll take care of you."

I didn't want to sleep. I wanted to get up and find her. But it was as if I was caught in a powerful undertow, and in spite of my desires, in spite of how hard I tried to cling to consciousness, it pulled me under, submerging me completely.

I don't know how long it was until I woke again. I know it was late, way past dark. I hadn't eaten any dinner, and though my stomach lurched with hunger I didn't want to eat.

The light was on in the kitchen, but the family room where I lay on the couch was dark. James was across from me in the recliner with his feet pushed up. He was asleep.

I rolled over onto my side and waited for my eyes to adjust to the dark. I blinked a few times. The ringing in my ears was still there, but it was fainter now. The house was quiet.

I managed to sit up. Nausea rolled through me, but it wasn't as bad as before, either. Once I was sitting I stayed very still, letting myself adjust to the new position.

James must have heard me stirring. He woke up with a start, jolting upright.

"You okay?"

"Yeah. Yeah, James, thanks. I'm better, I think."

He nodded and rubbed his eyes. "You hungry?"

"What time is it?"

James looked at his watch. "Ten-thirty."

"Where did everyone go?"

James shrugged. "Pete had a date with Melissa, I guess. He left to meet her at the store around nine."

"Where's Lala?"

"With Hog Boy."

"With *Hog Boy*?"

"Yeah. They borrowed Pete's truck."

"Did they say where they were going?"

"Lala wanted a ride somewhere." He paused. "So is she your girlfriend?"

I wasn't sure how to answer. "I don't know, James. I'm leaving in a couple of days for college. She lives in Portland." Or she did, anyway. After the scene out at the mine, I wasn't sure if she lived anywhere anymore. The weight of this realization was almost enough to knock me out again. Lala without a home—without anyone to protect her, to watch out for her. It scared me. In a way I guess I was going to be homeless, too, when we all left Gypsum. But compared to Lala's situation, mine seemed laughably easy. I might be leaving these four walls, but I'd still have people watching out for me, cheering for me. She would have nobody.

It was all too much to think about with my head pounding

the way it was, so I focused instead on what James had asked. "Why do you want to know about Lala?" I asked, trying to joke with him. "You think she's pretty?"

"She's beautiful." James's voice was serious. "But not my type, you know."

Maybe it was the concussion that got me to ask the next question. I remembered what I'd thought before—that maybe part of where I'd gone wrong with James was in the things I *hadn't* said. "What *is* your type, James?"

He shrugged. "I dunno. I'm only twelve."

I had to laugh at that, even though it hurt my head. "But you know your type isn't female, huh?" It was getting easier to talk about it, now.

"Well . . . yeah. I do." There was something in his tone— a defiance, that's what it seemed.

"How do you know?"

"How old were you when you first wanted to kiss a girl?"

The answer came easily. "Four. Preschool. Tara Wilkinson. Her family moved her away in the third grade."

"And how old were you when you first wanted to kiss a guy?"

"I'm not gay, James. I've never wanted to kiss a guy."

There was a smug satisfaction to his silence.

I waited a long time before I spoke again. I didn't want to say the wrong thing, or hurt his feelings like I knew I had the other night. Maybe he even thought I'd gone back to sleep, that's how long it was before I talked.

Finally I said, "It's just that I worry about you, James. You're my brother."

He sighed, and when he spoke again he sounded a lot older than twelve. "I know. Mom does, too."

"*Mom?*" Honestly, this was news to me. I'd never flat-out discussed James with Mom and Pops; I figured they didn't really see James, not clearly like I did. My mom did get kind of a weird look on her face every now and then, like when James had wanted to buy those sandals . . . but for the most part she seemed to take the things he did in stride.

"Yeah," said James. "We talk about it sometimes. She used to worry that I wouldn't meet anybody like me in such a small town, and now she worries that I'll have a hard time in Reno."

"Mom never said anything about it to me."

"I guess she figured I'd talk to you myself."

"How come you never did? Until the other night, I mean?"

"Oh, come on, Ben. I never kept any secrets from you."

I wanted to argue with him, but then I thought back. It was true—James had never tried to lie to me about who he was. I'd just refused to talk about it.

"Aren't you afraid?"

"Of what?"

"Of being made fun of, to start."

"Ben, I know you think getting in fights kept people off my back, but it just made them whisper their insults instead of shout them."

"Who?" I said, angry. "Who insults you?"

"It doesn't matter, Ben. You can't fight everyone. Anyway, like you said, you're leaving for San Diego in three days. And I'll be going to Reno."

I felt sick again, but it was guilt this time, not the headache, that caused it.

"I don't have to go," I said. "I could defer enrollment for a year. You know—help you guys get settled in Reno. Maybe get a job and save up some extra cash—"

"No way," James interrupted. "You're not going to get any faster hanging around Reno for a year. And how cool do you think that would make me, if my big bad brother walked me to school every day of the week?"

"I wouldn't have to do that," I said. "I could just . . . be there. I *should* be there, in case you need me."

"San Diego's not that far, Ben. If I really needed you, you'd come."

"Would you call?"

He shrugged. "It'd have to be pretty bad." After a minute he added, "And Ben, it's not like I'll be alone. I'll have Mom and Dad. A few of the kids from my school here will be moving to Reno, and I know for sure my friend Katie will be going to the same school. We'll probably have a class or two together."

The thought of my brother being protected by a girl named Katie didn't make me feel much better.

James must have sensed this because he said, "You know, Ben, I can take care of myself."

"Can you?"

"I've done all right so far."

"James, you haven't been on your own a day of your life. I've always been there to scrape you off the sidewalk when you fell down."

226

"Well, I guess times are changing, because tonight I've been taking care of *you*."

I laughed a little. "Yeah, I guess you have." It was nice, sitting there in the half-lit room like that, talking with James. I felt really sad that I'd waited this long to do it.

What *had* taken me so long? I guess it was just that James had always seemed like such a *kid*—the six-year spread between us had seemed impossible to bridge. He was always this dorky little guy who wanted to tag along.

Until he hadn't wanted to tag along anymore. When had that happened? I guess it was when I was about thirteen and he was seven or so. Nothing really drastic had happened; I guess he just finally got the clue that I didn't have time to hang around with him. I was running by then, and I had my little group of friends that I did things with.

I guess I didn't know all that much about him, if I forced myself to really see the truth of the matter. I knew he liked to play video games, but I never paid attention to which ones. I knew he was still into drawing, like he'd been when we were younger, but I would have been guessing if I had to say whether he preferred pencils or charcoal.

And I had no idea what he drew. It had been years since he'd shown me a picture.

It must have been the concussion, but suddenly my eyes filled with burning tears. I felt weak and weepy like a little girl. James was looking at me, his head tilted a little to the side.

"I'm sorry, James," I said. I wasn't sure what I was sorry for, but I was really, truly sorry.

He smiled at me. "That's okay," he said. "I forgive you."

And there it was—the same expression I'd seen on Lala's face out at the mine. Peacefulness. I'd seen it on James's face before, but I'd never stopped to name it, to recognize it for what it was. A sense of peace.

I wanted to feel like that.

"Hey, James," I croaked, my tears constricting my throat. "How come you're so well adjusted?"

He shrugged again. "Someone around here's got to be. Come on," he said, getting up. "I'll make you a sandwich."

CHAPTER SIXTEEN

LALA

It was generous of Pete to give me the use of his truck, and kind of Hog Boy to drive me. I would be eighteen in a matter of days, but I had little experience driving and did not have a license. I had never had need of one: I did not go out alone. And in a large family such as mine, there was always someone who could give me a ride.

But now I felt hobbled by my inability to operate a car. I resolved that I would learn.

We did not leave Ben and James until it was fully dark. Pete and Hog Boy had watched something on the television—a sitcom, something with a laugh track that told you when the jokes were funny. James seemed to pay no attention to the show. His focus was on his brother, as was mine.

Surrounded by *gazhè* on the couch in the small room, softened by the blue light of the television, I thought about what I had done.

I had kissed a *gazhò*. I had made marriage with Romeo an impossibility. I had waved my skirts at the men of my *kumpànya*. I had, in effect, exiled myself.

People make choices every day. Some of those choices are made through action; others are made through inaction. I knew much about human nature, learned from all the people I had seen at my table, their hopes and fears laid plain to me like the cards on that table.

I have always known that there is no magic in the cards. I think even that I have always known that there is no magic in this world. There are only choices. Many times a woman has sat across from me, tears running down her face as she wished desperately—like a child—for a magic solution to a problem she herself had created.

These women wanted me to give them something I could not give, no matter how many bills they pressed into my palm. They wanted me to rearrange past events, or restructure the future so that it would shine for them like a newly minted coin.

The *gazhè* come to us—me, my sisters and mother, others like us—for counsel, much as they go to their expensive psychologists, looking for easy answers and willing to pay for them. So I place their cards on the table and I show them what I see—what I need no cards to see. The truth is in their faces.

I felt the truth of my own situation as well. I had made a choice. I had stepped off a cliff. If I did not entirely like where I now found myself—well, there was no one else to blame for that.

But some choices necessitate other actions. And there were some things—some *people*—that I was unwilling to give up.

So I left Ben Stanley in the care of his little brother. It

seemed to me that Ben perhaps overworried himself when it came to the question of James. There was intelligence in his eyes, and real humor, and warmth. In my estimation, James Stanley was perfectly able to look out for himself.

"Your dad's not gonna be too pissed?" Hog Boy asked once he got the engine running and had pulled away from the curb in front of Ben's house.

"My father? He will not yell at me." I told my half-truth smoothly. Not everyone needs to know everything, and I saw no reason to show my hidden heart to Hog Boy.

"He sure looked pissed out at the mine."

I did not answer.

"And those guys? What about them?"

"They will not bother me, either."

"Huh." He did not use his turn signal as he turned onto the highway in the direction of my family's camp. "Pretty strange, if you ask me."

"I did not."

He chuckled. "True enough."

The silence as we rode together was not uncomfortable, though perhaps it should have been. Other than the time I had spent alone with Ben Stanley at the mine, I had never before been alone with a *gazhò*, and I had only rarely found myself alone with any boy who was not my relative, and never more than for a few minutes.

But Hog Boy's energy was so straightforward, so uncomplicated, that it seemed very easy to understand him. I was safe with him; he had determined that I was Ben Stanley's girl, and so he would keep his distance.

This should not have riled me. But it did. Not that I would have welcomed an advance from Hog Boy; of course I would not. It was his understanding that I was in some way marked—that was what irritated me. All my life I had been marked. All my life I had been someone else's girl—first my father's, then Romeo's. Now I had been free of my engagement to Romeo for less than four hours, and already I was labeled as another boy's girl.

I thought again of the story of the mouse girl. I am not a mountain, I thought, I am not a mouse.

"Pull over here."

"There's still like a quarter of a mile before we get to your camp."

"This will do."

Hog Boy slowed the truck and pulled it to the side of the road. He looked doubtful. "Listen, I don't know if Ben would like me to just dump you here."

"You are not dumping me here. I am getting out here."

"Let me drive you the rest of the way. I should make sure you get inside."

I smiled at him. "You are kind," I said. "I promise not to tell anyone." I pushed open the door of the truck. "Thank you for the ride."

He shrugged. "All right," he said. "Whatever, I guess."

I shut the door and watched as he turned the truck around, and I stared after it until the red taillights disappeared.

. . .

Never had I felt so utterly alone. It was an uncomfortable feeling. All around me the desert seemed completely barren, desolate. For the first night since we had been here, there were no stars out. Even the moon was obscured by the thick clouds that had gathered as day ended. The night was flat and black.

It had not taken us nearly long enough to drive out of town to this place. I had not yet had a chance to arrange my thoughts. I had wanted to come here, but now that I was close I was afraid. I felt my heart beating hard in my chest. My hands shook.

My father was not a violent man, by nature. He was a negotiator, and this is what made him such a strong *rom barò*. Men from our *kumpànya* came to him with their disputes and he considered all the sides of their argument. He rarely handed down a decision without inviting the men who had come to him into a discussion, attempting to find common ground, a place where each party could leave feeling as if he had won.

This situation was nothing like those. There was no middle ground here. There would be no forgiveness. Maybe if I had just ridden on Ben Stanley's motorbike, if I had not gone swimming with him in the pond, if I had not waved my skirts at the men of my own *kumpànya*, perhaps some negotiations might have been possible—the end of my engagement to Romeo, certainly, but still a return to my family.

Was that why I had gone so far—stripping myself of my clothes and entering the water with Ben? In part, certainly it was. It had been coming at me for a long time. Many years, I think. This desire to step away.

My father was not a violent man, but to him I was no longer one of his own. I was worse than an outsider. I was a traitor.

There would be no discussion with my father, no peaceful resolution. And though he was not the person I had come to see, if he were to find me entering his camp, I could not know for sure what he might do.

Perhaps it was this fear of his reaction that slowed me; I found that I was not going forward, toward the dim light of my family's camp. Instead, walking slightly away from the road, I settled myself on the ground. The air was not hot, that was a blessing. I stretched my legs out in front of me and lay back on the hard dirt, crossing my hands behind my head. A car drove by. Its headlights blinded me and the sound it made was terrifying. In its wake I felt the earth beneath me shudder slightly. Whoever was riding in the car—wherever they were going, wherever they had been—I would never know their story. They would never know that I had lain by the side of the road on this night as they drove down this anonymous stretch of highway. For them, I was less than a ghost. I was a nonentity.

Little Stefan. That was how I would be to him. Less real than Ana was to Anelie. I experimented with lying as still as possible, breathing little shallow breaths, pretending that I was not there at all.

The temperature of the air was exactly that of my skin. If I was very careful not to move I could not tell where the separation came between the outside of me and the beginning of the universe.

Is this what it meant to be *marimè*? To be unnoticeable, completely indistinguishable from the world around me? No—*marimè* is worse than that. It is not neutral; it is absolutely negative.

And the ground was there still beneath me; I felt the sharpness of little rocks and pebbles under my back, my hips. Above, though the sky was black and murky with clouds, there were occasional pinpricks of starlight that I could see if I looked carefully into the velvet depths.

I had often wondered what it would be like to be Ana, to be *marimè*. When she had left the circle of our family, had she truly continued to exist? It seemed difficult to imagine, her continuing to *be* without the rest of us. Like the old philosophical question: If a tree falls in the forest and there is no one there to hear it, will it make a sound? My visceral, immediate response would have been *no*. Without someone to hear, the sound of a tree's fall is so meaningless that it need not even happen. Without a family to speak her name, to evoke her memory, Ana, like the fallen tree's crash, lacked the context necessary for existence.

But though I was now *marimè*, I still somehow was myself. I breathed in and out; I enjoyed the slight breeze that cooled my skin; I even smiled, alone, into the night.

Perhaps I was *marimè*, but I was not dead.

I stood and wiped dust from my skirt. Blinking against the dark, I walked forward, up the road toward my family.

．．．

I crept toward my family's encampment like an enemy spy, careful not to make a sound. It simplified matters greatly that even though the night air was temperate and the motor home must have been hot, none of my family was outside.

I felt terribly nervous and unsure, a sensation I was not accustomed to and one that I did not like. I could not stop seeing in my head Ben's fallen body, his arms across his face, as Romeo and Marko kicked him again and again. There was a palpable weight in the air, a heaviness like death.

There was an electric lantern on the little picnic table just outside the entrance to the motor home. It threw shadows across the hard, flat ground. No lights were on inside. I stood near the cold fire ring, looking down at the circle of stones.

Had it been just a week ago that we'd foraged for stones together, laughing and comparing who had found the biggest? Anelie and I had found many rocks shot through with streaks of white. Together we had built the ring, layering our stones one atop another until we lost sight of who had found which. Our stones had each been pretty in their separateness, but together they were better than pretty—they were useful, a single unit with a purpose.

I, too, was many things, yet nothing—a ghost, a loose stone, a broken girl. A flood of shame washed through me and I felt it in my spirit—*marimè*, unclean, no good anymore at all. It was incredible, the fluctuation of my emotions. Lying on the desert floor, I had felt a flash of happiness, but now that seemed impossible. Cut loose as I was from my family, it was as if my body no longer had a center, a force of gravity to comfortably weight it.

I did not wipe away the tears that slid down my face, though I choked back my sob so as to not be heard. There would be shame in that, as well—to be caught like this with tears on my face.

There was the tent where I had sat with Ben and looked at his cards. Could I blame him, claim it was his fault that I had been tempted away from my family? I could, I suppose, pin everything I had done on a female weakness, an attraction beyond my control.

But that would be a lie. Ben Stanley had not made me do anything; every choice I had made had been of my own volition. I turned away from the motor home and walked to the tent. Quietly, in case my sister was sleeping, I pulled back the flap and stepped inside. For a terrible instant I imagined that Romeo and Marko were just inside, waiting for me.

The tent was empty. Of course it was; my father would not allow Anelie to sleep out here alone. I must have known that she would not be here, but I had not allowed myself to think it, almost as if to think it would make it so.

There was the table where I read fortunes. My cards were still there, wrapped in their velvet bag as if I had just stepped out. Each of us—my mother, Violeta, and I—had our own set of cards. On the days when we were the busiest we would do simultaneous readings. These were my cards. They had been given to me by my mother.

It was dark in the tent. I found my little reading light

behind the screen and turned it on its lowest setting. Then I pulled back a chair and sat down. The cards slid from their velvet into my hand. Face up, I flipped through them, sorting out the cards Ben had drawn and re-creating his reading. Since I had first thought of it—that he had not cut his cards, and that in a way that might mean that the drawing was mine as well as his, since I had shuffled them—I had wanted to see the reading laid out again.

First the Situation, represented by the Tower. This was topped by the Crossing Card, the Five of Cups. Above them was the Crowning Card, the Three of Cups. And beneath was the Root of the Matter, the Hanged Man. To the left lay the Recent Past, the Eight of Pentacles. Opposite, to the right, lay the Immediate Future, the Page of Cups. Next came the Questioner—the Fool. Above this lay the Views of Others, the Seven of Swords. Next came Hopes and Fears, and above them all was the Final Outcome.

I did truly believe that there was no magic in this world. So why, then, sitting alone in the tent with these cards laid before me, did I look to them for answers? Some part of me wanted desperately to find answers in the spread of cards on the table. I wanted things to *make sense*. Looking at these cards and imagining that they were mine, I wanted to believe—to hope, to wish, to pray that answers were there for me, and I yearned to doubt my own convictions, my own surety. Might I find my fortune there, if only I looked hard enough?

The Tower—my situation. I had read it to be Ben's falling town. Surely it was. But might not this situation also be mine, though I had not seen it as such? The tower could be my engagement to Romeo, something that had seemed secure but in reality was not. The lightning striking it, the figures plunging from it into the crashing sea—that was the reality. A crumbling edifice from which I might escape, but not unscathed. And like those figures, I had jumped—I had not been pushed.

The Crossing Card—the Five of Cups. Was that me, a hooded figure sneaking home to look at what I had spilled? Here I was, a trespasser, and the spilled cups could easily enough represent my lost family. I remembered how Ben had reacted to this card during his reading—yes, not all was lost, some cups retained their contents, but what comfort can that be in the face of what is irretrievably gone?

Looking at the Crowning Card, the Three of Cups, I could not help but draw a parallel to what might have been had I stayed the path and married Romeo. That was all I had thought I wanted, if I did not think about it too carefully—to follow Violeta into marriage and lead Anelie into womanhood. The three of us would dance, always together, forever linked, our cups overflowing with fortune. A child's way to look at the world.

Then came the Root of the Matter—the Hanged Man. This could be me also—hanged, as it were, by actions of my own, a willing sacrifice. And the Eight of Pentacles, the Recent Past? Clearly all the work I'd done for my family, with my family.

And then the Immediate Future—the Page of Cups. An apprentice on the verge of self-discovery. I supposed this could be me; certainly I was discovering much about myself, what I was capable of doing and what I was not. But this interpretation seemed too easy and not quite right; I set this card slightly to the side to think further on later.

Ah, the Fool—that was who I had wanted to be, was it not? I had asked for it, even welcomed it. And now here I was. It is funny how you can think you know what you are asking for, but of course you do not know at all until you get it. I had wanted to step off a cliff, and so I had. Was this where I had intended to land?

Of course I knew that any cards I might have pulled could have meaning for anyone who chose to look for it. These cards or an entirely different spread of cards could equally reveal something to me if I wanted them to.

I heard the tent's flap rustle and I turned to find Anelie staring in at me. Ah. This was who I had come to see, and she had found me. I smiled tentatively and held my arms open for her, unsure of her reaction. I feared she might scream at me out of fear or anger, or the way one might scream at the appearance of a ghost.

"Lala," she said, and she ran to me. We embraced and said nothing for long minutes, until her sobs had quieted. I did not allow myself to cry; what right had I to tears, when I had chosen my path?

Instead I stroked her hair and concentrated on memorizing the smell of her, warm and sweet in my arms.

"Is it true what they say about you?"

I nodded into her hair. "Most probably," I said, "if what they are saying is that I was alone with a *gazhò*, and I let him touch me, and I waved my skirts at our own men."

"That is what they say." Anelie was miserable. "But Lala, why?"

Such a simple question. But such a complicated, twisting and turning answer. "I would not have been happy, Anelie." That was the best, truest answer I could give.

"Are you happy now?"

Ah, Anelie. Such a smart girl. Such a quick learner. I remembered then the card I had set aside—the Page of Cups. An apprentice, in my Immediate Future. And here she was, arrived to me as if I had called her. There is no magic in this world—that I knew to be true. And yet, perhaps . . .

"Do Mother and Father know you have come out here?"

"Father is sleeping. Mother sent me."

"She sent you? What for?"

"She saw the light. She wanted me to give you this."

Anelie held out a bag to me. It was my own leather satchel.

"She wants you to know that she loves you. She says— she will miss you."

"But not that I should stay."

"No. She did not say that."

I nodded. I felt terribly, terribly sad.

"What will you do, Lala?" Her voice was anguished.

What *would* I do? What would I become? I did not wish to show my fear to Anelie. Hers was too great already; I would not make it worse, if I could help it.

"Anelie," I said forcing lightness into my voice, "do you not know by now that I am like the cat that lands always on its feet?"

She shrugged a little.

"Do you remember the time," I said, "when Mother was ill with her pregnancy and had to be taken to the *gazhikanò* hospital?"

"How could I forget? She was gone for close to a month."

"That is right. And how did Violeta, who should have shouldered Mother's responsibilities, react?"

"She spent most of her time in the bathroom," Anelie recalled, "styling her hair and painting her nails."

"That is right. Who prepared the meals? Who took care of the laundry and the cleaning?"

"It was you, Lala. And I helped you."

"Yes. I am the type of person, Anelie, who rises to a challenge. You are, as well."

"But where will you go?"

I remembered Portland, our rainy home. I would not return there; this was certain. "I do not yet know," I admitted. "But Anelie—this I do know. It is not necessary that I disappear from your life, if you do not wish it. I am not Ana. And we are not children."

"I'm only eleven," Anelie said. Her voice quavered.

"Eleven is old enough for many things," I answered. "Not that many years ago, eleven could have seen you close to becoming a wife."

She nodded. "I do not want to lose you."

"Enough to defy Father and Mother?"

I was asking something terrible of her. To defy our parents—this was no small thing. How could I ask it—that she risk her role in the family because of a choice I had made? It made me a terrible person to do this, and yet I did.

Her face disintegrated into tears. "Oh, Lala, I am so afraid!" she cried. "Why did you have to do it? How can you leave me? Doesn't it matter to you *at all* that I will be alone?"

So much pain. I welcomed it like lashes on my skin, her words whipping me just as painfully. I deserved it, all of it. It was impossible that I should escape without scars; had I stayed there would have been scars, as well, but different ones—and perhaps I could have borne them myself instead of sharing them with Anelie.

I could not undo what I had done. I could not spare Anelie.

"I am sorry," I whispered. She cried quietly so as not to draw attention to us in the tent. Then she managed to control her tears. It was a glimpse into her future—she would cry for me, and she would contain it.

"I will not make you choose," I said, even as I did just that. I wrote for her on a scrap of paper my email address. She did not yet have one; it might be months before she would be able to create one, if she ever manifested the courage.

She took the paper from me, but she did not look at the words on it before she tucked it in a pocket of her skirt. Still, she had taken it. That was something. A hope, at least, that she would one day find me.

"There is money in the bag," Anelie said. "I saw Mother slip it in."

Incredulous, I opened the bag and felt through the clothes

to the bottom. There was an envelope. I looked inside it; it was thick with bills.

"This is a lot of money," I said. "I cannot take this."

"Of course you can," said Anelie. "You earned much of it yourself."

I thought of the next card in my reading, the Views of Others—the Seven of Swords, a hunched figure sneaking guiltily away from a city of tents.

Ben had seen himself in that card; I saw myself, as well. Might they see me that way—my parents, my siblings, Romeo and Marko—if I were to take the money, if they were to know of it?

Another choice. To take the envelope or refuse it. Anelie was right; I had earned the family much money over the years, far more than I could have used in room and board. But to think about my relationship with my family this way—as a business transaction—made me feel guilty anew, and full of shame.

It did not please me to push the envelope back into my bag. But I did it anyway, avoiding Anelie's gaze.

When I looked up at her, I could not read the meaning in her expression. It was possible that she had expected me to refuse the money, in spite of her encouragement to take it. Taking it came at a cost, another cost that I alone would not bear. My father would be very angry when he learned that my mother had sent it to me, that Anelie had delivered it.

Again, others would suffer on my behalf.

But without the money I would be dependent entirely on the kindness of others. I was not yet eighteen—still a minor.

I could have gone to the *gazhikanò* authorities and found a place in one of their foster homes. Even with the money nothing was certain; surely it could not be more than a few thousand dollars, which would not get me terribly far.

"I should go back," Anelie said, "before Father wakes."

We embraced. When I saw her next—if I ever saw her again—she would be a woman.

I watched from behind the tent's flap as she ran, light and filly-like, the short distance between the tent and the motor home. And then she opened the door, and then she was gone.

My cards still lay spread on the table. I slowly picked them up, one at a time, and replaced them in the velvet bag. I came to the second-to-last card of the reading, Hopes and Fears—the Lovers. Ben Stanley had asked me a question about this card.

"Didn't you say that the Major Arcana . . . that the cards in it can, you know, represent actual *people?*"

There they were, a light-haired man with a dark-haired woman, so clearly him and me. They stood naked together under a tree, faces up and shining, no shame, no regret.

And there was the final card. The Three of Swords. A rounded red heart, floating against a rainy sky, pierced through by three swords.

Outside there was still no moon, no stars in the sky. I stood looking at my family's camp. Just as I was about to turn and leave, the door to the motor home opened. Out stepped my mother. She walked down the two metal steps and stood very still. I was obscured by the dark, but I think she felt me out there. She could not see me, but I could see her face in the circle of light thrown by the lantern. Her expression revealed nothing. She looked just as usual—a little lined, a bit rumpled, her streak of gray pulled away from her forehead with the rest of her hair.

Then she reached out for the lantern and switched it off. And I could not see her anymore.

Shouldering my bag, I walked along the highway's edge. The picture on that card—the Seven of Swords—that was how my father would see me, and Romeo as well. Perhaps all of them would, even Anelie, though she would want to the least.

I had no power over this. If I was a thief in the night to them, so be it. Would I believe it, though? Would I accept their vision of me as the thief on the card?

Part of me did. The weight of my pack seemed overwhelming as I thought about the envelope tucked inside it. What hypocrisy, to take what served me while denying the rest of it—the union with Romeo, the pressure of my family to conform.

But I could do it. I could choose to take some of it with me—the money, yes, but not only that. The memories, too, of my childhood—I would take those with me as well. The incredible closeness we had shared, the indulgent love my family had lavished on me when I had been a child—all of that would stay with me forever, even as I walked away from them.

And the condemnation of being marked *marimè*? Would I accept that as part of the burden I carried away from here? Or could I refuse it, if I chose to?

That was a choice, and I could make it. My family might call me *marimè*, but perhaps I did not have to accept it as my own truth. My people believed that—that there is not just one truth, but rather many truths that at times contradict each other. Perhaps it was true that my actions had made me *marimè*. But equally true was that I was *not*. It depended entirely on which side of the table I chose to sit on. It spread through me like sunshine, this dawning of the idea that I could *choose* whether I would be *marimè*. I could shoulder that burden and accept it, or I could shrug it off.

This would be my choice. I did not know everything—indeed I knew very little about the world I was choosing to enter—but I felt the lightness of hope growing in my heart.

And I knew where I would go tonight.

As I walked, it seemed to me that I was in a different place than I had been in earlier that same night. I was still in the desert, yes, but barren? Suddenly, it did not seem so. Over my head I heard the flapping of bats' wings. Somewhere, not too far away, an owl called. Around me on the sand insects rustled by. Life was all around me. Even out here, where life seemed impossible, it found a way.

Perhaps I had no right to happiness. Others might say that a girl such as I, one who had shamed her family, should have no claim to joy. Yet I felt it in my breast, a beautiful clarity, and when the heavy clouds at last opened above me, I smiled widely as I turned my face up to receive their rain.

CHAPTER SEVENTEEN

It was the rain that woke me. I guess I'd been sleeping again—real sleep this time, no more crazy hallucinations. I was still on the couch and James was spread out on the carpet nearby.

Maybe it was close to midnight. I sort of remembered my parents coming home, asking James what was wrong with me, my mom peering into my eyes and making me track her finger as she passed it back and forth in front of my face. She must have decided I was all right, because I was still home—they hadn't loaded me up and driven me into Reno.

The rain was intense, pouring down, and actually I was surprised I was the only one it woke. I stood and tried to stretch, but a sharp pain in my ribs on my left side stopped me short.

My jaw was sore, too, and my stomach felt like I'd done about a thousand sit-ups. I stepped carefully over James, not wanting to wake him, and made my way into the kitchen. The clock on the microwave read 12:32.

Saturday, then. Two days until the move.

On another day, this thought would have been enough to slap me with another round of anxiety. But my problems—my guilt over going away to college, the fact that I wouldn't be in any shape to run when I got there, and what my new coach might think about that—none of that seemed important just then. I stared out the kitchen window at sheets of rain and wondered about Lala.

She was out there somewhere. I couldn't imagine that she could really be at home with her family. The angry faces of Romeo and his brother flashed in my head and I felt a jolt of fear. They'd had no qualms about taking me apart out at the mine. Did that mean that they might be willing to hurt *her*, too?

I couldn't just leave her out there, not without knowing that she was all right. Maybe she didn't want to see me ever again. Maybe that was why she'd left. If that was the truth, okay, I'd deal with it. But without knowing that she was safe . . . I couldn't just pretend that nothing had happened.

Outside, I stood on the front porch, shielded from the rain by the roof's small overhang. The rain was torrential. Our little front yard was dotted with puddles, the ground too dry to gulp up so much water.

One of my favorite smells—the rain. Probably because I didn't get to experience it very often. I breathed in deep now, filling my lungs with the damp, earthy air and ignoring the uncomfortable twinge in my ribs. I was a little dizzy, so I held on to the porch rail as I stood there. Our narrow street was a slick ribbon of rain, the gutters overflowing. And as I watched it seemed that the rain started coming down even harder.

I couldn't ride the motorcycle in this weather. Dad's car was in the driveway, but the keys would be in his room. If I went in there to get them, he'd wake up. There was no way I could possibly skateboard all the way out to Lala's, not in the rain.

I guess it was because I still felt so loopy that I just stood there, full of indecision, watching the rain fall. At last I left the porch and walked down the steps, through our yard, and onto the sidewalk.

No shoes. Damn. And it only took about thirty seconds before I was soaked through. The sky was as black as I'd ever seen it. More than half the houses on my street were vacant, and none of them were lit. Maybe my dizziness contributed to the feeling that I was terribly, horribly lost in the rain— usually I had a really good sense of direction, but tonight I didn't even feel sure which way to turn to head out to the highway.

I was shivering; I heard my teeth chattering together. I don't think I made a real conscious choice to do it, but I began running—Lala, Lala, Lala, her name in my head like the beat of a drum, thrumming out her name with each step, and I wondered if I would ever run again without hearing her name. I breathed deeply through my mouth, the rain streaming into my eyes. As I reached the corner I picked up speed, thinking maybe I could run to her, maybe I could find her out there in the rain.

And then there she was.

The rain was so heavy that I didn't see her until she was practically under me, right around the corner from my own house. She reached out her hand and touched my arm, stopping me in my tracks. She was soaked through, too, and carrying a pack on her back. Her hair, straightened and flattened by the rain, was pushed back from her face, and her teeth flashed at me in a broad, almost triumphant-looking smile.

"Ben Stanley," she said.

The pack slipped from her shoulder and she wound her arms up around my neck, and we stood there together, alone in the street, the falling rain our only music, and I held on to her tight as I could, as if I would fall down without her there to keep me on my feet, and her face tilted up to mine and we kissed, our mouths warm in spite of the cold rain, and I lifted her feet up off the ground to get her closer to me, the satisfying weight of her body in my arms pressed up against my chest making me suddenly, brilliantly happy.

After a while I lowered her back to the ground and picked up her pack. I wouldn't let her go, though, and I wound my arm around her waist, leading her home.

We stood dripping wet and kissing just inside the door. I could see James's feet; he was still sleeping on the family room floor.

"Come on," I whispered to Lala, and I led her into the bathroom. There I switched on the light and cranked the shower to hot. She stood next to me in the narrow bathroom, her skirt heavy with water, a growing puddle at her feet.

"I'll wait in the other room," I offered, "while you shower. I'll bring you some dry clothes."

I turned to the door to leave, but Lala's hand on my arm stopped me. "Stay," she said. Her voice—it was clear and strong, like the rain outside.

Our bathroom was tiny, and it was already filling with steam. Slowly, gently, I closed the door and pressed the button to lock it.

In the light of the bathroom I looked carefully at Lala. She hadn't been hit; her face was unmarked, beautiful as ever. But there was a difference to her, something I couldn't quite name. She looked—lighter, I guess. Not skinnier— *lighter*, like she'd set something down, or let something go.

I wanted to ask her where she'd been, and what had happened with her family, and if she was all right.

But then she started taking off her clothes and I forgot all that.

Each thing she took off she dropped in a pile in a corner— first her sandals, then her shirt, and then her belt and her skirt, and then she reached behind her back to unhook her bra—a little hesitation here, as if for a second she considered leaving it on—but then the hook came free and the straps slipped from her shoulders and her chest was bare.

Her breasts were beautiful. Round and heavy, with dark pink nipples that stood up because of the wet and the cold. And then she pushed down her panties and stepped out of them.

I'd never been in the same room as a naked girl. She

stepped past me into the shower and pulled closed the curtain behind her.

It felt a little like déjà vu, like I was reliving our swim down at the pond. I wondered briefly if her family was going to storm in again like they had then, but I'd locked the front door when we came in, and anyway I don't think they knew where I lived.

Shaking myself out of my soaking wet jeans wasn't easy, but I managed and piled my wet clothes on top of Lala's. I thought for a second that maybe this was another dream, like the one of me and Lala under the tree, and decided that if it was I wasn't in a big hurry to wake up.

The shower was pretty small, but there was room enough for us both inside it. I pulled the curtain closed after I stepped in and then it was just the two of us in this little rectangular enclosure, not enough room for us *not* to touch, with warm water raining down on our heads.

Lala touched my chest with her fingertips, my shoulders, the line of my arm. I saw her looking down between my legs, but she didn't touch me there. I lifted her hair, so heavy with the water, and kissed her gently on the cheek. Even wet like this she still smelled spicy and sweet all mixed together.

When we kissed again I was careful not to press up against her, though it was really hard not to—all my testosterone, I guess, urged me to push into her, but I didn't. I touched her so gently, kissing her as softly as I could, trying to show her that I wasn't going to make her do anything she didn't want. Hell, I figured I was the luckiest guy alive to be standing right there, under the hot waterfall, with her. If this was it, I'd have nothing to complain about.

Lala had come back to me. That was the best part of all of this. She wanted to be here, with me.

We kissed until the water started to lose its heat. Then, reluctantly, I turned the shower off. The first towel I wrapped around Lala, and I rubbed it against her skin—her arms, her back, her belly, drying her off. She laughed quietly and let me.

Then I grabbed another for myself. We tiptoed past my parents' closed door to my bedroom. I could hear James breathing in the family room.

"Do you want a T-shirt or something?"

Lala stood with her back to me, looking at the boxes that lined the far wall. Her towel was looped loosely around her, falling low across her naked back. She had twisted her hair into a knot after the shower, baring to me the long expanse of her back, the gentle inward curve of her waist.

I waited for her to answer my question, wishing with everything I had that she might say no, she did not want a T-shirt.

"So many boxes," she said. "A whole lifetime's worth."

"Yeah," I answered. "I guess between the two of us, James and I managed to collect a bunch of stuff."

"Everything I have is in that satchel by your door," Lala said. She turned to me. "I do not want a T-shirt."

And this time it was Lala who kissed me first, and she didn't seem to mind when I pressed into her, the urge too strong to deny.

254

We made our way to my skinny single bed. She climbed in, dropping her towel on the floor. I slid in next to her and tucked the sheet around us both. Her skin was so warm and soft up against my body.

But as much as I wanted just to lose myself in her skin, I had to ask. "You can't go home?"

Our mouths were only inches apart. "Never."

I wanted to say something else, but I didn't know what to say, and anyway Lala was kissing me again, exploring my body with her hands. Finally I pulled away just a little and said, "It's my fault."

"You are silly," she said, propping herself up on one elbow. "You think you are handsome, and you are right."

I felt myself blustering, not really sure what to say.

"Yes, you are handsome. Very handsome, that is true. But I know my own mind."

"I shouldn't have taken you to the mine."

"You may have been driving," Lala said, "but I was no passenger. I knew where that ride would lead—away from my family. It was no mistake. I think it has been coming for a long while, though I was not brave enough to look it in the face. Ben Stanley, you have done nothing wrong. I knew exactly what I was doing when I climbed onto your motorcycle."

"You knew your family would react like that?"

Her forehead creased. "I feel badly that they hit you," she said. "I did not imagine they would follow us. I assumed that once I left with you, I would be dead to them. It took slightly longer than I had thought, that is all."

I shook my head. There was nothing I could do, nothing I could *imagine* doing, that would make my family throw me out. I told Lala this.

"And your brother, too?" she asked. "Is there anything he could do—anything he could *be*—that would cause you to no longer call him your brother?"

I thought of James, sitting up with me, bringing me Tylenol and making me a sandwich. And I felt it so strongly right then—my love for him, the entirety of it. "No." My voice was firm. "James is my brother. He always will be. As long as he'll have me."

She sighed. "Then you and James are both fortunate. That is how it should be." She kissed me again, this time feather light. When she spoke, her voice was different. Less certain. "Ben," she said. "There is something I want to do with you."

It wasn't that I *didn't* want to have sex with Lala; more than anything ever, I did. But I didn't want to cause her any more trouble. I didn't want to start something that I couldn't do the right way.

I started to say this, but Lala stopped me with a finger to my lips. "Let me speak."

So I listened.

"For my people much of a woman's worth is bound up with her virginity," she began. "Do you remember what I told you about the bride price—the money the groom's family pays the bride's?"

I nodded.

"If it is revealed after the wedding night that the girl had not been a virgin, the groom's family has the right to demand the return of the bride price. The girl and her family are shamed. Of course, no such equivalent punishment is meted out if the situation is reversed."

"So you want to have sex to piss off your family?"

"No," she said. "It is not that. I want to have sex—because I want to share this experience with *you*, Ben Stanley. And I want this to be *my* decision. *Ours*. No one else's."

I was kind of embarrassed to tell her what I said next. "But, you know, Lala . . . I've never done it before, either. I probably won't be very good at it."

Her laugh was husky and beautiful, but quiet, as if she was being careful not to wake my family. "Probably neither of us will be," she said. "But we will learn together." And then she said, her voice a little singsong, "Can a body meet a body, coming through the rye?"

I caressed the curve of her breast, and pressed my face into her neck, murmuring, "Can a body kiss a body—need the world know?"

And then we didn't talk anymore.

I don't know why people would ever want a bed any bigger than the one Lala and I shared that night. Lying on our sides, my body curved tight behind hers, my arm tucked under her head, there was just enough space for the two of us.

Her head was heavy on my arm as she slept, and the wild tangle of her curls tickled my face. But it was perfect. I could finally breathe in her spicy sweetness all I wanted. It seemed almost to hover in a cloud, the smell of her skin, and I felt a little drunk on it.

Or maybe it was what we had done together. Or maybe it was the concussion.

Probably it was all of it, everything—but most of all having her here in my bed, in my arms, asleep and soft and wonderfully bare.

I guess I'd slept enough earlier, after Romeo and Marko had laid me out, because I wasn't tired now. I was happy to lie awake and listen to the steady rhythm of her breaths, the quieting of the rain and finally the silence when it stopped, and remember again and again what we'd done together.

Around five a.m. I heard other people stirring in the house. I heard the bathroom door slam and remembered with a start that our wet clothes—Lala's and mine—were still on the floor in there.

And a little later I heard James banging around in the hallway and my mom's voice hissing at him, "Don't go in there!"

I laughed a little into Lala's hair. Even though I had no desire to unwind my body from hers, it seemed like I should probably get up and explain a little bit to my parents about whose clothes they'd found.

So I slid my arm out from under Lala's head and untangled myself from the sheets. She rolled over, still sleeping, and I forced myself to tuck her in rather than stare at her naked body.

I felt better this morning for sure. My headache was just

a dull pounding and I wasn't dizzy anymore. In some ways, I felt clearer—happier, definitely, and more hopeful—than I could remember feeling since I was a little kid.

My mother was sitting with a cup of coffee and the newspaper from Reno when I walked into the kitchen, running my hand across my hair.

She looked up over the edge of her reading glasses. "You look better than you did last night, at least," she said. "Sleep well?"

I grinned, a little sheepish. "Good morning, Mom."

"Coffee?"

I wasn't in the habit of drinking the stuff; mostly just water and juice. But I poured myself a cup anyway before I sat down across from her. "Anything interesting in there?" I asked, tapping the newspaper.

"Not as interesting as what's in *there*," she said, indicating the dryer that was running in the corner of the kitchen. "Whose clothes?"

I burned my mouth with my first sip of coffee. "Lala's," I choked. When I'd recovered, I elaborated. "Lala White. The Gypsy girl I told you about."

I had to hand it to her; if she was surprised, she hid it pretty well. "I didn't remember Cheyenne ever wearing a skirt longer than six inches," she said, "so I supposed it wasn't hers." But then she looked at me more seriously. "I hope you were smart."

It made me uncomfortable, but there was no getting around it. "Yeah," I said. "We were careful."

She nodded. "Well, that's good, at least."

"You're not mad?" I blew a little on my coffee before taking another sip.

"Mad?" she asked. "No. Not mad. You're a grown man. High school graduate . . . off to college . . . eighteen years old. I guess you're old enough to make your own choices. If anything . . ." She shrugged. "I guess I would have hoped you would have chosen someone who was . . . special. A girlfriend, I guess. Someone who meant something to you."

"You're wrong." My voice came out harder than I'd meant it to. "Lala isn't like that. There's never been another girl— who I felt like this about Who's been special like she is."

Shit. I hadn't exactly wanted to spill my guts to Mom at the breakfast table. But I couldn't stand the thought that she might get the wrong idea about Lala, so I went on. "You'll really like her, Mom," I said. "She's smart. Whip smart. And she sees things, you know, about people. She isn't someone who just gets blown around, you know? She . . . chooses things. And then she does them."

That was the best I could do to explain how I felt about Lala. I don't think it was the words I'd used that made the expression on Mom's face shift; I think it was the sound in my voice. I heard it, too.

"You really like this girl."

I nodded.

"That will make things harder for you."

I didn't tell her everything I'd been thinking in the hours between Lala's arrival and sunrise. I wasn't through working it all out yet. So I just nodded again.

"This won't—change anything for you, I hope." Her voice sounded anxious now. "You're still getting on that bus to San Diego."

I shrugged.

"You can't *not* go to college." Her voice sounded a little panicked now. "Not because of a girl."

"I thought I was all grown up," I said, a little angry.

"I thought so, too," said my mom. She was more than a little angry.

We both needed some space, I thought, so I asked where James was.

"He's with your dad. They're helping the Wilsons load their truck." She wasn't anxious for me to change the subject, because she said, "Ben, there will be lots of girls."

"There's only one of *her*, though, Mom." I wanted to find the words to explain how I felt. "Do you know how you're always telling me and James about you and Dad? About how he was *the one*?"

Mom took off her glasses and rubbed the bridge of her nose. "Ben," she said, "you know I love your father. I wouldn't undo what we've made together, not for anything in the world. But Ben, I don't think I ever said your father was *the one*."

I blinked. "You mean there was someone else? Some other guy you wanted to marry?"

She laughed. "Sure, Ben, there were a few of them."

"I don't get it."

She sighed. "You're eighteen, Ben, and you're going off to college, but in some ways you're still a boy."

"Okay, fine, I'm just a big kid now. Is there something you're trying to tell me?"

"Sweetheart, I don't think there *is* a 'one.' Your father probably doesn't either, though he'd never admit it in front of me. There are lots of paths," she said, "lots of people. Probably there are *dozens* of men—maybe even hundreds—I could have fallen in love with, married, even raised a family with, given the right set of circumstances."

"Real romantic," I scoffed.

"Maybe not," she said. "But I would have thought that would appeal to you."

"To *me*?"

She nodded. "Crossing the finish line is pretty romantic," she said, "but I've seen you after practice. Nothing real romantic about that—the sweat, the stink of your shoes."

"What's your point?"

"My point? Anyone could break the ribbon if you set him down magically right in front of it. But that's not how you get there."

I didn't like the way she was using my running as a metaphor for whatever point she was trying to make. Lala was just a couple of walls away, still sleeping, and what I wanted was to crawl back into bed with her.

"No, Mom, I get there by running. I get it."

"Do you? I don't think so. A successful long-term relationship, Ben, is about a whole lot more than sex, or even finding the right person. It's about a hell of a lot of work. Even when you feel like walking away."

"I'm not afraid of work."

"I know that, sweetheart. We've all seen how hard you've worked—on your running, your grades, all of that. Now imagine all that work times about a hundred, and you'll have the beginning of an idea of what it means to be a husband and a father."

"Who said anything about me being a *father?*"

"Condoms break."

"Well, ours didn't."

"Not this time. But they do break. I can promise you that."

It took me a minute to figure out what she meant. But then I saw it. "You mean—you and Dad—"

"That's right."

"But I thought you were high school sweethearts. That you loved each other."

"Absolutely we were—off and on. And after I got pregnant with you, we got married. We moved to Gypsum. And I wouldn't undo it, Ben, like I said, not for anything. That's not what I'm trying to say. What I want to say is this—choose your path, Ben, and choose it carefully. Don't lie to yourself about where it might lead."

"Dad couldn't have known moving here would turn out like this," I said, gesturing to the boxes everywhere.

"No, that's true. And it could have turned out differently, if the housing market had held." She sighed, and for a second she looked lost. "I don't know, Ben. I don't have any of the answers. I guess any path could take you places you might not expect. Hell." She laughed. "I never thought I'd be moving back to Reno."

Mom looked at me like she wished she had something more to offer me, and I thought of that stupid story she used to read me about this tree and a boy. The tree just gave and gave until it was a stump, until it had nothing left. I thought about Pops, out in his garage, reorganizing his stuff for a life he never intended.

Maybe I would have said something more, but then I heard something from my room. Lala was awake. Drinking the last of my coffee, I pushed back from the table.

Mom smiled at me wryly, and I wondered why I had thought about the tree story. She wasn't anything like that, not really. "You're a good man, Ben. I'm sure you'll do what is right—whatever that means for you. Now, why don't you see if Lala White would like some breakfast?"

CHAPTER EIGHTEEN

LALA

I woke to sunlight streaming through the windows. The rain was gone.

I was alone in Ben Stanley's bed, and I was naked. Perhaps I should have felt shame, but I did not. Sitting slowly and stretching, I considered how I did feel.

Like a cat with milk on its whiskers.

My clothes had been left in the bathroom the night before and my satchel still sat in the hallway. Perhaps I could find something to wear in the dresser. Before I looked for clothing, though, I wanted to see something else.

I stood and turned back the blanket to gaze down at the bottom sheet.

There it was—smaller than I would have expected, an uneven rust-colored stain. Proof of my virginity lost.

It was funny; I did not feel that I had lost anything. Quite the opposite, I felt as if I had gained—experience, independence.

I remember my sister Violeta's wedding—the food, the music, the dancing and excitement—and the white flag carried by the men of Marko's family, a symbol of the sheet on which her virginal blood would be spilled that night.

She had blushed as she looked at it, and though no one had displayed the actual sheet the following morning, Violeta did share with me that her new mother-in-law had inspected the marriage bed before pronouncing the wedding officially consummated.

Violeta had seemed to feel mostly relief that she had indeed bled—we knew that some girls, despite insisting on their virginity, did not have any proof of it, much to their and their family's shame.

I had been angry on her behalf, even though Violeta was not at all angry. More than anything else, this was something I dreaded—that specific lack of privacy, my future mother-in-law's right to see my blood.

But not now. I looked carefully at the stain.

My phone had given me a secret window into the world. Through it I had seen many things—glimpses of other cultures, other people, their past as well as their present.

One day last spring, I had come across a story. I think it was fiction, but perhaps it was based on fact. It was about a Catholic nunnery in Portugal, and so involved a country—and a religion—about which I knew very little. I had even suffered under the misconception that Spanish is spoken in Portugal until I began to research it a bit.

I had known that Catholics have a practice of celibacy among their priests and nuns, but was surprised when I read that some of their nuns wear wedding rings, and all consider themselves married to Jesus Christ. For my people, a life without sex and childbirth is not a whole life; bearing children within the confines of marriage is what truly transforms a girl into a woman, more even than beginning her monthly blood or becoming a wife.

This was what the story had said: The convent in Portugal, where their nuns lived, had a special kind of collection. Down the walls of a long hallway hung a series of beautifully framed linen fabric squares. Each square bore the proof of a royal woman's deflowering, proof that she had entered marriage pure, untouched, a virgin.

And people visited this nunnery, and they wandered up and down the long hallway looking at each fabric square, commenting on what shapes they imagine they see in the stains, much as children gaze into the clouds.

But there was one framed square at which everyone would stop and stare the longest, imagining the story behind that woman's wedding sheet: it was unmarked, perfectly white, clean.

If my blood were to be added to that collection, this is what it would be. Small, pleasingly dark, one edge smeared, the rest distinct.

It would never be displayed for anyone—not a husband, not a mother-in-law, not a hall full of tourists. It was mine. Mine alone.

There was a knock at the door.

I sat back on the bed, pulling the blanket across my body.

Ben came in carrying my satchel and my clothes from last night, dry and folded, smiling at me as if he was not sure what kind of reception to expect.

"Good morning," I said, and patted the bed next to me.

He sat down and leaned over to kiss my cheek. Such a sweet, sweet boy.

"Did you sleep all right?"

I nodded.

"Do you feel . . . you know, okay?"

"I feel wonderful."

His face split in a grin. "Really? That's great. Because I was worried. . . ." Here he trailed off.

"I have no regrets." I could have said more, but there was no need. He looked into my eyes and saw what I was feeling, that my words were sincere.

"Neither do I."

He took my hand in his lap and traced his thumb across the lines on my palm. "So what do you see in your future?" It seemed to me that he tried to inject humor into his voice, but there was a real seriousness there that I was not yet ready for.

"I believe a shower," I replied. "And perhaps something to eat."

He did not look entirely pleased with my answer; it seemed he wanted to talk more. But I did not yet feel like talking.

"Okay," he said. "I'll be in the kitchen if you need me." He kissed me again, this time on the forehead, and then stood. "Um—my mom is out there, too. She says she can't wait to meet you." His grin was apologetic, and then he left me alone.

Ben Stanley's mother. No doubt her opinion of me would

not be good; I had gone out with her son unchaperoned, my people had injured him, and then I had returned to spend the night in his room. There was a word my people reserved for girls such as I had become—*curva*, whore.

When I went to the bathroom, I took the sheet with me. I had stripped the bed entirely and put the blanket and the top sheet in a pile. The bottom sheet I wrapped around myself. Then I took my clothes and peered carefully into the hallway. No one was there, though I heard movement in the kitchen. I moved quickly up the hall into the bathroom and locked the door behind me.

First I started the shower, turning the temperature to hot even though I could see, through the bathroom window, in the bright flash of sunlight, that the day was already heating. Then I unwound the sheet from my body and looked once more at the stain.

It did not look like a blooming rose. It did not look like a heart, or a bird, or a flowering tree. It looked decidedly like a spot of dried blood—nothing more, nothing less.

And when I held it under running water in the sink, adding a bit of soap and rubbing the fabric back and forth, it faded away, darkening the water for just a moment before it ran clear.

Then it was gone.

When I entered the kitchen, dressed once more in my red skirt and white blouse, my damp hair tied behind me, I felt the coward's relief that I did not find Ben's mother alone at the table. The entire Stanley family was there—Ben, whose smile upon seeing me was heartbreakingly honest, James, who looked at me with open-faced curiosity, and Ben's parents, his mother in front of the stove preparing a pan of scrambled eggs and his father pouring out cups of coffee.

Ben stood up quickly when I came in. "Hey, Lala," he said, and he came around the table to take my hand. It felt like a message—he was showing his parents what I was to him. And perhaps he meant to show me, as well, for he pulled back a chair for me at the table and offered to get me a drink.

In my family men did not serve the women. It was not done. But I was not at home anymore, and so I asked Ben if I might have a glass of water.

"Sure," he said. And then he said, "Mom, Pops, James—this is Lala White."

"We met yesterday," said James. Then he asked, "Are you really a Gypsy? Can you tell me my fortune?"

His father made a sound into his coffee cup as if perhaps he would choke. "Nice to meet you, Lala," he said. "Would you like a cup of coffee?"

"Yes, thank you." I watched in wonderment as he poured it for me.

"Sugar?"

"Yes, please." I grew bolder. "And milk, if you have some."

He poured a generous dollop into the cup and scooped in sugar as well. I decided that I liked this man—generous, slow to make judgments, and gentle with his boys. He ruffled James's hair as he passed, drawing a steely-eyed gaze from his younger son, who quickly repaired the damage with a pass of his hand.

Ben's mother—I was less certain of her. She had set the table for five, I noticed, and she did not look unkind as she spooned the eggs onto our plates. At home, or at a home of any in my *kumpànya*, I would have immediately offered my help. But these were not my people, and I was unsure of what might be expected of me here.

Nothing good, most likely, at least when it came to Mrs. Stanley. Though she doled me out a generous portion, the tightening of her jaw revealed that she was not pleased by my presence.

I did not blame her, of course. But I saw what she perhaps did not see—Ben watching her, his face tensing up as well, in response to her measured politeness to me.

"So Ben tells us you're from Portland?" Mr. Stanley asked after we had all had several bites of our food.

I wondered what else Ben might have shared with his family while I had been dressing.

"Yes," I said. "Being in your desert has been quite a shock for me. I am used to the rain, as you might imagine."

"When are you heading back?" Mrs. Stanley was fairly successful in making her question sound innocuous, but I felt waves of heat radiating off Ben at my side. His mother might not like me, but it would be in her best interest not to make that fact too plain. Ben, I could see, had cast himself in the role of my protector.

My actions were indefensible, perhaps. Truthfully, I had no desire to defend them. And they had led to a rift with my own family that I could not undo, even if I so desired it. But to see that my choices were creating further ripples, shifts in this other family . . . why had I not considered this?

It was because I had not wanted to see it. I should not claim to be surprised that what I had done would affect these other people, as well as mine. But my desire to be with Ben, and the urgency I felt to part from my people, was like a stone cast into a pond. The wake of it was no longer in my control.

James appeared oblivious to the tensions at the table, carrying on a chirpy monologue about what he had seen on television the night before—a new game show that involved people throwing themselves off large objects in an attempt to win money and prizes—but I could see that his chatter was deliberate. His role in the family dynamic was to act as a diversion. He was the entertainer, with a wide smile and a smart, witty tongue. He was in his element, recreating the expressions of the game show contestants as he told us all about the show.

Mr. Stanley seemed willing to listen and laugh, to be entertained. Ben and his mother were involved in a silent discussion of which I was the clear subject, casting weighty looks at each other as they ate and sipped their coffee.

This family was no more perfect than mine. As in my family, each person at this table had a job to do. James was the entertainer. Ben was the achiever. Mrs. Stanley was the backbone. And Mr. Stanley? I believe his job was to love, unequivocally and without restraint, each of the others.

I alone at the table lacked a function. Like an unnecessary cog added to a machine that otherwise worked quite serviceably—not perfectly, but well enough—I was complicating matters.

"Mrs. Stanley," I said, "thank you for breakfast. It was very good." Though the eggs had been overcooked, rather rubbery in texture, of course I had eaten every bite in front of me. "May I help with the dishes?"

"No, that's fine," she said. "It's James's turn."

When we returned to Ben's room after breakfast, he tried to close the door behind us, but I stopped him.

There was an awkwardness between us that had not been there before we spent the night together. It seemed that he did not quite know where to put his hands or what to say to me. He sat on the edge of the bed and watched as I opened my satchel to see what my mother had sent for me.

There was my phone, wrapped in a plastic bag to keep it safe. She must have anticipated the rain. It was lucky that she had—the other things in my bag were damp. She had included two of my skirts and several shirts, along with a thin sweater. And the envelope with the money, the bills slightly wet even though they had been tucked at the bottom of the bag. I had not yet counted the money; I did so now, as Ben watched.

It took me several minutes. As I counted I separated the money into four piles—tens, twenties, fifties, and hundreds.

When I was finished the tallest stack was the hundred dollar bills. Altogether it amounted to fifteen thousand dollars. The exact amount of my bride price.

"That's a shitload of money," said Ben.

"As you say," I agreed. But I did not feel any joy. Instead I saw what was *not* among the bills—a message from my mother.

In spite of myself, I had hoped that perhaps she might have slipped in a letter—just a little something, perhaps *I love you* or even *You will always be my daughter*.

I was not as impressed by the sight of all this money as Ben was. All my life my family had preferred to deal in cash, and at home my father had a hundred thousand dollars or more tucked away in various locations. He did not trust the bank, nor the government, and when we traveled to purchase cars he always brought cash with which to pay for them.

Ben had slid closer to me. He was thumbing through the bills, a look of wonder on his face. To him, this amount of money represented a fortune. In some ways, Ben Stanley was still a child. Fifteen thousand dollars was something, but a fortune it was not.

A beginning, perhaps.

"Hey," said Ben, "this one has something written on it."

He handed me the hundred-dollar bill. There, printed across the bottom edge in my mother's unsure script, was one word—*Korkoro*.

Ben asked me something, but I was far away. I was with my mother in my home, and I was nearly thirteen. Separated from my family because I had begun my first blood, I felt burdened by a confusing mixture of pride and shame. I was alone in my room—everyone else was in the kitchen eating dessert and drinking coffee.

My mother entered my room and sat with me on the bed. She stroked my hair and kissed my cheek. Then she leaned in close to me and whispered a word into my ear—*Korkoro*. Freedom.

My people do not have just one name. Of course we each have the name our families and friends know us by, and often we have another name, one by which the *gazhè* know us. But there is another name—a *first* name, whispered by a mother into her baby's ear, a name that no one else will ever know. Our traditions tell us that keeping this first name a secret will confuse the spirits that might otherwise steal away a baby. This secret name is spoken only twice, each time whispered by the mother to the child—first, at birth, and later, at the change of puberty.

Korkoro. For reasons she had never explained, my mother had named me Freedom. And here it was, my secret name, printed on a dirty piece of currency.

"It means 'freedom,'" I told Ben, my throat burning and closed with unshed tears. I did not tell him any more.

I needed to breathe, and so Ben and I went outside. I carried my satchel with me. In it were all my possessions, my money, my secret name. I did not wish to put it down.

There were not many places to go in Gypsum. There was the little store where I had gone with my family—was that just yesterday? It seemed a lifetime ago—and there were churches, and other homes. We walked slowly down the town's main street. It was early in the day still, but like every other day that I had been here in the desert the ground was dry and the air was terribly hot. One would never guess that the night before there had been a terrific storm.

Sometimes that is how things are. Something can occur—something that feels earth shaking, monumental, life transforming. But then the clouds clear and all seems normal again. The great change one had expected is not there after all.

And yet other things—other occurrences—can indeed shift irrevocably the entire trajectory of one's life. The storm might have brought with it lightning that could have struck me as I walked the long highway into Gypsum. This could have happened, but it did not.

"Ben," I said. "Have you ever gone to the festival—the Burning Man?"

"No," he said. "I never had the money for that sort of thing."

"Would you like to go?"

"I dunno. I guess I wouldn't mind seeing what it's all about. And tonight's the big night—when they burn the Man."

I must have looked shocked, for he laughed. "Not a *real* man," he clarified. "They build a giant wooden structure, and on Saturday night—tonight—they spray it with kerosene and light it up. Watch it burn."

"This," I said, "is something I would like to see."

Of course Ben did not like the idea of me spending my money on a ticket for him. But once I had gotten the idea in my head of going to see the Man burn, I did not wish to let it go. It was not in my habit to insist on things, but I felt as if I were stretching my wings. I wanted to see how far they could spread.

We walked to the store to purchase supplies before we left. Pete's Melissa was again behind the counter. Ben introduced us, and she rang up our items as we laid them on the counter.

"Five bottles of water, beef jerky, mixed nuts, four apples," she said. "Going somewhere?"

"We thought we'd check out Burning Man," Ben told her.

She nodded. "I hear it's pretty wild this year. Hog Boy'll never forgive you, Ben, for going without him. He and his folks finished loading the U-Haul last night."

"Have you been to this festival, Melissa?" I asked.

She wrinkled up her nose. "No way. All that sex and drugs. Naked chicks everywhere. I don't think it's really my speed." And from the expression she gave me—inquisitive—it seemed she did not think it would be mine, either.

Most probably she was right. But that was precisely why I wanted to go there. I wanted to see what was *other*, outside of myself. Foreign.

"I've gotta go by Hog Boy's place before we leave," Ben told me after we had made our purchases. "Pete's sticking around until Monday, but Hog Boy and his folks are leaving today. I want to say goodbye."

We left our supplies at Ben's home before walking the short distance to the house that Hog Boy was leaving. He was standing in the front yard, looking depressed. A moving truck sat in the driveway.

"Hey, Ben. Gypsy chick. What's up?"

I stood back and let Ben step forward to his friend.

"Hey there, Hog Boy. Cleaning out the sty?"

Hog Boy laughed, but there was no humor in it. "Yep. Watch out, Reno."

Ben nodded. He lifted his hand to pat his friend on the shoulder, but it hovered there, as if he was not sure whether or not to make contact. Finally he lowered it.

"I'm gonna miss you, Hog."

"Sure you are, off in the fucking land of milk and honey."

Ben took those deep breaths I knew him for, and when he replied his voice was kind. "I wish you were coming with me, you know."

Hog Boy turned to Ben. He smiled. "Yeah, I know. You'd take the whole goddamn town if you could."

Hog Boy's parents came out of the house. His father held the door open for his mother, who was carrying a table lamp. It was porcelain with a white shade and the figure of a little shepherd girl with a crook and bonnet. He locked the door behind her.

"Hello, Ben," said Hog Boy's father. "When are you leaving for college?"

"Monday." Then he said, "This is my friend Lala. Lala, these are Hog Boy's parents, Russell and Judy."

We shook hands all around.

Russell said to Ben, "Well, make us proud out there."

"I'll do my best."

Hog Boy's father clapped Ben on the back and then tossed a set of keys to his son. "Your mom and I will take the truck. You follow in the car."

"See you there," said Hog Boy.

Judy placed the lamp carefully in the center of the truck's cab before climbing in. Russell slid behind the wheel and they drove away.

Hog Boy spun the key chain around his finger. "Time to go," he said.

"I'll see you at Christmas, all right? I can't come back for Thanksgiving, but I'll check out your new place in December."

Hog Boy looked as though he might say something hurtful to Ben and I felt myself bracing against it. But then his face softened.

"Okay, man. Hey—Knock, knock."

Ben rolled his eyes, but he answered. "Who's there?"

"Boo."

"Boo who?"

"Stop crying, you pussy. It's not the end of the world."

Ben laughed. So did Hog Boy. They laughed and laughed, and there was nothing but their laughter and their friendship. All their problems, all their differences fell away, and I saw the little boy in each of them.

"Get out of here, then, and go show your Gypsy girl a good time," said Hog Boy. They shook hands, and then embraced.

Hog Boy climbed into his family's car, a tired-looking brown sedan, and we watched as he drove away, his hand stretched out the window to wave goodbye.

Ben put his arm across my shoulders and I leaned my head against him. So many goodbyes. And more still to come. I remembered it—our last card. The pierced heart, the driving rain.

It was in my future. Ben's, too. Yet it was not necessary to rush to greet it. We could tarry first. There was time still for us, and I intended to enjoy it.

Korkoro.

CHAPTER NINETEEN

BEN

The salt flats of the playa are an ideal place to do things you can't get away with doing practically anywhere else. The long, flat expanses make it perfect for going really, really fast—the land speed record has been set, broken, and set again in Black Rock Desert. And unlike a highway, it's not just a long, straight strip; you can go in any direction. But also unlike a highway, the surface isn't grippy, so your tires can slip out all haywire without any notice. More than a few amateur speed freaks have rolled their cars out here by turning too sharp.

You can burn things out here, too. With no vegetation to worry about, pyromaniacs have a monster hard-on for the place. That's half the reason some of these pyros travel all the way out to the playa for what they call Burning Man— for the pleasure of the burn. They burn a lot more than just the effigy on Saturday night; all week long the partiers light bonfires, send up rockets and flares, explode shit just for the hell of it.

Lala wanted to see Burning Man, and I wasn't about to

let her go to that freak show alone. It was true that I'd never been inside, but I'd seen some of the characters who pass through town for supplies. Wild eyed, half the time done up in some crazy costume or another, usually stoned or baked or drunk.

If Lala wanted to go, I'd take her there. But I had made a decision, during the quiet hours that she'd slept in my arms. If her family wasn't going to protect her anymore, if they'd really thrown her out for good—then I would take care of her.

I hadn't told Lala yet how I felt, but that didn't make it any less real. I knew what I felt. It was love.

Pete drove us out to Burning Man. I sat in the middle so that Lala wouldn't have to be jammed up against him. Lala kept her window down and watched the desert.

Pete had the music turned way up and was beating his thumbs against the steering wheel. He sang along with the song every few words, but he didn't really know the lyrics, so half the time he just sort of hummed the tune. I'd thrown my backpack into the bed of the truck, but Lala kept hers tucked down by her feet.

I felt myself tensing as we neared the place on the highway where Lala's family had camped, but I don't know which was worse—the anticipation of seeing their motor home and tent or the shock of realizing they weren't there anymore.

"Stop here, please," said Lala.

Pete didn't seem to hear her, so I shoved him in the ribs. "Hey, pull over."

"Huh? Here?"

He parked, and Lala climbed down out of the truck. There was nothing much to see—her family had cleared out pretty thoroughly. I couldn't really remember where exactly the motor home had been parked, where the trailer and tent had been. There was sort of a circle of rocks that had been their fire pit, but it was all kicked around like someone had wanted to mess it up but hadn't taken the time to do it right.

This was where Lala went. She knelt down at the edge of the circle. Her skirt trailed into the ashes. Pete and I sat in the truck, watching her. I wanted to go out to her because she looked really sad, totally alone, but I thought maybe she needed a little time to herself. I felt myself getting really mad at her family. Who the fuck were they to leave her here like this, in a strange town, even worse, a town that wouldn't even *be* a town in a couple of days? Abandoning her in the middle of the desert . . . bizarre.

"What do you think she's doing?" Pete asked. "Some sort of weird Gypsy ritual?"

Her back was to us, but I could see it moving a little, like she was shaking. "I think she's crying," I said.

I left Pete in the truck and walked up behind her. She'd sat herself all the way down at the edge of the fire pit, and she had a rock in her lap. As far as I could tell it didn't look any different from any of the other rocks.

I knelt down next to her. She was crying, all right, but she didn't make any sound, which in some way was even worse. Tears poured down her cheeks and her shoulders moved up and down like she was trying real hard to hold it together but she couldn't quite do it.

I didn't know what to say. What *could* I say? But I felt like I needed to say something—I mean, here was this girl—a girl I *loved*—who was crying like her heart had broken.

I wished her dad was there so I could punch him in the face. And Romeo, too, and his brother. Some of these rocks that made up the fire pit were just the right size to fill a fist, perfect for a good face pounding.

But there was no one to hit. There was just Lala and me, and Pete waiting for her to pull it together.

There was no way *I* was going to leave her, too. That was what I had been mulling over the night before—how could I possibly walk away from Lala, after what we'd shared, after what she had given me? That would make me just as bad as her family—maybe worse. Where would she go without me? What would she do?

It didn't matter, because it wasn't going to happen. I was with Lala, and I wasn't going anywhere. Not without her.

When I put my arm around her shoulder Lala seemed grateful for it. She turned her face into my shirt and cried a little more, but I could tell the worst was already past. After a minute she dried her eyes.

"Thank you, Ben Stanley," she said.

"No problem." I stood up and gave her my hand. "Are you sure you want to go to Burning Man? We don't have to. And I really don't think it's gonna be your scene."

"That is exactly why I want to go." She was holding one of the rocks from the fire pit. It was just a rock, but she looked down on it as if she saw something I didn't see.

And when we climbed into the truck, when we pulled back onto the highway, she didn't look back. Not one time.

I'd been out to the entrance to Burning Man a few times over the years. I didn't have Hog Boy's voyeuristic obsession with the place, but he'd managed to drag me out to see the sights at least once a year all through high school. So I knew what to expect when we drove up: We crested a little rise in the road and then, all of a sudden, instead of blank desert there was a city in the middle of nowhere.

A strange sort of city—ringed by a fence of four-foot-tall orange plastic netting, the city was formed of tents, lean-tos, RVs, and tent trailers. From the road you couldn't see the details, but I knew that when we got up close Lala would be getting an eyeful.

That orange plastic fence seemed like a little glimpse into the future; in just a couple of days a fence would go up around our town, too. But there wouldn't be anyone inside, and the fence the mining company was erecting would be topped with barbed wire.

This fence was designed to go up fast and come down fast later, when the week was over. The one around Gypsum—who knew how long it would stand? Probably until the elements eroded it, along with everything else.

Pete pulled his truck up toward the main entrance. I knew

that on the first couple of days, cars and trucks formed a long, winding line as greeters checked tickets and inspected vehicles to make sure no one was hiding in the trunks of the cars and in the showers of the motor homes, trying to avoid the steep price of entrance.

But this was Saturday; everyone coming to Burning Man was already here. We were the only car driving up to the entrance, and unlike the other times I'd been out here, always toward the beginning of the week, there wasn't a big group of greeters gathered around the entrance gate. Actually, it looked pretty deserted.

It was early in the afternoon and really, really hot; probably anyone with any sense was inside a tent or an RV trying to avoid the sun.

"How are you guys gonna get in?"

I shrugged. "Lala says she's going to buy the tickets."

Pete whistled, impressed by the idea of so much money being shelled out for a single day. "I could try to drive around the perimeter," he suggested. "We could see if there's a place where you could climb in without anyone really seeing."

Lala shook her head. "We will go in the main entrance."

I shrugged at Pete. He was smart enough not to argue with her; Lala had a way of talking that pretty much let you know she wasn't opening up a discussion.

"You want me to wait to make sure you get in?"

This didn't sound like a bad idea to me, but Lala refused. "We will be fine, thank you. If you would just drive us to the front."

"Well, I've got my phone if you need anything," said Pete as we got out of the truck.

"Thanks, man. I'll give you a call when we're ready to head out."

"Thank you, Pete," said Lala. "I appreciate your kindness."

"No problem," said Pete. He looked a little embarrassed. "I'll see you guys later. Have fun."

Every year Burning Man had a theme that sort of guided the art projects people brought and also created kind of a vibe. In the past the theme had been all kinds of things—Rites of Passage, the American Dream, and Evolution are a few I remembered. This year I guess it was New Horizons. There was a big banner across the entrance, a picture of a desert landscape with a rising sun exploding into fire, NEW HORIZONS printed in big, bold letters.

Hog Boy had told me about the time he'd gone to Burning Man, all the half-naked chicks and guys in skirts and costumes lined up to tear tickets. But today there was just one guy in the front, sitting on a folding lawn chair with an umbrella stuck into the back. Not far away were a couple of ladies, probably in their fifties, each with the leathery skin of a lifelong tanner. They were stretched out in a patch of shade and looked to be asleep. Either that or dead.

The guy was wearing a big, broad-rimmed straw hat and some khaki shorts and a tank top. Nothing like the people Hog Boy had described. Behind him I could see the layout of what they call Black Rock City, a big, horseshoe-shaped curve of campsites and art displays. Straight ahead was the Man himself—a giant wooden effigy, maybe eighty feet tall, that would burn later that night after being stuffed with fuel.

One year some guy managed to set the thing on fire like four days early. Hog Boy said he wished *he* would have thought of that, but it seemed to me a pretty lame thing to go to jail for.

Pete drove away as we walked up to the guy in the lawn chair. For a second I thought maybe he was just going to watch us walk on in. But then he said, "You guys miss the bus back or something?"

Every day of the Burning Man week, a bus carried loads of people into and out of our town, keeping Melissa pretty busy down at the Gypsum Store. This guy must have thought we'd gone into town on that bus and hadn't made it back on board.

"We did not miss the bus," said Lala. "We have just arrived."

"Just arrived?" He sat up straighter now, looking us up and down. "You virgins?"

I felt Lala next to me take a sharp breath. "What did you say?"

He smiled at me like an idiot. "You virgins?" he said again. Luckily, he added before I punched him in the nose, "This your first time here?"

"Oh," I said. "Yeah."

"Well, welcome to Burning Man," he said. "You got money?"

Now I felt like a piece of shit as Lala nodded yes. I'd only been on a few dates, but I'd always paid.

"I could pay you the entrance fee," Lala said, "but perhaps I could offer you something of more value instead."

"Hey, I'm all for barter," said the man, "but they're pretty strict about the entrance fee. No exceptions."

"Tonight the Man burns, does it not?"

"That's right."

"And for you especially that ritual must hold special meaning."

"What do you mean, for me especially?"

"You find yourself here, outside your element, yearning for something you think you have not yet found. Perhaps you came here looking for answers . . . but you have not been successful in finding them."

The man pushed his hat up on his forehead. It fell backward and dangled against his back, held in place by a string around his neck.

"Who've you been talking to?"

"If you will allow me . . ." Lala reached out with both of her hands, gently taking his and turning it palm up. "Perhaps I can help you find direction toward the answers you seek."

He wasn't saying anything now. Behind him I heard guitar music, some sort of folk song, the kind of slow, easy music that's just right for a hot day.

She looked into his hand and traced its lines with her finger, as if she were reading Braille. "I can see that you are a person who strives for balance," she said. "You believe in the value of practical work and do not shy away from it. Still, your mind is your best tool when it comes to earning a living. You are a man of solid values—and solid energy. And it would not surprise me to learn that you are a leader, and usually the man in a room that others turn to."

"How do you know all that?" His voice was full of wonder.

"It is all there, written for any who knows how to read it," Lala answered. "Would you like to know what else I see?"

He nodded, totally under her control now that she'd earned his belief. I stood quietly and watched her work.

"This is your Life Line," she said, tracing a line that began at the edge of his palm and extended up across the middle of his hand, wrapping around the base of his thumb.

"Do I have a long time to live?" He tried to make his voice sound like he was joking around, but I heard something else in it—fear, maybe, definitely a sense of awe.

"Oh, yes," Lala said, "but longevity is not all we can learn from a Life Line."

"What else?"

"Look," said Lala, "the line can be divided into three parts—your youth, your adult years, and old age. See how the line is long and deep? This shows your life will be long and largely full of health."

"Well, that's not really true," he scoffed.

"I did say *largely* full of health," Lala said. "You have battled illness."

She did not say it like a question, but he nodded just the same. "How did you know?"

"You see how the line has a chained quality here in the

middle—it begins deeply, but then seems more shallow, and then deepens again?"

By now I was into it as much as the guy. I looked over his shoulder to see the line.

"This represents the struggles you have had with health. But look—see how deep and clear the line is from middle life into old age? Your health problems are behind you."

The guy smiled, a big, beaming grin full of teeth. "That's a relief," he said. "What else can you see?"

"This here is the Head Line. It indicates your basic belief system—your philosophy, the perspective with which you look at life." Lala indicated a line just above the Life Line that stretched horizontally across his palm. "This too is a long, deep line, in your case. See how straight? You are a logical man, not given to emotional outbursts. You are a realist."

He laughed. "I used to think so," he said. "So what in the hell am I doing here?"

"As I said, searching for answers. But perhaps looking in the wrong places? And look here," she said, indicating a place on the line where it looked a little broken, like part of it was missing, "Do you see this? A broken line tells us that you have come to question your way of thinking. Perhaps something has happened to make you shift in this way?"

"You could say that."

"I thought so," Lala said, "and I imagine it has something to do with this line here. . . ." She pointed to a line above the Head Line. "Your Heart Line."

"That one must be broken into a million pieces," the guy

said. His voice had that weird edge to it that people's voices get when they're trying to joke about something that they don't think is really funny at all.

"Look here," Lala said. "Do you see this little constellation of lines that crosses your Heart Line? These indicate happiness in your romantic relationship."

"Well, that's wrong," said the man.

"Let me finish," said Lala. "The cluster of lines is *here*, early on the Heart Line. There was happiness once, wasn't there?"

The man kind of cleared his throat. "Yeah," he said. "There was."

"There can be again," said Lala. "It is all here, written in your own flesh—your suffering, your ability to rebound from it. You were sick once, were you not, and now you are well?"

"Never healthier. But how could you know that?"

Lala ignored the question. "Your marriage is ill, too. But it is not dead. There is still time to heal it, if you wish."

The man blinked, looking into his palm as if he could see what Lala saw, if only he stared hard enough. Then he looked up into her face. "Listen," he said, "I don't know who you are or where you came from. But thank you." He closed up his umbrella and folded up his chair. "I've got to go home," he said. "You kids have fun out here."

He took his chair and umbrella and turned to the two browning women, nudging the nearer one with his foot. She grunted and sat up. "These kids are all taken care of," he said. "Take over the gate, will you? I've got to go."

Then he headed into the city, picking up a jog in spite of the heat.

"What the hell just happened?" I asked Lala after we'd walked through the entrance, smiling at the women who were now in charge of the gate.

"I believe we just had the entrance fee waived," said Lala. She sounded a little smug.

"How the hell did you *do* that?"

She smiled. "I told you once before—you need to pay attention. Then you will see."

"*What* did you see, exactly?"

"I saw a man whose ring finger on his left hand still bore a pale stripe where a ring had been for a long time, and until very recently. I saw a man with well-manicured fingers, no calluses, and a fine, expensive watch."

I hadn't seen any of this. To me, he was just a guy. "But you said he'd been sick. How could you know that? He looked perfectly healthy."

"You are not serious," she said.

"What?"

"Ben Stanley, did you even *look* at that man?"

"Of course I looked at him." I was getting a little upset. It seemed like Lala was laughing at me.

"Did you see his bracelet?"

"His bracelet?" I thought back. "He had one of those rubber things. The ones people wear for causes."

"Did you read it?"

"No. What did it say?"

" '*I am stronger than cancer.*' "

"No shit."

"Absolutely none."

"Huh." I shook my head. "Okay, then."

So we were in.

Even in the middle of the afternoon, when the day was at its least tolerable, the place was crazy. After all those years of living just outside the gates, it seemed surreal to be here now, inside them, and ironic that I was here with Lala when I'd rather have been anywhere else, alone with her.

The people, I guess, impressed me more than anything else. Name an outfit, someone was rocking it. Bunny ears, capes, body paint every color of the rainbow, ridiculous platform boots, and full-on naked. There was a dude in vampire teeth and black leather being pulled around on a *leash* by a blond chick in a black corset and heels.

And they were riding bikes and unicycles and contraptions of all different kinds, and some of them were playing instruments and others were carrying around drinks.

Lala's eyes were wide open. She kept swiveling her head back and forth like she was trying to take it all in at once.

Hog Boy hadn't been lying about the girls. All kinds of them—tall, short, fat, thin, old, young, beautiful, and somehow beautifully ugly—were out there on the playa. I was with Lala, and she was who I *wanted* to be with, but even so I couldn't help but see all the flesh on display, and a small voice in my head couldn't help but wonder what it might be like to touch them, to have them touch me.

The thought gave me a flash of guilt, and I hoped Lala hadn't seen what I was thinking. Because more than any of them—more than *all* of them—it was Lala I wanted.

No one really even seemed to notice us. I guess it was because we were just wearing regular street clothes. So we were free to look all we wanted.

We wandered through the streets of Black Rock City, holding hands.

So Burning Man is divided into different theme camps, each with its own flavor. The theme camps are created by the campers, and I guess people join whichever camp seems the most fun to them.

Each camp is supposed to give something away to anyone who wanders over to visit it. Lots of them give away cold drinks, but not all of them. Others give out snacks or even experiences. There was a bondage camp where girls dressed up in leather skirts and heels—and one guy who was in the exact same getup—were hard at work spanking any camper who announced he'd been bad and needed punishment.

There were a few body art camps where you could get something airbrushed or hennaed onto your body, anywhere you wanted.

One camp we saw was full of instruments. People came and went, adding their sounds to the music.

There was a place to do yoga, a place to create "vision boards," whatever those were, a spot for adding to a giant clay statue display, a place where people would apply *lotion* for you, a confessional where the leaders were dressed like priests from the waist up, naked from the waist down. There was a place to make sock monkeys.

I found it hard to believe there could be enough people interested in a golden shower camp to fill a whole section on the playa, but there they were.

After Lala got over her initial shock, she seemed set on seeing as much as she could. Honestly, I would have preferred to go somewhere we could be alone together.

There was this one theme camp that was set up as a little chapel. It seemed kind of out of place, out there among all the naked sparkly people and booze, but there it was: several rows of benches half-full of people, none of whom looked really dressed for a wedding, watching what was happening on a little raised platform at the front, and a five-foot wall at the back decorated with all kinds of religious symbols. There were a couple of crosses, a Star of David, one of those Muslim crescent moons, a yin and yang, and some other symbols I'd never seen before. A bunch of white sheets were suspended by ropes to form a little enclosure around the whole thing, making it kind of private. The wind was picking up and the sheets fluttered a little. It was kind of nice.

There was a couple—a man and a woman, both pretty young, in their twenties, I'd guess—standing up on the platform. He was wearing a kilt and flip flops and had this crazy beard, long and tangled, and a head full of dreadlocks. She was wearing a wedding gown, sort of; it was white, and she had a little tiara in her brown hair with a veil, but the dress was way shorter than most churches would be okay with.

And there was another woman, short haired and bare faced, dressed in long, rust-colored robes, who was facing out at the audience and the couple. She was smiling.

Lala joined the crowd, sitting on the bench farthest back from the stage. I sat next to her.

Actually it was a pretty normal wedding ceremony, considering how crazy the venue and the guests were. I couldn't stop staring at the guy. It was the way he looked at the girl he was marrying. Like he was totally gone on her, like he couldn't even see anything else.

That was how I felt when I looked at Lala.

At the end, right before they kissed, the guy said this little poem to his new wife:

> *"From this day forward,*
> *You shall not walk alone.*
> *My heart will be your shelter,*
> *And my arms will be your home."*

When they kissed, the whole audience burst into applause, and I was right there with them, slamming my hands together. It's embarrassing, but I almost could have cried.

Lala smiled and laughed a little when she saw how . . . I don't know, *affected,* I guess, I was by the whole thing. It was just so *hopeful,* so *unexpected,* to see love out here, of all places.

"You enjoyed that," she said to me after the couple was

gone and the crowd had dispersed. We were alone, just us two. The wind had picked up a little more and set the white sheets to dancing.

"It was nice," I admitted. "I guess I'm more romantic than I thought."

The word "romantic" reminded me what my mother had said to me that morning back in the kitchen, when Lala was still in my room. About her and my dad. About why they were here, in Gypsum, in the first place. I'm not proud to admit it, but for a quick flash my thoughts went to some of the girls I had seen that day at Burning Man—and to Cheyenne, too. A question came to me, uninvited—could it be true, what Mom had said? I pushed it away.

"Do you think they will be together very long?" Lala asked.

It was like she was reading my thoughts. And even though I had just been thinking along similar lines, I felt compelled to hide that fact.

"Who? The couple who just got married? I guess so—they looked pretty happy."

Lala seemed unsatisfied with my response, like maybe she knew that I was thinking more than I said. "Most people look happy at a wedding," she said. "It is later that things can fall apart."

"I liked what he said to her," I told Lala, and this was the whole truth. "About being her home, you know, her shelter."

"Yes. It was pretty."

"Lala," I said, "I want to talk to you. About what we're going to do next—now that your family is gone."

"What *we* will do?"

"Well, yeah." Regardless of what my mom thought, regardless of what I might even be thinking, there was more that I needed to say—that I *wanted* to say, in spite of anything else. "I don't like it, Lala. Your family abandoning you like that . . . just freaking taking down camp and driving off. It's not right. And I want you to know that you're not alone. You never will be, Lala. I love you." It was the first time I'd ever said those words to a girl. It felt good to say them. Really good.

She smiled at me sweetly and patted my arm. "You are a good man, Ben Stanley," she said. "But you owe me nothing."

This made me kind of mad, like she misunderstood me. "Owe you? It's not a matter of *owing* you anything. Lala, I love you." The more I spoke, the more I got kind of caught up in what I was saying. "I'm not leaving you. Listen—this is what we'll do. Come with me to San Diego. I don't have to live on campus. We can get an apartment. I'll get a part-time job. We'll be together. We can make it work, Lala. I love you." I knew I was kind of rambling, and I felt all worked up, like I'd been running a race.

She looked for a minute like she was going to say something, but then she stopped and just touched my cheek. I wanted to say more, so much more, but I didn't have the words. Everything else fell away. UCSD, my family, my fears and hopes—none of it mattered anymore. All I knew was that I needed her with me. Even though I hadn't known she existed a week ago, now that I'd held her in my arms, now that I'd felt her skin and smelled her hair, I didn't know if I could live without her.

Lala tipped her mouth up toward me and I kissed her in that little chapel in the desert, and it felt so good to hold her like that, to shelter her with my arms, to know that I wouldn't leave her, I wouldn't walk away—that this was where I belonged, with Lala forever.

We kissed and kissed, and when the windstorm began, swirling around us and stirring up gypsum dust into the air, I held her even tighter; when the white sheets flapped angrily in the wind, coming loose and flying across the playa, when the air grew so thick with dust that the whole world turned white, even that was all right because Lala was in my arms and I would never let her go.

CHAPTER TWENTY

LALA

After the windstorm died down, together Ben Stanley and I explored the festival—the art projects, the musicians, people kissing and touching in ways that should be private but here were on display for anyone to see. Ben did not wish to wander through the festival; he wanted to exact a promise from me, one I was not willing to make.

But I had pulled him from the little chapel and he followed me as I explored, full of wonder at the strange sights and even stranger people.

It was clear to me that these people were playing at being Gypsies—not true Gypsies, as my people were. There would be little pleasure in pretending to be that. No, they play-acted like children, like the Gypsies from the movies. I even saw a woman dressed in a long skirt, red like mine, with a belt of gold coins circling her waist. The coins were not real, of course, but little wafers of painted plastic. She wore no shirt and her nipples were pierced, something I had never before seen. Her hair was long and dark, like mine. Then I realized it was a wig.

The people at this festival were on vacation from their realities, living for a week or so as if they had no home, as if the silly clothes they wore had meaning of some kind.

But then, of course, they would return to their real homes, their true lives.

My people, too, had homes. It had been decades since most of us lived on the road. In a way, I supposed, being cast from my people would bring me into closer union with my roots. As the sun went down I considered this—how it felt to be homeless, a wanderer, like my ancestors.

Ben Stanley had offered me a home. He said I could come be with him, I could follow him to his college and live with him. Perhaps we would marry, or just live together in the *gazhikanò* way as husband and wife without commitment.

I could look into my future and imagine how this would go. We would move together into a little apartment near his college campus. During the day he would be gone, busy with his classes and his running. I would find a menial job and prepare meals for us. At night we would make love.

And what would happen then? Most likely I would get pregnant. I would be in a different town, with a different man, in a different life. But still I would not be free.

Ben had been moved by the little poem we had listened to at the wedding ceremony. It appealed to him, how straightforward it was, how simple it made love seem to be. I saw that he did not truly trust the simplicity the poem promised, but that he wanted to choose to believe it.

I knew a poem, also. This poem was about a Gypsy girl. It came to me now:

Said the gypsy girl to her mother dear,
"O mother dear, a sad load I bear."
"And who gave thee that load to bear,
My gypsy girl, my own daughter dear?"
"O mother dear, 'twas a lord so proud,
A lord so rich of gentile blood,
That on a mettled stallion rode—
'Twas he gave me this heavy load."
"Thou harlot young, thou harlot vile,
Begone! My tent no more defile;
Had gypsy seed within thee sprung,
No angry word had left my tongue,
But thou art a harlot, base and lewd,
To stain thyself with gentile blood!"

It was called "Song of the Broken Chastity." I used to wonder, where did the girl go when she left her mother's tent? My best guess was that she had gone to the lord who rode the fine stallion and that he cast her out as well, leaving her to wander the streets, poor, alone, heavy with child.

Had Ben Stanley been the handsome lord, he would most certainly have offered his arms to the girl. So I imagined that Ben was the stallion-riding lord offering me, a poor disgraced Gypsy girl, a home, a safe place, a loving heart.

Would it be terribly wrong if the girl refused to feel shame and left him, too, *choosing* solitude over companionship, freedom over love?

We wandered through the festival and drank our water, ate our snacks, waiting for nightfall to come to the desert.

Always Ben Stanley was at my side, waiting patiently for me to answer him.

I tried to look boldly at the people I saw, but embarrassment colored my cheeks. The way they touched one another seemed very different from how Ben and I had come together.

Night came, of course, as it always did, the sun disappearing into the horizon.

NEW HORIZONS, the sign at the entrance to this festival had read. But there is only one horizon. There is nothing new about it, just the inevitable cycle of the sun rising and setting and rising once again. That is the Fool's Journey—to choose a path and set out on it, to take it to its end, to find that at the end is another beginning.

Perhaps that is where our choice lies—in determining how we will meet the inevitable end of things, and how we will greet each new beginning.

With night's fall the debauchery began in earnest. I had never experienced such a crowd, so many bodies in so tight a space—everyone came out for the burning of the Man.

There were drumbeats, there was dancing and singing.

Ben kept his arm around my shoulder, the weight both constricting and a comfort. Part of me wanted to huddle close to him; part of me wanted to throw off his arm and dance and dance and dance.

I thought again about how Ben Stanley had touched me—at the mine, with the horses as our only witnesses, and later in his bed. There was beauty in the way Ben and I had touched. There was beauty, too, in the wild horses. Beauty in the way they ran.

A dozen men had stuffed the Man full of explosives, and a dozen more wet it now with gasoline. The air was pungent with the smell of it and the crowd was hungry for the destruction it knew was coming.

This is how it was. Something is built—something beautiful, something you love—and then, inevitably, it falls.

Look at Ben Stanley's town. Look at this wooden Man. One was falling without the consent of its people; the other would go out in a blaze of glory with an audience cheering for its destruction. Is it better, perhaps, to light the torch yourself than wait for it to be lit by another hand, even the hand of Fate?

Soon the effigy would be lit. I knew this because the crowd was growing louder, more rhythmic in its celebration. It was almost as if the energy of the crowd by itself would be enough to combust the wooden figure.

They had loved their Man all this long week and now they would watch him burn.

This thought recalled to me the final card of Ben Stanley's reading: the Three of Swords. Is it better or worse when the hand that holds the sword is the hand of someone we love, someone who loves us in return? For swords do not find their way into the meat of a heart all on their own; a hand must wield them.

That hand, I saw, was mine.

There are many truths in this world, and perhaps also there are many paths. I could see before me the path I had already chosen not to walk—the path that would have kept me close to my family through marriage to Romeo. And though I had chosen not to take that path, there were things along the way I certainly would have loved—being always near my sisters, the birth of a dark-eyed child who would look so clearly like my own people.

Here was another path, down which I knew some certain happiness would await. Ben Stanley was a kind man, and I loved him as best I could for only having known him these few days. Already I was regretting that I would not be accepting his proposal. But I knew with a cold certainty that I would not.

I wanted to tell him now, before the fire was lit. It seemed important to do so, as if perhaps I might hurt him less if I did it quickly.

I turned to him and tilted my face upward for him to kiss. His mouth was tender and warm against mine, and I did not doubt that he loved me, or that I loved him. But when our mouths parted, I whispered to him, "I cannot go with you," and I watched his face as the swords pierced him through.

"But—what? What do you mean?"

"I am sorry, Ben, but I cannot."

"Lala," he said, and his voice sounded tinged now with despair. "You can't do that. You can't just—take off. It isn't safe. There won't be anyone to take care of you."

True. That was the truth. There would be no one to take care of me. But I was days from my eighteenth birthday, when I would legally become an adult, and my knapsack was full of money. Perhaps—the idea so fragile still that I hardly dared to voice it, even inside my own head—I could take care of myself.

"I am not your responsibility, Ben." I tried to make my voice gentle.

"It's not—just that. It's not about responsibility. I *want* you to come with me, Lala. I don't want to lose you." His hands gripped my arms tightly, too tightly.

Always I have been very good at listening, and also at truly hearing what is said. He meant his words; he wanted to do what was right. Most likely he thought this was all he wanted. But there was more there, in his voice and in his face, something he would most likely not acknowledge. I think it was relief. Just a shadow of it, but there.

Around me I heard the crowd's excitement cresting; the burn was close.

"Lala, please—"

Whatever he said next was lost in the roar of the crowd. I saw his lips moving still as he spoke, but heard no words. Behind me I felt a flash of heat as the Man was lit, as it caught and flared.

In Ben's eyes I saw twin fires, the effigy aflame. As the dry wood exploded into fire, crackling and lighting the sky, I saw the Men in his eyes blur with his tears.

I think often there is no good way out of something. No nice, easy ending or neat resolution, no clear way to set things right. That works in stories, in children's fairy tales, but not in real life.

Not everything can be fixed. And perhaps not everything *should* be.

Maybe it was all right to let things be broken for a while. Would I be doing him a favor to follow along as he lived his life?

I leaned toward him and spoke into his ear. "Do you remember the story—of the mouse girl?"

He nodded.

"I know what I am not—I am not a mountain or the wind or the sun. And I am not a mouse, either."

"So you're not a fucking mouse, Lala. Okay. I get it. But Lala, you can't just—take off. It's not safe. It's not right."

"This could be true," I admitted. "I cannot know the future."

He laughed, but it was bitter. "Not even you, huh?"

"No," I said. "Not even me."

"I don't want to lose you, Lala." His voice sounded anguished.

I tried to be gentle as I said, "But, Ben Stanley, I am not yours to lose."

I turned and clasped his hands about my waist and let him hold me. He held me so tightly it almost hurt, but I knew this too was temporary and so I did not protest. We watched together as the Man burned, and each of us saw what we saw. Perhaps Ben Stanley saw the fall of his town, the end of his childhood, the edge of a cliff. I cannot know; I am not Ben Stanley.

But I know what I saw. In the burning figure, bright against the black of the night sky, I said goodbye to the life

I would have had. I breathed deeply the smell of heat and gasoline; I opened my heart to all of it—the beauty that awaited me, and also the pain.

I spread my arms wide and imagined I was on fire as well, and the heat from the flames felt as if it could be radiating from my core.

I was Lala White. And I was free.

ACKNOWLEDGMENTS

Maybe some books can be written single-handedly. *Burning* wasn't one of them. I relied on the expertise of many people to write this book. First, Dr. Anne Sutherland, professor of anthropology—thank you for your guidance and for your careful reading of my book. Richard Taylor, agronomist extraordinaire, the information about gypsum mining and the photos of the mines you provided helped shape some of my favorite scenes in the book. Thank you. I'm also grateful to Robin Wood, who created the tarot deck that inspired the cards Lala uses. And I owe a big thanks to Google—without the modern magic of the Internet, the research for this book would have been much more difficult. Truly, we live in amazing times!

Of course I am so grateful to my wonderful agent, Rubin Pfeffer, whose comments helped shaped the characters' voices—and who, once again, came up with the title. Rubin, you're the man. Françoise Bui at Delacorte Press, your enthusiasm for *Burning* thrills me. Thank you for loving my book. Stephanie Moss, I love the cover of *Burning*. Thank you for its beautiful design.

And my family of readers—Nana, Dad, Sasha, Zak, and Mischa—I write for you first of all. Thanks to each of you, especially Sasha; your help in creating the tarot reading was invaluable.

Keith, Max, and Davis . . . thank you for putting up with my obsession with this book. I know you ate sandwiches and eggs more often than you would have liked while I wrote it. I love you all.

ABOUT THE AUTHOR

Elana K. Arnold writes curled up in a corner of her couch with a cup of coffee—heavy on the cream and sugar—perched nearby. She finds the words flow more freely if the house isn't too quiet and if there is the promise of chocolate in the near future. She lives in Long Beach, California, with her husband, two children, and a dozen pets. Literally a dozen of them. Her previous novel is *Sacred*. Visit her at elanakarnold.com.